WOLF CREEK

BASED ON A TRUE STORY

A novel by William J. Pardue and Patrick J. Pardue

William J. Pardue

Ordering Information:

Books to Life Marketing Ltd
70 Coulson's Road, Bristol BS14 0NW, UK

Printed in the United States of America

Previously published works include:

- *Visionary Perspectives on the Good Life, 1999*
- *Why God, 2012*
- *Visionary Perspectives Reincarnated, 2013*
- *A Mystic Guide to Spiritual Evolution, 2021*

DEDICATION

This book is dedicated to all the "boys" who survived the ordeals which they encountered in the back woods of East Texas with green horn counselors and nothing but the hard ground to sleep on and the starry canopy as a roof. Thank you for the lessons you taught me. They have lasted me a lifetime and been of great value.

It is also dedicated to my son Patrick for his patience in transforming the first draft into a manuscript which for the first time held promise and to my wife Patricia who assisted me in infusing life, heart and a sense of the boys as individuals into this story. I would also like to thank my son Bobby for his un-failing encouragement and support of this project. This story would not have been possible with all of the above I was merely a grateful recipient of their guidance and insight.

PREFACE

I n 1971 the author graduated from the University of Texas in Austin with a degree in Zoology. In an impulsive moment he applied for a job as a wilderness counselor in a program for emotionally disturbed delinquent adolescents. He had no idea what that meant nor where it would take him. He sensed however that it would be a great adventure and his passion for life drew him to the remote East Texas woods where life was about to deliver a chapter which would forever stand out as perhaps the most transformative year for the author and the group of discarded outlaw youth that survived that year in the best spirit of "*Lord of the Flies*".

The story is in its entirety seems unbelievable and hard to imagine especially in this time when we are all so careful and guarded about everything from bicycle helmets to how many calories we consume every day. These boys did not have the luxury of those worries they worried instead about survival about not being stabbed by the fellow campers or being drowned in the raging rapids of a flash flood in Arkansas. Many could not even read or tell time for they had never spent enough time in a classroom to acquire those skills. Instead they spent their youth incarcerated being bumped from one institution to the next searching for a home a place where they could co-exist with others and stay out of jail.

The story is based on the author's experiences. There are however six chapters which have been introduced within the book which attempt to give a background, a history, a sense of the drama which these boys dealt with before the found themselves in the East Texas woods. These chapters were composed with particular boys in mind however the "unknown" details of their lives have been created by the author. It was the author's intent to communicate the "sense" of each boy and what it was that drove him to his fate not necessarily a factual rendition of the boy's history.

PROLOGUE

The Orphan

When the child arrived at the hospital or better yet was discovered curbside wrapped clumsily and hastily in a soiled dishrag the nurses thought there was no hope of survival. The baby was no more than one month old yet its small body carried the indelible markings of hate, desperation and the hopelessness of the miserable poverty of Chicago's South Side neighborhoods. It arrived without fanfare, without any signs of parental love or a mother's ominous vigilance for her newborn. It could easily have been a crumpled wrapper with meat gone bad thrown from the window of some passing car except for the almost silent mewing, the lost forlorn wail of souls hell bound which arose from the shit stained rag. The janitor had found the boy not so much on the curb but in the gutter amongst the trash and putrid city run off which gathered around the babe. There were no shepherds or three kings or bright stars accompanying the manifestation of this baby on that dark and cold concrete bed. There was no frankincense, no myrrh, and no gifts for the un-named child. There had been no innkeeper to turn the mother and father away as they sought shelter for their child, the warmth of hay and the company of beasts. The infant's mind paralyzed with fear and beat down by the horror into which it was born curled up in a tight ball of panic and waited unconsciously for some miracle.

The janitor, an old Negro, stooped over from years of hard work in southern cotton fields and then gut punched by the city's grinding jaws of hopeless brutality, was the child's savior. Although his hearing was failing and the incessant city noise was deafening, he sensed the babe not so much with his ears but with some sixth sense which pulled him to the ragged bundle. He thought at first that it was an injured animal, some discarded housecat or dog which had been the victim of an accident but the matted infant hair blacker than the night and the round old man face darker than coal looked at him through crusted eye lids. "I am no housecat" it shouted silently into the night. Tears gathered on the windowsill of his eyes when he pulled the corner away and the child welcomed him with a broken cry a plea for help. The old man rested his push broom against the grimy bricks of the arthritic hospital edifice and he lowered himself to the curb where he could more carefully examine his find.

The child was naked. Its lower body crusted with feces and dried urine which exuded a stench, making the man's stomach rebel. He covered his nose and turned away instinctually. He felt sick. His heart was torn apart by the tortured innocence the heartless brutality, the wanton depravity which the child's presence shouted. A cruel wound slithered below the baby's hairline to his cheek bone, still raw. A jagged scar an object so foreign so unexpected on the canvass of infant skin that the old man had to look twice had to touch it gently with his old wrinkled hands to confirm its reality.

It wasn't until he unwrapped the child completely that he noticed the cigarette burns mostly on the baby's back randomly scattered, assiduously applied that the tears poured forth. The old janitor's entire body shook with great shock waves of grief in a silent memorial to the loss of innocence, the evil of man. He pried loose the last remnants of the dishrag and threw it to the ground. He tucked the infant into the welcoming warmth of his great coat against the beating of his heart now racing with urgency a need to get this child some help. He raised himself from the mindless concrete carefully cradling the fragile flickering flame of innocence against his body. He moved through the glass doors his mouth already forming the words, "Help me I have a baby here" his words partially drowned by the emotions the love the hate the anger which overwhelmed him simultaneously which made him dizzy with anguish. Before he handed the child to the ER nurse he carefully raised its head to his lips and placed a lingering kiss there. He couldn't be sure but he thought he heard a small sigh rise from the child's soul as his lips brushed across the battered forehead. He silently whispered in response to the child's pleas, "I love you" before he handed the child over.

Rowena, the infant's mother was huddled in the doorway of the abandoned building across the street from the hospital. Her thin cotton dress soiled, torn and then mended haphazardly by the fourteen year olds untrained hands proved no barrier to the cold winds which swept hopes from the squalid streets. Her makeshift blanket coat pulled tight around her small frame gave some warmth but it was her heart that suffered most that felt frozen. She saw the old janitor discover her child watched him carefully inspect her baby and she looked heavenward and gave thanks. She smothered her cries in the worn blanket and as the old man's body wracked with great waves of grief so did her young frame resonate with a great sobbing an inconsolable emptiness. When he left her sight and entered the hospital she merely slumped over and lowered her old-young body onto the concrete mattress. Her cries more subdued now but no less painful. She cried for her baby for the child that she was for the childhood which she never had. She cried for the fool she had been hoping for love and understanding for a warm safe bed and a mother who was not a whore who could talk to her, protect her. The last of her innocence passed that night into the dark streets blown by the wind into dead end alleys where hobos drank cheap wine and waited for death. She would never again have young girl thoughts, innocent dreams or cherished hopes. At that moment her life was crystallized from amorphous unknown ooze into a granite hard product of destiny wed to fate and defined by violence. Her last hope destroyed as her child disappeared into the vacuum of the future. She would often wonder years later what had happened to him just as her son would wonder who his mother was and why she abandoned him on that street in that gutter without any concerns for his safety.

Years later in his short life the infant would as he lay dying in the river bed wonder if his mother ever cared for him if this hate he harbored for her and for the whole world which defined his life was all the world ever had to offer him or if perhaps things had been different he would have found love experienced the joy of being wanted. With his last breath of life a great grief heavy as a mountain descended on his soul and he heard his mother's cries from so long ago.

CHAPTER I

Charlie stood in the mild, mid-June, central Texas heat, stretching his thumb out to Highway 35, which ran from the pristine lakes, hidden valleys, and limestone cliffs of Texas hill country to the party-ravaged campus of the University of Texas in Austin, on through Dallas and into the heavily-wooded forests of East Texas.

Charlie looked each passing motorist directly in the eye, attempting to draw the drivers over to him. More often that not the technique had worked, as it had only been a short time between rides. If he couldn't get a ride now he would walk the whole three hundred miles to Jilma, Gilmer—or whatever the hell the name of the town was where he was headed.

He was beginning again to reflect on the college life that lay behind him. It hadn't gone exactly how he'd imagined, with all the girls and fun which he could have sworn at some point had been whispered to him as the rewards of being a hardworking college man.

The college experience had been different, yet no less interesting in an odd sort of way. There had been lots of work, morning, noon, and night, any job, anytime, just to pay the rent and buy some food, a few drugs to hasten the spiritual process, girls—only one—but more than a handful, and still a factor in Charlie's life that he had to contend with. It had been a time of learning, about life, people, women, emotions, of growing up and still not being grown up, searching and not finding, and finishing and not feeling finished.

A long, sleek Cadillac, new year model 1971, pulled over to the sound of crunching gravel and Charlie ran for the car as if hesitating too long would make it vanish. The trunk popped up and the driver waved Charlie to put his things in the back. Charlie put his battered old boy scout pack in the trunk and bounded around the car. He let himself in and was immediately enveloped by the interior opulence of the Cadillac and the old world charm of the middle-aged driver.

"Hey man, thanks for stopping. I was starting to think I was gonna have to walk it," Charlie rattled out as he oriented himself to the luxury of the Cadillac.

"Well you looked like you needed a ride. I don't usually pick up hitchhikers, but you don't look like the kind that does this all the time. By the way, my name's Jim."

Jim extended his hand to Charlie, who grasped it solidly.

With a succession of subtle, sidelong glances, Charlie guessed his chauffer was a businessman. Tie, neatly folded jacket on the back-seat, briefcase to match. He appeared to be thirty-eight to forty years old, probably enjoying a good income.

"Where are you goin son, and what are you doing out here in the middle of nowhere in this heat?" said Jim.

"I'm coming from Austin, where I graduated from the University, and I'm headed to Gilmer, for my first real job."

"Gilmer? I think we can manage that." Jim started up the car. "First job huh? College man." Jim laughed and pulled out onto the road. "I can remember my first job, never was fortunate enough to go to college. Guess I missed the fun. I'm sure you can tell missing college never held me back though. This car alone cost me over eight thousand dollars, new too only a hundred and fifty eight miles on it." Jim's face lit up with the pride of achievement.

Charlie agreed that the car was indeed a beauty and wondered if such richness was in store for him. After all, he was just beginning. The future—even tomorrow—was unknown.

Jim began summarizing his career in the shoe business. He described the struggle it had been, giving tidbits of advice here and there when he felt they would be most appropriate and appreciated by a young college man just starting out. Charlie was congenial as usual, a skill he'd learned growing up to adapt to life. Let them talk, see their side of things, empathize, make them like you. Jim soon found himself expounding on more personal matters: trouble with his wife, kids not appreciating him except for what he meant to them in dollars and cents.

"You know son, I wish I was in your shoes—new start, fresh ideas, places to go, optimistic, the great unknown to be met and beat. It seems so long ago. The force of youth, no obstacles too big. I could use some of that myself right now seems like I have enough trouble just getting it up anymore, much less tackling the world." Jim stared straight ahead as the highway was sucked under the hood of his car. "But don't let me get you down. I'm just getting to that age where dreams become scarce or even extinct. Whatever you do, don't let that happen to you."

Charlie offered his thanks for the advice and pondered the notion that not everything in life is as it seems. Jim certainly couldn't be called unhappy, yet despite his wealth he did seem sad somehow, perhaps empty—was it lost youth, or as he said, lost dreams?

"You got a girlfriend?" said Jim.

"Well sort of, there's been this girl. We're both just doing different things now," said Charlie.

Charlie's thoughts drifted to Linda. He had met her under circumstances which at the time hadn't seemed particularly ominous, yet which in hindsight had set the embattled tone of their entire relationship.

*   *   *

It was a clear, crisp Saturday in October. Charlie had just finished his noon stint of dishwashing at the campus dorm and was taking a circuitous walk through downtown Austin.

The first he recalled seeing of Linda was her flying, shoulder-length red hair, trailing behind her like a warning flag. She was tall and slim, with a light complexion speckled with traces of childhood freckles around her nose. Her gray eyes were never still and seldom trapped even by a direct gaze. She was hurrying toward Charlie from up ahead on the sidewalk. Tears streamed down her face as she glanced down in order to avoid the looks of passersby.

She looked familiar to Charlie. He'd seen her before, at the University—the girls' dorm—always by herself, looking somehow different—misplaced.

"Excuse me," said Charlie, "but can I help you? Is something wrong?"

"No, just leave me alone, I don't need anymore crap from anyone today."

Charlie instinctively grabbed her arm and held on as if he were saving someone caught in the throes of a hurricane. "You live at Samson House, don't you? I've seen you there. I work in the kitchen."

Linda looked her would-be rescuer in the face for signs of recognition. He didn't look familiar. She studied him more carefully. He was attractive. Actually cute was more accurate—dark hair, dark penetrating eyes, a bit taller than her. He had a hesitant but determined air about him. The boy, as his features were still more round than square, obviously meant well and wanted to help, even if he wanted more.

"Yeah, maybe you can help. Those bastards, assholes over there…" said Linda, wiping her tears and pointing to a large group of black men assembled two blocks down on a corner.

Charlie turned his attention toward the gathering. The group was noisy, excited, probably spreading some brand of politics.

"What happened, what did they do?" said Charlie, his anger beginning to boil.

Linda took a nervous drag on her cigarette and, still shaking, began to relate her story.

"I was just walking down the street, minding my own business, when that guy there, the one at the table, grabbed me by the arm and started raving about white honkies like me and how we were gonna get ours. Before I could shake loose I was being cursed at by a half-dozen of those fuckers."

Linda discarded her half-smoked cigarette and embraced herself as if it would help control her trembling. Before she knew it, Charlie was heading for the group of probably thirty black men, assembled around a folding table. The small black man whom Linda had indicated had grabbed her stood in the middle of the group. The deference with which he was being treated obviously marked him as the leader of the group.

Charlie forced his way through the crowd. He leaned on the table and pointed at the accused. "A friend of mine says she was down here a few minutes ago and that you accosted her, gave her a really bad time. Is that how you treat women?"

Unbeknownst to Charlie, a crowd of supporters had begun closing in behind him.

Suddenly the table ended up in the street and the leader caught Charlie in the side of the head with a glancing roundhouse punch. Charlie recovered from the punch and felt the crowd behind him. A spark of common sense alerted him to the danger of the situation.

"Hey my man, cool it, I didn't want to fight," said Charlie, trying to keep his voice at a calm tone. "Looks like I'm outnumbered anyway. I just think you owe an apology to the young lady."

"Fuck your apology you white motherfucker!" said the leader as the group began to shout and holler.

The crowd suddenly opened up and a six-foot-two black man weighing in the vicinity of one-hundred-and-ninety-five pounds approached Charlie. The man was built like a prize fighter, with the assured air of one who wins more than he loses. He grinned at Charlie.

"You want to fight somebody whitey, then you're gonna have to fight me. Why don't we just step around behind this building here and settle this like it should be settled—bare knuckles."

A motorcycle accident the week before had left Charlie with a pair of almost useless arms bandaged from wrist to elbow. The prize fighter seemed to be enjoying the predicament Charlie had found himself in, and Charlie's ability to resist squirming under his adversary's stare was waning.

Charlie quickly assessed his odds of survival in what might prove to be his Waterloo. He politely declined his opponent's challenge and gingerly backed out of the gathering. Once safely out of the crowd, he turned his eyes from the hornet's nest which he had so successfully stirred up to the maiden whose honor he had tried so disastrously to preserve.

*   *   *

The Cadillac pulled to a stop, jolting Charlie from his reminiscence. Jim reached over and touched Charlie's shoulder.

"You alright? Looked like you were a thousand miles away. Probably thinking about that sweet girl you left back in Austin."

"Matter of fact I was. That's on the back burner for now though. I should start being more concerned about what happens tomorrow."

Anxious to be on his way, Jim extended his hand for the second time. "This is as far as I go my friend. You're almost there anyway. Best of luck to you."

Accustomed to the trouble-free luxury, Charlie hesitated for an instant before taking Jim's hand. "Thanks for the ride, I appreciate it. Good luck to you too."

Charlie stepped out of the car. Jim accelerated into the lane of traffic and disappeared out of sight.

Charlie once again found himself alone, looking east. Ten miles stretched between him and his future.

CHAPTER II

After one more free ride, Charlie arrived near Daingerfield State Park, in Gilmer. He approached the entrance to the park, secluded in the far East Texas woods, with a degree of trepidation. He knew very little about the career upon which he was embarking. The few phrases he was able to recall from his interview two months earlier didn't offer much substantial information.

"There will be a lot of camping, a good deal of adventure, backpacking into wilderness areas, canoeing, and you will be your own boss."

Charlie had recalled and repeated these words to himself continually when feeling doubtful about the job, like some sort of mantra, to raise his spirits and prepare himself for the adventure which awaited him.

He recalled seeing the advertisement for the position posted on the job listings board at the student employment office, hidden among numerous other more proper and dignified callings: electrical engineers, we offer you the world; education majors, save the globe's ignorant, teach English to Malaysian pygmies so their children can one day read the Wall Street Journal.

The ad had merely read, as nearly as Charlie's memory served, "wanted: young male, college graduate, preferably social services major, for work with teenagers in unusual setting. Must like the outdoors."

Enjoying the outdoors wasn't a problem. Charlie had always wanted to go to Boy Scout camp. His brothers had gone, giving him that disdainful look that children even slightly older than their peers cultivate and use effectively when receiving some special privilege. Perhaps it was that burning frustration of always being left behind that had made Charlie desire to indulge himself in what he had unconsciously fantasized as a fulltime holiday at Boy Scout camp with pay.

Charlie crossed over the perimeter of the campsite where he had been instructed to rendezvous. He recognized Mr. Johnson up ahead, who had interviewed him for the job. Johnson was an older man, probably in his early sixties, tall and skinny, almost gaunt—his appearance on the whole suggested only a slight variation on that of Ichabod Crane.

At Charlie's interview, he and Mr. Johnson had taken to each other after only a short exchange. Considering the episode upon the moment of his arrival at the campsite, Charlie realized that it was Johnson's warm personality which had pulled him towards a strange job and an indefinite future.

"It doesn't even sound like work. What are you paying us for?" Charlie remembered remarking at the close of the interview.

Johnson laughed and put his hands on Charlie's shoulders as if reassuring his own son. "Now that you put it that way, I'm not sure." Johnson's amusement was suddenly replaced with a serious air. "Remember that you will be responsible for the lives of ten teenage boys. Mind you, not your everyday variety, but a rather special brand requiring the kind of energy and personality which I sense you possess."

Johnson's words made Charlie feel confident, as the social worker had credited him with a sense of character that few others had acknowledged before.

Mr. Johnson waved as Charlie approached the edge of the campsite. He grasped Charlie's hand and wrung it thoroughly while thumping him on the back—enthusiasm more fitting the reunion of a beloved family member after years of separation.

Charlie scanned the campsite. It was one of those typical vacation pull-ins that state parks throughout the country were noted for, containing the standard four foot high barbecue perched atop a steel well secured by cement in the ground. The camp was situated within a small grove of mature pines, which had deposited their needles over the years, creating a natural carpet of scented pine. There were several logs ringing the campfire area itself.

Four men, two about Charlie's age and two older, maybe mid to late thirties, were seated upon the logs, scrutinizing the new arrival. As they rose and introduced themselves, Charlie's nervousness at meeting new people prevented him from catching any of their names. A natural reserve also hindered him from taking in their overall appearances. His curiosity held in check for a more surreptitious moment.

One of the men stayed behind as the greetings came to an end.

"Well I guess we'll find out what this is all about tonight," said the stranger, feeling his way around Charlie. "What do you know about what's gonna be expected of us?" He hesitated, anxiously awaiting a reply.

"Nothing really," said Charlie, taking in the stranger with a more studied gaze.

Duane, as Charlie later found out, was of a different breed than Charlie. His eyes possessed the look of the hunted, easily discernable even behind the glasses. They roamed ceaselessly, not resting too long on anything, darting about as if wary of some unknown. Duane's body spoke of a sedentary character: hips and shoulders in line, heavy posterior, underdeveloped arms, and a head which appeared difficult to control due to its weight. He fell in the class of shy wallflower—a studious, responsible, intellectual type, who had been condemned to a life of loneliness in high school, and had had his first date as a sophomore in college, a blind one set up by a friend of his older brother.

Duane's life had been full of bullies. One could sense a paranoid wariness in his company. He wasn't a ladies man, nor the star of the football team—not even in the band. He was just a regular nice guy.

Charlie heard his name being called. He turned to look back up the road and saw a familiar face approaching, hidden under a wide-brimmed black felt hat.

"Charlie my man, how you doin? When did you get here? Bet you didn't expect to see me, did you?"

"Hooper! Looks you did go down and talk to Johnson after all..."

Charlie and Hooper threw their arms around each other in a friendly embrace.

"By the way Hooper, this is Duane. We were just getting acquainted."

Hooper and Duane shook hands.

"Hooper and I've known each other for a few years. We both just graduated from the University of Texas this summer."

"Old rock hounds."

"What happened to the Geology? Did you finish?"

"Yeah I did, but this sounded so great that night you told me about it at Linda's party. I remembered how jazzed you were by the camping."

Ole' Hooper, Charlie thought, ready to try anything different.

"I hope this doesn't mean that if things don't work out here, I'll have that burden to bear the rest of my life," said Charlie, shooting Hooper a sly look.

"Well if it does, that's your problem, isn't it?" Hooper laughed.

This grinning coyote was a refreshing sight for Charlie's eyes. Hooper was taller than average, with a slender build and a sinewy strength that could be seen when he was in motion. He wore wire-rimmed glasses which accentuated the sharpness of his features. His dark hair, which seemed to look longer now than Charlie had ever remembered seeing it, completely covered his ears as it escaped from under his hat. He had an easygoing, no-rush, things-will-wait-until-tomorrow mentality and partook in simple pleasures which were meant to be enjoyed at one's leisure, like drugs. It was this luxury which brought he and Charlie together, for the known drug culture consisted of only a small group of people who indulged and even fewer who enjoyed indulging as much as Hooper and Charlie. Hooper, because of his open nature, abandoned himself more regularly, while Charlie, answering to the call of a more conservative strain, would only allow himself so much fun.

As his reunion with Hooper died down, Charlie found a quiet moment to study the rest of his companions. His attention was first drawn to a dark figure seated directly across from him. A certain stillness surrounded the man and his chosen color scheme heightened the atmosphere. A black cotton T-shirt covered his thick chest. The short sleeves were forced upward to his shoulders by the girth of his upper arms. A pack of Camels rested squarely in the front pocket. His black aesthetic carried over into a wide leather belt with the name "Bud" engraved on the back in bold letters.

Suddenly Bud seemed to sense the attention and he slowly raised his head to establish its source. His eyes met and locked onto Charlie's. Charlie withdrew his gaze and fixed it once again in the direction of Bud's black jeans ending in matching cowboy boots.

Charlie sensed that Bud was a product of the early '50s. A hot rod '56 Chevy, four-speed 327, could easily be pictured as his choice of cars as a young man. He reminded Charlie of Elvis and James Dean. His well-controlled, dark shock of hair glistened dully as the Brylecreem clung to each strand; the beat of Jailhouse Rock was almost audible when one was held in the trance of that oily sheen. His attractiveness was of the earned variety, each year adding a subtle new tone to the tough guy image.

Charlie had surmised from their short eye contact that he would definitely want Bud on his side in any grudge match. Upon the lower part of his exposed forearm Bud sported a tattoo, a pair of twin parachutes with what looked like an outfit identification below. The tattoo wasn't one of those oversized eye-grabbers that shouted to the world, but rather the subdued type that spoke softly of experience.

In Charlie's continuing inspection, he recognized a certain country-boy ease in Bud's demeanor, the way he sat way back on a log or slowly turned his hands over, studying first one then the other. He seemed to have no interest in studying the other members of the group and spoke only when addressed. Charlie guessed that as with many men of such a reserved temperament a cluster of thunder clouds lay just below the calm exterior.

Bud and Mr. Johnson seemed to know each other, although they appeared to be from much different backgrounds. The few words Bud had spoken had been addressed to the elderly social worker.

Sitting on the far side of Duane was Mark, a philosophy student turned dropout. The only skin above his shoulders which was not covered with a prodigious growth of curliness was the top of his head.

Mark was even quieter than Bud and appeared to be in his own world somewhere theorizing and expostulating to himself.

The last of this little group was La Mar. He had proven himself to be outspoken and gregarious by attempting to draw the others into an initial group dialogue. At six-foot-five and two-hundred-and-seventy-pounds he was easily the biggest of the group, yet contrary to the impression his bulk created he exuded a sense of feminine compassion—often expressed in the weeks to come in the form of big bear hugs. There were some, Charlie thought, who might question Lamar's masculinity, but certainly not to his face. His manners and speech indicated a family background in the more cultured and wealthy classes. He could very easily fill the role of resident bon vivant.

Mr. Johnson approached the campfire with a clipboard and a look of unconcealed satisfaction. His eyes traveled the circumference of the group, searching each individual's face while communicating a silent message of support and approval. The group fell silent as Johnson faced them, all intent upon learning a little more about what they were in for.

"I'm glad to see that you could all make it. It was a long selection process and we talked to large number of applicants before we decided on you six men in particular."

The soft cadence of Johnson's voice worked like a sedative on the collective anxiety of the group.

"As you all know, my name is Bill Johnson. I prefer being called Billy. I would like to welcome you all wholeheartedly to the adventure which awaits you. From the very beginning I would like to officially be on record as wishing you all the best of luck. This isn't to say that you will all make it here." Johnson became aware of the sudden increase in tension from the group. "Because, I'm sure some of you will come to find out that this is not what you are looking for. Simply not your cup of tea."

Johnson paused to let his words be absorbed.

"So just remember that if you do make that decision and you are absolutely sure that this isn't what you want, please don't hesitate in letting me know. After beginning on a negative note I would also like to add that, for those of you who do find that you enjoy this type of challenge, the rewards couldn't be greater. You will have the elusive and rare opportunity of changing the lives of young boys—bringing them back from the brink of destruction to a point where they can develop their constructive sides. If I seem like I'm lecturing, please forgive me!"

Johnson's supplication filled the attentive ears. His features suddenly became melancholy.

"We will be talking more about the boys later. By the way, the first group is scheduled to arrive at the end of the week. This is Sunday night. Friday afternoon, three of you fellows, which three we don't know yet, will be receiving a busload of ten boys who will from that day on become your responsibility. As far as living arrangements are concerned, the site we occupy now will be ours until Wednesday, at which time we will break camp and move to Lake of the Pines State Park, which will be your and your group's home until we feel everyone is prepared to move to the acreage which has been purchased in the country outside of Gilmer."

As these salient facts emerged, the group leaned forward, anxious for details.

"Tomorrow you will all have an opportunity to inspect the country and make preliminary plans for establishing two permanent campsites. Until then, I want you all to just relax and get to know one another."

Hooper and Charlie exchanged glances, each anxious for three unobstructed days of leisure.

"From now on you will be preparing all of your meals outside, so please schedule yourselves for cooking and cleaning duties as needed."

Before the group dispersed, they quickly drew up a schedule which covered each shift through the week, with pairs taking responsibilities for cleaning and cooking chores.

Duane edged close to Charlie. "Sounds like he's warning us about something. He made it sound like this job is gonna be dangerous." Duane hesitated. "Hey, how about you and I pairing up as counselors if they give us that choice. I mean, if you want to of course."

"Sure," said Charlie. There was something about Duane that read responsible, and from what Charlie was beginning to assume about the job, responsibility would be essential.

The first night the group spent together proved to be uneventful, with the exception of Charlie singing his hair and arms in an inexperienced attempt at starting a cook fire with large quantities of Coleman fluid. The incident quickly established his lack of Boy Scout credentials. Later in the evening, those members of the group who enjoyed the use of mind-expanding substances found themselves perched on a grassy, gently-rolling hillside which dipped quietly into the crystal clear waters of the lake. They lay on the grass into the small hours of the night, looking for shooting stars and traveling to the moon and back. The small group of lawbreakers included Hooper, La Mar, Mark, and Charlie, with Duane and Bud abstaining.

Eight o'clock Monday morning found the group huddled around the campfire, gorging themselves on fried eggs and sausage. As Bud and Charlie worked together to prepare breakfast they quickly established an unspoken understanding with one another.

Bud placed a bucket of hot, soapy water on the end of the bench and glanced at Charlie's singed arm. "How's the hair? That's bound to keep the girls away for awhile." Bud chuckled.

Charlie was cleaning off and stacking the plastic plates. He turned and passed a friendly grin as a prelude to his reply. "Oh, it's not too bad, mostly bruised ego. I felt like such a dim wit and obviously played the part well. First day on the job and I set myself on fire. I guess Johnson didn't realize how quickly some of us would start eliminating ourselves."

"We all make mistakes and if ever you're going to be in a situation where you'll need to understand that, it's what we're headed for come the end of the week."

"Yeah, sometimes I have a hard time recognizing that I make mistakes like everybody else. Maybe that's why I have to set myself on fire occasionally, just to remind myself that I'm not perfect."

Bud laughed.

"By the way," Charlie continued, "rumor has it that you've done this sort of thing before. What's the deal with these kids? Information's kinda scarce around here."

Charlie directed his full attention to Bud, attempting to glean information from the nuances of the veteran's expressions.

"Just hang in there Charlie. There's really no way to explain anyway, believe me. If you tough it out, I promise you'll understand why I say it can't be explained."

Charlie finished the last of his morning chores and climbed in the back of Johnson's pickup truck. His thoughts returned to the mystery at hand. There were indeed facts available about the job; the sheer absence of specific information on the boys was itself the most important fact. For the most part, the information that he had acquired thus far was purely geographical. He knew for instance that his journey had taken him deep into the wilds of East Texas.

The most populous city in the area was Longview. It sat astride Highway 80, where as a hub of activity it offered a mild dose of city living to a flock of country towns nestled within its rim. Charlie had already passed through Big Sandy, New Hope, Sand Flat, and White Oak. These hamlets were large enough to support only one entertainment concept. Daingerfield had the movie theatre, Big Sandy the roller rink, and Gilmer the Dairy Queen. An eastward beeline from Dallas would take one to the Longview exit, which if utilized would put one on State Highway 259, which unfolded to the north. Approximately forty-five miles north lay the heart of East Texas, Daingerfield Lake, and the beginning of the group's Monday morning trek.

The pickup truck made passage along Highway 155 some thirty miles, then turned down a dirt road hidden within a forest of weeds and wildflowers. This one-lane road, pitted with ruts, rocks, stumps, and all variety of natural fallout, came to a Y about a half mile in.

The truck came to an abrupt stop at the edge of a steep incline which protruded down some thirty yards, leveling off into a large, cleared area lined with spindly, skyscraping pine trees, the kind only one generation away from the logger's death grip.

The passengers exited the truck amid dust, sweat, and the sound of hacking lungs battling upturned dust.

Mr. Johnson herded the group together in the manner of a down home preacher welcoming his flock into Sunday services.

"This is it fellas. This is where you will begin building your new home. We are now standing in the northwest corner of a parcel of land that covers twenty seven acres, which the boys' ranch has purchased in order that we might undertake our project."

While Johnson warmed to his topic, his dusty congregation began to pull their thoughts from the overwhelming isolation which greeted them to the tones of the spoken word.

"What we propose to do today is to take a look around the area, keeping in mind possibilities for establishing permanent campsites. Remember, this will be your home.".

A small whirlwind of dust settled over the silent group.

"I don't see any water or electricity in here," said Hooper with a quizzical look.

"That's because there isn't any," said Mr. Johnson, his face set stiff in a salesman mask. "What you see here is potential and what you are able to do with it is totally up to you and your ability to motivate not only yourself but others whom you will come to depend on."

"Just what'll be expected of us Mr. Johnson? We really haven't heard much about our real duties or about these kids," said Duane.

"I'm glad you asked Duane. What we are talking about is two groups of ten teenage boys, average age fifteen. Officially they are called emotionally disturbed delinquents. In reality they are a group of adolescents who have severe problems with the control of their basic emotions. They are kids many of whom have never known either parent. A good percentage of the others wish they hadn't. They can be, at times, extremely violent and aggressive as well as passive and withdrawn. A good number have never even completed first grade, not because of lack of intelligence, but because of the inability of school personnel to deal with them."

"What do you mean when you say violent?" Duane sputtered as his blood pressure rose.

Johnson leaned heavily against the truck, preparing his answer.

"I'm not trying to soft-pedal this issue at all. I just prefer not dwelling on it as I don't want to establish stereotypes so early in the game."

Johnson halted momentarily, considering how best to proceed.

"There are two occurrences, however, which I offer to you as examples of what we are talking about."

The group formed a tighter circle around the social worker as he began.

"From the first group of ten children we know for certain that there has been considerable violence related to animals. In one instance, a horse on the ranch was exposed to a cigarette lighter inserted into its nostrils. The horse was scorched badly. The second concerned a pet dog found bleeding to death under a bed with all four legs amputated at the knees."

Charlie didn't hear much after that—his sensitivities shrieked within him at the thought of such violence. Being an animal lover, especially dogs and horses, the information was particularly hard for him to hear. He had difficulty imagining anyone who might be capable of committing such acts. The description of inconceivable violence rang a strange note that affected the entire group.

CHAPTER III

Despite the excitement over the new camp and the pleasant weather of the first two days at Daingerfield, with light, high altitude clouds obscuring just enough of the sun's rays and southerly fall breezes bringing just a hint of coolness, Charlie had been experiencing a growing feeling of depression. It started, as best he could recollect, when he had set himself on fire. After that, a series of small incidents had seemed to snowball.

There was the twisted ankle which he had acquired the day the campsites were selected. Apart from the physical maladies there was Mark. Even though Charlie had tried to avoid spending time with him a seed of animosity had grown between the two that seemed to get nourishment at each encounter. Their limited contact had consisted mostly of nightly trips to share a little weed with the others.

Wrestling with his despondency, Charlie recalled a story he had been told once which seemed to have relevance to his situation with Mark. The main thrust dealt with reincarnation and how all imbalances eventually right themselves. He remembered clearly the portion that dealt with enemies or friends made in past lives and how they were again destined to cross each other's paths in future lives. This reunion took place in order that debts could be repaid or simply so the saga could continue until it had run its course.

The antagonism with Mark had begun to cause Charlie to doubt his ability to deal with what lay ahead. Would he be one of those left by the wayside, unable or unfit to cope with this particular chapter in life? Now, when he needed all the strength he could gather, his doubts had suddenly coalesced into a potent force within the darkness of his unconscious.

The trick was to never give up. Seven times down, eight times up. Losers never win, winners never quit. Even these worn out cliches could better his mood if recalled enough—or so he convinced himself.

The tedium of the days had only added to Charlie's despondency, for very little of any significance had occurred since the counselors' trip to their future campsite.

Johnson had issued everyone a new bedroll. They were the standard model, cotton with a side zipper. Their length allowed room enough to get all the way inside and their width offered spacious accommodation for one and, if entertaining, would be suitable but cramped for two.

Everyone had been issued a regulation pup tent. Front to back they measured seven feet. They were supported by two upright poles approximately three feet high. These were located inside the tent, one fore and one aft. The aft support stood above the head, and formed behind it a small space of approximately a foot square, which proved convenient for storage. The canvas sides, when pulled taut, supported to a frame structure. Four tent stakes on either side created the required tension across the support poles in a lateral direction. The balance of the structure was held in place by a longitudinal tension created by two nylon ropes extending directly from the front and back of the tent and secured to the ground by stakes.

Charlie had discovered that these tents were quite comfortable for the average-sized adult. They also offered a degree of privacy which could be easily regulated by the combination of a screen and canvas flap in front, both of which could be secured from the inside. This particular feature would surely prove indispensable to the maintenance of sanity as time wore on.

The counselors had begun to learn the routine of securing tents, sleeping bags, and other essential equipment: Coleman stoves, lanterns, cooking and eating ware, and personal items. Among the last could be found a broad range of reading materials. Hooper kept a few well-worn issues of Playboy while Charlie's library consisted of "How to Survive in the Woods" and "Walden Pond."

Charlie received a lift in spirits when Johnson confided to him that he would be a counselor for the first group, along with Bud. Bud later told Charlie that he had personally requested this arrangement, but didn't mention why. Charlie imagined his own reasons, conjuring up a long list of his own outstanding qualities.

Charlie, true to his promise, requested Duane as the third member of the team. The suggestion met with Johnson's wholehearted approval. Bud, on the other hand, although too polite to state the obvious, wavered slightly.

"Do you know Duane very well?" Bud drawled as he studied Charlie. "What I mean is, have you had an opportunity to get to know him?"

"No, not really, but I do have a feeling there's more there than meets the eye. I'm not sure why or what, but I do have a feeling."

"Just remember, even though there are three of us, only two will be working at any one time." Bud cast a knowing look at Charlie. "So if I'm gone, you and Duane have full responsibility and vice versa. We won't always have each other there."

"I know that, but I still think he's stable. Definitely more so than some of the others." Charlie's primary concern with the others was the vast amount of time they spent getting high. Even Hooper, whom he favored, fell into that category. Charlie's more cautious nature warned him that such patterns of consumption while working might prove hazardous.

Time, however, would be the ultimate judge of the counselor's merits. The overall plan was for two campsites staffed by three counselors each. Both sites were to be located within two hundred yards of each other on the twenty-seven acre site. That was where the rules ended. From there on, each site was on its own.

The camp at Daingerfield was moved smoothly on Wednesday. Lamar, Hooper, and Mark were not included in the move. They continued to enjoy the amenities of Daingerfield and the lower levels of anxiety that their situation provided.

The move took the campers fourteen miles southwest from Daingerfield to a campsite bordering the shores of Lake of the Pines, chosen by Johnson because of its remoteness and isolation. The nearest adjacent camp was located one hundred yards southeast. The compensating element was that the recreational and swimming facilities at Daingerfield were only a short drive away. The lake stretched forty miles northeast. The newly established camp was located approximately at midpoint on the south side.

As usual, a picnic table and a small barbecue pit built on the ground were located in the center of the camp. The water supply consisted of a single faucet located at the entrance to the camp, to one side of the dirt road leading in. Toilet facilities were twenty yards north on the gravel road which encircled all the campsites.

On Friday, Charlie, Duane, Bud, and Mr. Johnson assembled for a lunch of peanut butter and jelly sandwiches, potato chips, and Kool-Aid—standard fare in the months to come—and waited for the arrival of the boys.

"Before the boys arrive, I would like to add just a few more formal comments about them and what the ranch expects," said Johnson.

Duane swallowed hard.

"The boys you will be meeting tonight are what most people would call losers. Just for a moment I would like to trace the institutional trail which lies scattered behind each one. To begin with, you will find that the typical boy is from the south side of Chicago. His history shows he ran with street gangs and eventually became involved with the law and ended up in a reform school of some sort. Now, these particular boys have been kicked out or shall I say removed from at least three in-state institutions. None of which could cope with their erratic behavior. After meeting these qualifications they were sent to the ranch located outside of San Antonio, which is set up to handle this kind of youth."

Johnson paused momentarily, and when no one chose to interject, he continued.

"Our boys, however, have also been rejected from the ranch. The most glaring reasons being disruptive and uncontrollable behavior. There have been repeated instances of physical attacks on teachers, including a desk being hurled at one. What we hope you men will be able to do is harness that erratic behavior and carefully guide it into more constructive areas."

Johnson turned his attention to Bud. "Now Bud, as you probably already know, has had similar working experience. Perhaps he would like to share some of his knowledge with you."

Bud shifted self-consciously under the weight of the attention. His powerful arms rested on the picnic table. "It's not really that they're bad kids," he began in a slow, emphatic cadence. A look of sadness came over his face, lending a shade of softness to his otherwise hard features. "It's mostly that they're unwanted, they've had shitty lives, always being dumped on. They act like loners, but they're really searching for companionship. They'll take any they can get, not particular as to where it comes from." Bud halted abruptly and looked out towards the lake, entering a private place within himself where no one else was allowed admittance.

Charlie and Duane exchanged puzzled looks.

"Just don't give up on them, whatever you do, because they can sense it in as little time as it takes to think the thought," said Bud. His brooding eyes bore into Charlie and Duane.

Duane postponed meeting the boys until after his vacation. He departed abruptly.

The first indication of the boys' arrival was the cry of grinding gears pulling the last hill into the campground. Charlie watched the small school bus approach at a rapid pace along the main campground road, his eyes subdued by inner doubt. The time for preparation gone, he was destined to meet the unknown in a state of less confidence than usual.

The school bus pulled to a stop in front of the picnic table and a group of young boys poured forth like a school of sharks. Their keen senses picked up the smell of fresh blood and in a frenzy they began to sniff out their prey.

Charlie was seated on one end of the picnic table while Bud was on the other. Bud had his back turned towards Charlie and his eyes focused on the new arrivals. In the immediate confusion that ensued the two men were given a few minutes to scout the boys.

The main body of the boys, obviously familiar with Mr. Johnson and knowledgeable of his influence over their lives, formed a circle around him and began shouting disparate demands. From Charlie and Bud's vantage point Johnson appeared to be handling himself well enough. Considering his position as the potential granter of certain privileges, he was treated by the boys with all the discretion they could muster.

From his still somewhat protected position, Charlie identified two blacks, one olive-complexioned youth, obviously Italian, and six white Anglos. Their sizes ranged from five-foot-two to five-foot-ten and maybe one-hundred-and-ten to one-hundred-and-sixty pounds. Two common traits which Bud and Charlie readily identified were a vast supply of energy and a blind hunger for acquisition. Within the first two minutes of the boys' approaching Bud, Charlie could see that he had gone through a whole pack of Winstons. As soon as one had been given, word had spread and it had become obligatory to supply the entire group. Charlie was also briefly scouted out, but when it was discovered that he didn't smoke, interest quickly faded.

Johnson had begun to receive a rougher handling. A bevy of queries demanded "Where are my fucking letters, my money?" and "What in the hell am I doing way out in the boonies?" Johnson cleverly fielded all the questions with a patient smile and elusive rhetoric. The boys, apparently familiar with this variety of answer, persisted. Aware of the futility of their quest for an answer to all their problems, they hammered even harder.

Charlie remained rooted to the end of the bench, feeling lucky that he didn't have to deal with the initial onslaught. The Italian boy, David, as Charlie later learned, sauntered towards the bench directly opposite Charlie.

Charlie remembered seeing this one emerge from the bus. He clearly recalled that he had come through the front door, taking his time. He had been the first one off and none of the others had attempted to hurry him. He was a handsome young man, probably fifteen, with dark hair and dark eyelashes, the kind girls love to coo over. His olive complexion covered soft features and a finely sculptured nose. His immaculate hair and clothing displayed an obvious pride in appearance. Charlie quickly gathered that the boy devoted a great deal of attention to personal grooming. He studied Charlie carefully with what appeared to Charlie to be a total lack of self-consciousness and shyness. The boy's general demeanor was what Charlie would expect of a Mafioso boss, patiently judging the character of an adversary whose fate was already sealed.

The table was rapidly filling and Charlie could feel himself being nudged closer and closer to the end and a hard spot on the ground. Meanwhile, David, in his position across the table, seemed to gain space in direct proportion to Charlie's losing it.

David bummed a light from the boy sitting on his right, who obviously heaped authority on David. David took a deep drag on his cigarette, then slowly turned his full attention to Charlie. The rest of the boys followed in turn, each broadcasting his lust for a quick and bloody showdown.

"What's your name twerp?" said David.

David's words, accompanied by the swarm of mocking faces, burnt Charlie like a hot iron.

Charlie's voice shook noticeably as he replied. "Charlie, my name is Charlie you little asshole. What's your name?"

Charlie, as a general rule, was well-mannered and self-composed; however, when pushed to the point of anger, he could be dangerous. He could never recall using that particular expression with a kid before, but there appeared to be very little of a kid left in his antagonist other than the lack of his full growth.

The sound of jeers passed quickly around the table.

David took a second deep drag, coolly leaned forward, and blew a large cloud of smoke in Charlie's face.

A chorus of ridicule descended on Charlie. Attempting to control his rage, Charlie noticed Bud watching him intently from the other end of the table. Bud offered no assistance, yet somehow his watch was a candle in the darkness of ridicule which surrounded Charlie, and it clearly shouted: do what you have to do my friend, you are on your own.

The smoke cleared and Charlie fixed a flat, stone-hard gaze on David. "Don't ever do that again, friend, or I'm gonna have to kick your ass just for the fun of it."

The audience feigned terror simultaneously.

David took another long drag and nonchalantly exhaled it into Charlie's face.

Charlie felt his body release its pent up rage as he leaped over the table, knocking the cigarette from David's mouth and dragging him to the ground. The young tough was subdued after a short flurry of attempted punches, all of which went wide of Charlie's face and head.

The boys shifted to gain a better view, but none moved to help David—obviously they adhered to the philosophy of every man for himself, no matter whom.

Charlie sat astride David's chest, pinning his arms to the ground. Charlie's position of superiority subjected him to a flurry of profanity from the powerless boy. David quickly wore himself down in his unsuccessful attempts to remove the weight. Being an intelligent kid, he realized his efforts were in vain and cooled off rapidly. Charlie watched the transformation take place before his eyes. David's physical violence was absorbed into his eyes and face until the cold presence of hate had swept away all other emotions. Charlie clearly recalled, as he replayed the scene later in his head, a total absence of fear in David when he was obviously overpowered.

Charlie released David and allowed him to get up off the ground.

David turned to Charlie, the audience of boys looking on, and thrust his outstretched finger in Charlie's direction. "You just wait you motherfucker. When you're asleep tonight, I'm going to get an axe and cut your fucking head off!"

"I'll be waiting friend. Just be careful, cause I wouldn't want to see you get hurt. Just because I think you and I are really going to get to like each other."

Charlie realized, as he watched David withdraw into the darkness of the camp, that he had weathered the first storm. Returning to his seat on the bench, which seemed to have grown since his sudden departure, he concentrated his full efforts on maintaining a semblance of composure.

"Hi, I'm Jerry. Old David, he sure got what he deserved. That dude is always screwin with somebody," came a small voice from near Charlie.

Charlie turned toward the voice. The first impression he formed of the boy was that of a small, scared animal. Jerry carefully watched his peers while he lavished praise on Charlie in a low, confidential tone. He was much smaller than the majority of the others, probably five-foot-two and one-hundred pounds, with the slim figure of a boy. The breadth of manhood which could already be discerned in several of the others was absent in this one. His small, thin hands were naturally drawn to his face as his fingernails were to his teeth. The nails had been chewed down, leaving red and decimated fingertips. His tinkling laugh delighted the listener with its simple charm, but was boxed in by a wariness which strangled all ease and spontaneity out of his personality.

"You'd better be careful though. These guys mean business. They never screw with me though, they know better," continued Jerry.

The incongruity of the remark's issuing forth from such a defenseless form immediately set Charlie on guard. He studied the boy carefully, wondering how best to proceed.

"Well, I'm glad to hear you can take care of yourself," said Charlie.

"Oh sure, you don't have to worry about me." Jerry jumped slightly when one of the larger boys walked behind him and thumped him on the head. The bravado rapidly left his voice. "That's Roy, he's just kiddin' around is all."

Charlie saw Jerry, from the first moments of their acquaintance, as a frightened boy, a youngster surrounded by forces which continually threatened his well being and from which there were few places to hide. It was obvious that his physical powers were no match for the others'. He relied instead on other shields. Manipulation, assisted by a studied insight into others strengths and weaknesses, helped him to survive. He was a miniature con man, a liar, hustler, and smooth talker.

"You got a cigarette?" said Jerry. "I had one but fuckin Roy took it from me. He's always fuckin around with me. And by the way, if you hear any of those guys telling you things about me, don't believe it. It ain't true."

"Like what?" said Charlie as he scrutinized Jerry's small, ferret-like features. A dapper golf cap was perched at a slightly cocked angle over his left eye.

"Oh, nothing really, you know, just the kind of crap these assholes talk about."

"Kissin ass, huh? Rat fucker can't be here five minutes he's already suckin up to some counselor," jeered a black boy across the table. He had been surreptitiously observing the scene in front of him.

"Screw you Chuck, I can say whatever I want. Besides, I was just being friendly. It's none of your business anyway."

"It will be my business if I come over there and bust you in the mouth, you little rat, fuckin asshole."

"See what I mean Charlie? These guys are always looking for trouble."

"Yeah Dino, what the fuck you doin rattin on David? Just cause he's not here to kick your little ass. You better just keep your mouth shut or I'll do it for you," yelled a burly young man with a tough fighter's scowl hidden under his hood. Charlie recognized him as Jerry's previous tormentor.

"That's just Roy again, he's always calling me Dino or Rat. Usually it's rat. Dino's not bad, but rat." Jerry edged close to Charlie.

"What did you say rat?" yelled Roy.

Roy moved around the end of the picnic table, avoiding a pass by Charlie, and headed like a bull for Jerry. Jerry cast a succession of wary glances to his rear as Roy approached. Charlie sat rigid, unsure of his part in the imminent encounter. Roy dealt the cowering boy a resounding slap on the back of his head. Roy's actions spoke of a quick and sure retribution for all implied or overt attacks on his character. His sloping forehead descended into a pair of deep-set eyes, which were punctuated by a broad, fleshy nose. A rock-like jaw jutted forward, framed by a pair of elongated sideburns. They had been allowed to grow into a curly mat that spilled over his jaw and down his neck.

A second blow, harder than the first, landed squarely on the back of Jerry's head. Jerry sat hunched over the table, edging cautiously toward the protection of Charlie.

"Rattin again, huh Dino. I guess I'm gonna have to teach you another lesson, you little fucker," said Roy.

Roy grabbed Jerry viciously by the hair in an effort to remove him from his position at the table. The small boy refused to release his hold on the edge. Charlie jumped up with a sudden jerk and carefully but forcefully shoved Roy to the side.

"Leave him alone. If you want to pick on somebody, pick on somebody your own size," said Charlie, standing with his back to Jerry and the rest of the table.

Charlie quickly found himself warding off a frontal attack from Roy. The two combatants slammed into the table and rolled over into the dirt. Their fighting styles were similar: go for the throat, close in, no punches, just sheer strength, shoulder to shoulder, grunting and trying to gain control by finding that weak spot, that loose leg or arm which could be turned to the other's advantage.

Charlie and Roy tumbled their way to the edge of the campground and rolled down a steep incline, crashing into a tree at the bottom in a tangled heap of arms and legs. The two gladiators lay silent, Roy gripped in Charlie's iron-tight headlock, waiting for the last surges of aggression to pass.

Charlie could never remember a time when he hadn't had to fight; it seemed to be a part of his nature—either he attracted violence or it attracted him. He had grown up fighting his older brothers and had gone from there to the resident bully in each subsequent year of school. Contrary to the hostility which he attracted, his innermost nature recoiled at the thought of injuring anyone else. His fighting skills were geared towards subduing violence in lieu of inflicting injury.

Bud too had a few opportunities to establish his rank in the pecking order. In Charlie's estimate, he was much cooler and smoother in the process. He was no less convincing, however, for there was a sinister presence in his overall appearance and demeanor which quelled many a fight prior to its conception.

Bud gave Charlie a concerned, questioning look as they passed each other on the way to their tents for the night.

"So much for the first night. Get a good night's rest Charlie, you look like you could use it," said Bud.

Charlie crawled head first into his pup tent, set up on the outer perimeter of the camp, and zipped the nylon screen behind him. He lay in his sleeping bag, assailed by guilt and self-castigation. Was he a fool, an idiot? Was he was acting worse than the kids, rolling around in the dirt, fighting teenage boys? What had come over him?

His conscience accused and judged him. It was the combined voice of all the judges he had known in his life: parents, teachers, priests, peers—whoever it was that at the time felt they had the right to tell him what was best for him. These voices attacked the citadel of his self, that island within where he was able to justify all things to himself. On certain occasions, powerful currents of doubt tore at the shores of this sanctuary and threatened to undermine its very existence.

Charlie accepted his capacity for self-analysis and self-criticism as a vital function. It was essential to the growth process, for without it there would exist no check and balance, no avoidance of the same error twice. The problem arose, however, in what precisely constituted this corrective function. It was a dilemma that everyone faced, Charlie realized in a brief moment of clarity—who is to say what is right. Some relegate this responsibility quite readily to more institutionalized and dogmatic sources: church, society, parents, television, school, employers. Charlie had come to suspect, as he had compiled evidence through the years, that these so called authorities often as not were selling a shoddy brand of merchandise which seldom withstood the pressure of intense scrutiny. It was, as Socrates so aptly revealed, a curious penchant of mankind to forego the more time consuming and arduous task of employing one's powers of inquiry when there were others available who offered prepackaged formulas for all occasions. Fate had bestowed the malady of the empiricist on him. Perhaps it wasn't fate but learning which had bred the compulsion. He recalled desolate periods when his soul had wandered, lost on the arid terrain of self-reliance when he would have gladly welcomed any cup bearing the nectar of truth.

Charlie turned again, seeking the comfort of sleep, when a familiar scene came to his mind.

He was standing on the flight of stairs in his grandmother's house, looking through the railing. His father was backing out the front door, pulling it closed.

"Daddy, where you goin, can I come?"

"Not this time Charlie."

"Would you buy me some bubble gum?"

"Sure Charlie. You be a good boy now and I'll bring it right back."

"Right back" turned into four years. Accordingly, Charlie's tough self-reliance was bred, and his cynicism blossomed throughout the years.

Charlie's tossing and turning gradually died down and finally subsided sometime after midnight. His doubts became less pronounced as he carefully reviewed the other, less violent options for dealing with the boys' wild behavior and rejected them all one by one. He concluded that this band of boys had strict rules of conduct of their own. Their total repudiation of society's ethics left a vacuum which they filled with their own code—namely the law of the jungle.

Charlie wondered how Duane would have handled the situation. He was the lucky one who had left on vacation only hours before the boys' arrival. Mr. Johnson too had departed. He thought it best for the counselors and the boys to get to know each other with the minimum amount of distracting influences. The counselor who had driven the boys up had also left with Johnson. He had appeared under the weather and had been anxious to bid the boys farewell. The stage had been set for the debacle that had followed.

Then there was the mystery of the missing boy, for Charlie had been told that there were to be ten. He had counted only nine. He would have to ask Johnson about it in the morning.

In the solitude of his tent, Charlie hoped the worst was over. He ached in every joint and his ankle was swelling again. He reached inside his sleeping bag to assess the damage and winced with pain. Charlie stared up at the roof of the tent and began to fall asleep. On the border of the dream world, just before the last light of consciousness faded, a shadowy figure towered over his bed. Charlie's strength deserted him and as he was unable to move, the axe descended. Before the axe cut bone, Charlie was awakened by his own muffled screams.

CHAPTER IV

The Killer

The crushing weight of the boy's body sitting astride his chest kept him pinned to the ground. The boy was too big too heavy to move and he felt the hatred well up inside. He wanted to kill this boy his rat-faced meanness taunting him. He felt his will rise hard as iron. His eyes burned with the desire to destroy this fiend this neighborhood bully who fed on the frailest and youngest of the packs of wild children running through the back alleys and side streets of the city. "Fat Johnny" was what all the kids called him at least until he caught them and tortured them at will. At this particular moment he had succeeded in capturing his latest and until now his most elusive quarry. The pretty boy, the blonde headed foster kid from down the block had been hard to catch, too fast and too smart especially for eight years old. Fat Johnny had used all available means in his efforts to corral this little shit this thorn in his side but none had worked not until now that had all changed thanks to the boy's foster dad who wanted the boy toughened up and even suggested to Johnny that he was the one to do it.

The helpless boy had a shower of curls defining the contours of his face. He was almost as pretty as a girl but he had the vocabulary of a drug addict searching for his stolen stash. "Fuck you, you motherfucking cocksucker. When I get up I am going to kill you." Fat Johnny just laughed. The boy struggled under him as Johnny pulled the pliers from his back pocket. Blondie's' threats subsided suddenly as he focused on the rusty tool the terror of every kid in the neighborhood. These pliers had done more damage to more kids than any of their parents had done. It wasn't that the injuries were life threatening as some injuries sustained by way of parents or foster parents or step parents could be but they did permanent damage. "Fat Johnny" was never satisfied with injuries which healed and could not be detected after weeks or months. He wanted permanent evidence of his handiwork of his power. His cruelty was broadcast by mangled earlobes, disjointed fingers and scarred flesh where pieces had been pulled out with these same pliers now taunting the cherubic countenance suddenly quieted by the promise of pain.

Fat Johnny, his weight firmly planted on the boy's chest and his arms pinned beneath his knees, took his time. He used the tool to trace lines around his victim's nose then his mouth where it hesitated before it was inserted inside his top lip where the jaws closed on soft flesh. At first almost gently and then as the victim failed to call out to scream for his mother his father for God the torturer closed the jaws on yielding flesh and twisted and pulled until the lip tore and the once straight lines of the mouth hung flapping. The tear reminded Johnny of his torn jeans caught on a nail the denim hanging sadly in a triangular plea for help. Later Fat Johnny would have nightmares about this boy who failed to cry out but only stared vacantly ahead through his torturer. If he had known the hate that he had unleashed by that act he would have stayed clear of the blonde boy but how could he know the boy was so young.

When the boy arrived home this foster dad was sitting in the small living room surrounded by empty beer bottles and dressed only in his boxer shorts. He would sit there night after night drunk his private parts audaciously exposed to whoever glanced his direction. "Where you been faggot" he inquired as the boy, holding his lip together with his fingers walked stealthily past the time bomb he was told to call "Dad". He called him faggot because he thought he looked like a girl with slight features and a slim frame. His current "Dad" had been the neighborhood bully when he was young. He knew how to fight how to hurt to deliver pain. He could smell fear, all but his own fear of death of being nobody a nothing. The boys' silence mocked him. He grabbed his arm as he passed and twisted it behind his back into an impossible angle. His lip dripped blood on the worn carpet. "What the fuck, what happened to you faggot boy. Did you get your ass kicked again? You are a worthless piece of shit almost nine and you don't know how to fight. You make me look bad. I won't have a kid living in my house that is nothing but a pussy. I will not stand for that" The boys arm twisted into a vicious curve sent wracking bursts of pain through his shoulder until he all but forgot about the lip but he did not call out he did not cry.

Blondie knew pain. There was times when it was his best friend his only friend. He could always rely on it to be there. It never deserted him. It had followed him from foster family to foster family. It never came in the same way or size but it always attacked his mind sought to steal his sanity. Its gift was "hate". He could use this gift to forget the pain to pursue his desire to hurt to return the pain to watch others cry out to beg to bleed. It was his only lifeline to sanity to not being lost in the vast unknown of psychosis.

He would sit often alone in some dark corner of his current residence and recall his retribution his reckoning. He never forgot an injury a slight and he always, after that time with "Fat Johnny", retaliated. It may have not been immediately for the boy was patient he learned at a very young age the value of strategically waiting for there would always be an opportunity to strike back not with equal force but with the force of the devil. He carefully nurtured his hate and used it to clear his mind to focus his anger to plan his revenge. It fueled his young life gave him strength promised hope.

After the Fat Johnny episode he always carried a weapon something easily concealed and not necessarily recognized as an object of destruction. A toothbrush sharpened on the end was his favorite. He became friends with fire, a useful ally easily carried quickly discarded. He carried a book of matches at all times. He first experimented with it when he captured Fat Johnnie's scraggly cat taped its paws together and set it on fire on Johnnie's front stoop. They never suspected him when he was young it was only as he grew older that they looked more carefully at the coincidence of foul play and his proximity to the horror. The never ending transition from foster families helped to mask his tendencies but even his movement was not enough as he got older.

It wasn't until the busboy at the restaurant observed him setting Fat Johnny on fire while he lay recovering from drinking a pint of whiskey which he found half empty behind the restaurant in the alley. It was serendipitous that the boy walking by the entry to the alley glimpsed his nemesis lying helpless in the alleyway. He did not hesitate but without a second thought he approached him emptied the remains of the bottle on the boys clothing and set him afire. He was thinking about this as he placed the lighter carefully in the mare's nose and lit it. The same emotionless smile blossomed on his scarred lip as it had when he watched "Fat Johnny" burst into flames. The thought calmed him even as the horse screeched and bolted into the night.

CHAPTER V

The campers were greeted Saturday morning by the sounds of squirrels quarrelling in the treetops. Their incessant chatter signaled turmoil in the lower levels of the animal kingdom. Responding to the treetop alarm, Charlie listened carefully for the more complex sounds of his own species. Unable to distinguish any, he ventured a peek out the front of his tent.

The scene outside was peaceful, in stark contrast to the previous night's drama. Bud sat in thoughtful repose at the picnic table, his torso curved over his coffee cup and his forearms resting heavily on the table top, encircling his morning brew.

Charlie had noticed other men, usually those cut from a rough cloth, assume the same position. It reminded him of a bear hovering over a freshly killed salmon, warning all intruders to stay clear.

Charlie dragged himself out of his tent and stretched to rid his body of the insomnia-induced lethargy. His blue jeans and T-shirt were stained with spotty patches of blood. His hair was disheveled and in dire need of washing. Dark circles hung under his eyes, accentuated by the pallor of his face.

The campground was littered with the bodies of young boys contorted in every conceivable position. They slept under the bus, on the hood of the bus, under the picnic table, and wherever they had crashed the previous night. Various articles of the boys clothing lay strewn next to them.

Charlie approached Bud's smiling form.

"Good morning Charlie. You look like you kept vigil last night for axe murderers rather than getting any sleep."

Charlie thought Bud looked positively refreshed.

"Well, I have to admit that the thought did cross my mind from time to time. I trust you didn't have to abort any attempts during the night," said Charlie through a sleepy haze.

"No, I didn't. But David and I got together last night, late after everyone else had given up the ship and had ourselves a little talk. I think it really helped him. I think he's basically a good kid, smart and grown up in his own way."

Paternal concern came over Bud's face as he began to relay his meeting with David.

"The boy, like all of them, has had a hard time of it. He's only fifteen and they've had him locked up in one sort of institution or another on and off for seven years. He didn't say much about his parents. In fact, now that I think about it he didn't say anything. I noticed when he took off his shirt after your little tussle that he has a scar that runs from his shoulder blade down below his belt line and son-of-a-gun if it doesn't cover half his back. I asked him about it and he said he got in a gang fight. Said he was hit by a Molotov cocktail. He suffered third degree burns over half his body. After our talk last night, I think, or at least I hope, you'll see some better manners."

"Well, I didn't like doing what I did, but something had to be done. I want to survive too. If I'm in charge, then I guess I better take charge."

Charlie felt relief as he was presented with his first opportunity to talk to someone about last night.

"I guess you know I couldn't help you last night. With these guys you're definitely on your own," said Bud. "By the way, we better start thinking about organizing everyone today. Johnson will be out later and we need to get showers some place, and food, and generally start tightening up right from the start."

Thank God for Bud, Charlie thought, as the contemplation of a hot shower cleared his head.

The camp, now that it was almost fully populated, was in dire need of organization. Bud and Charlie spent the morning tending to the myriad details required for supplying the basic necessities.

Cooking and cleaning were in themselves major activities. All food was cooked over the campfire. The intricacies of starting and maintaining a fire required gathering the appropriate kindling and wood from the surrounding area. Stoking the fire until it reached the optimum level for cooking came next. It was a skill that would be perfected only after much practice. The fire pit was built on the ground and enclosed by rocks placed around the perimeter. A wire mesh was placed on the top of this structure to form a cooking surface for pots and pans.

All the basic utensils normally used in the kitchen were also used at the campsite and at the end of each meal they all required washing. Water had to be carried from the lone spigot at the front of the campground and heated until it was a suitable temperature for removing the remains of sausage and eggs from the dinnerware.

The cooking, eating, and washing exercise expended a full two hours. Pairs were established, including Charlie and Bud, with each having responsibility for the preparation, planning, and clean up of every meal for a week. Sundays were transition days when the next pair would assume the drudgery for their week.

Johnson arrived with a truckload of clothing, adequate enough for each boy to have three changes. They had arrived at Lake of the Pines with only the clothes they had on. New sleeping bags were distributed in addition to quantities of toilet articles, including soap, toothpaste, tooth brushes, and combs or picks, whichever the boys preferred.

Everything considered, it was a full Saturday morning, and as Charlie was soon to find out, the afternoon promised even more excitement.

It was shortly before one o'clock when Charlie heard the first screams issue from the interior of the school bus, accompanied by a torrent of swears. Danny, a curly headed boy whom Charlie had remembered meeting briefly the night before, ran out the front door of the bus and into Charlie.

Blood flowed down Danny's face and neck and onto his shirt collar. His tears and trembling form presented a picture of a hopeless victim after a vicious attack.

Danny's tormentors arrived quick on his trail, colliding with Danny and Charlie at the front of the bus.

"All right, what's going on here? Back off Vince, keep your hands off him. I want to know what's happening," said Charlie.

"The little fart stole my bugler and he won't tell us where he hid it!" said Vince.

"Yeah, I saw him rolling a cigarette about an hour ago and I know he didn't have any tobacco of his own, and when we went to look for ours it was gone. The little creep stole it and he's going to pay or else," said Keith, the other boy.

Charlie turned his attention to Keith, momentarily dropping his guard over Danny. Vince shoved forward and slugged Danny in the face. The blow unleashed another flood of blood and tears.

Charlie quickly pushed Danny behind him. He reached in and grabbed Vince by the shirt and threw him out of the bus.

Vince landed near the remains of the morning's campfire. No sooner had he hit the ground than he was up and armed with a cudgel-like stick snatched from the unused kindling.

Vince stalked toward Danny. Charlie stood braced for the attack as Danny cowered close behind him. Keith stood motionless in the doorway.

Vince rushed Charlie. Charlie ducked and the weapon smashed into the side of the bus. On its backstroke the weapon caught Charlie a glancing blow on his shoulder. The pain sliced to the bone.

Vince made for Danny, who was attempting to squeeze under the bus. Regaining his balance, Charlie threw himself on Vince's back and wrenched the stick free from his hands. Charlie jerked Vince around by his shoulders, grabbing two handfuls of his shirt, and slammed him hard against the bus. Vince stood struggling as his feet dangled off the ground.

"I'm going to kill that little bastard, you wait and see," said Vince.

"I didn't take your bugler," Danny whimpered from under the front wheel of the bus. "I never saw your damn bugler. You can ask Sherman, he knows."

Charlie kept Vince pinned against the bus as Keith looked on from inside.

"Keith, get Sherman, tell him I want to see him, right now," Charlie ordered in a razor-edged tone. His hard gaze ground into Vince, who struggled to free himself.

Charlie had only briefly met these three boys the previous night. It had become obvious that Vince, the boy who dangled at arms length, had acquired at some point in his short life a wild, hair-trigger temper. This attribute looked to be common to all these young men. Vince's face was hidden under a mass of thick hair which hung over his ears. A red bandana encircled his forehead, Apache-style. The boy's character suggested a young Indian brave whose dreams were full of hunting buffalo and scalping white men. His frame was well-defined and muscular. The young man appeared to own only a pair of pants, for he had worn neither shirt nor shoes since arriving at camp.

Keith presented a somewhat different picture. He was taller than Vince and could look Charlie level in the eyes. His large, hawk-like nose overshadowed a pair of narrowly spaced eyes. His appearance was not one of strength, for baby fat and a general lack of definition curtailed any such image. Excitability and a quick intelligence were his most readily identifiable traits, as well as an affinity for the sound of his own voice, which he preferred more than any other. Like Jerry, Keith was a natural born salesman mixed with a dash of a "momma's boy".

Charlie's attention was drawn to little Danny, still under the wheel of the bus, a head shorter than the others and worlds apart in experience. Danny's overall appearance brought to mind the fattened lamb thrown among the wolves. His entire defense mechanism consisted of tears and the ability to elicit sympathy and appeal to the higher emotions of mutual protection existing in the group. Even Jerry, the most diminutive of the group, could intimidate Danny.

Charlie lowered Vince to the stoop of the bus, admonishing him to keep still as he noticed Keith striding towards them with Sherman in tow. Sherman, like Roy, was powerfully built. He walked with a lopsided gait, first tilting to the left then the right.

"What you want? I ain't done nothing', I didn't steal nobody's tobacco. What you want with me?" said Sherman.

Charlie fixed his attention on Sherman. "Danny here says you can prove that he didn't steal Vince and Keith's bugler. He says you know something about the cigarette he was rolling this morning."

"That fucker stole my tobacco and I'm gonna kick his ass!" Vince said from his guarded position on the step of the bus.

"Cool it Vince. Let Sherman help us clear this up. Danny, you can come out from under the bus. Come on now and wipe that blood off your nose," said Charlie.

"Well yeah, I let Danny have some of my tobacco this morning, if that's what you mean. That's all I know about it, though Vince and Keith probably smoked all theirs up and just want some freebies," said Sherman.

"Shut up nigger, nobody asked you," said Vince.

"You're the one better shut up Vince, or I'll pop you one upside the head," said Sherman.

Vince and Sherman began to square off.

"Alright tough guys, stay cool or I'll knock both your heads together," said Charlie. "Now I want you guys, all of you—Keith, Danny, Sherman, and you too Vince—to know from now on that you are all responsible for your own stuff, tobacco included. This isn't kindergarten. If you think somebody's gonna steal your stuff, then you better put it where they can't. If you know for sure that someone did take something of yours, then you let me know. I don't want you beating up on each other, got it?"

The group of boys huddled around the door of the bus reluctantly nodded and assented.

"Alright, now try to be good little boys and not hit each other before dinner. And Vince, I don't want to see you picking on Danny, or else," said Charlie.

"Or else what," Vince spat through gritted teeth.

"Or else you'll find out! Now go amuse yourselves."

The boys drifted away, mumbling profanities and casting back contemptuous glances.

Danny and Charlie remained at the front of the bus. A satisfied grin had replaced Danny's frightened countenance.

"You all right partner? How's that nose? Looks like you might have a bit of a shiner there come tonight," said Charlie. His sympathy reached out for the small boy.

"Oh, it'll be all right. Those guys just like beating up on me 'cause I'm little. They wouldn't do that to Sherman."

Charlie was wiping the blood off Danny's face when Bud approached. He motioned Charlie to one side.

"You know, I haven't seen Russ all morning," said Bud. "I asked around and it doesn't seem like anyone knows anything about him. Even Vince, who he pals around with, says he saw him take off towards the lake this morning right after breakfast but hasn't seen him since."

Charlie tried to picture the missing boy. "What do you think happened? You think he ran away?"

"I don't know."

Bud looked toward the camp entrance. A brown and white squad car, a park police unit, pulled into the campsite and came to a dusty halt.

"Looks like trouble," said Bud.

"Sure does," said Charlie.

The ranger exited his vehicle. He approached Bud and Charlie, surveying the scattered clothes and the group of ragamuffin boys.

"Hi, how you all doin'? I'd like to have a word with whoever's in charge here," said the ranger.

"We're in charge," said Bud, motioning to Charlie as they both braced themselves for the ranger's inquiries.

"These all your kids here? Have they all been here all day?"

"Yes, as far as we know. They just arrived last night and we're in the process of getting ourselves squared away," said Bud.

"It just so happens that a campsite about a half mile from here was broken into a couple of hours ago," the ranger began as he motioned the two men towards the privacy of his patrol car. "Whoever broke in either had a strange sense of humor or is disturbed."

"What do you mean?" said Charlie.

"The tent itself was sliced from the back and entered. The couple, who have a young daughter about ten years old with them, were out with her at the time fishing."

The three men drew in close.

"All the women's underwear, panties to be more specific, had been smeared with peanut butter and jelly and strewn over the tent's floor. The only other thing which was touched was the child's doll, which had a knife inserted between its legs."

The ranger cleared his throat.

"Now, I'm not sure who did it or why. But I'll tell you one thing, it sure scared the hell out of that couple. The reason I'm here is that your campsite is the only other one occupied, other than the one broken into. I would appreciate it if you would let me know if you hear anything."

The ranger cast a scowl in the boys' direction. "No harm meant, but that's a rough looking bunch of kids you got there. Make sure you keep a close eye on them. We don't like trouble around here."

"Thank you officer, and you can be sure we'll let you know if we hear anything," said Bud as the ranger got into his car.

Bud and Charlie watched the ranger pull out of camp. They stood in silence, gauging the gravity of the situation.

"Sounds to me like we better find out what happened to our friend Russ. As far as I can see, everyone else seems to be accounted for," said Bud. He studied his partner's response to the first sign of real trouble which had visited the camp.

"You don't think he had anything to do with that, do you?" said Charlie.

"I don't know, but I do know we better find him as soon as we can."

"Alright, why don't we break into pairs, take different directions, and see what we can come up with."

"Sounds good to me. Let's get going."

Bud and Charlie began the process of organizing search teams.

Vince and Keith, Sherman and Danny, Jerry and Roy, Bud and David, and Charlie and Chuck headed in different directions. The search parties agreed to meet back at the camp in two hours with or without Russ. Charlie had chosen Chuck randomly, the urgency of the situation dictating his choice.

Charlie's selection proved fortunate, as Chuck was the only youth whom he had yet to become acquainted with. Chuck was a wiry-haired boy, lean, gangly, and second only to Keith in height. Since his arrival at camp, he had managed to avoid disharmony with the counselors and the other boys. He was well-liked and respected among the others.

During the search, Charlie maintained an increasingly self-conscious place beside the quiet boy, seeking an excuse to break the ice. In contrast to the boisterousness of the others, Chuck seemed to display a shyness and reserve which kept his personality hidden.

Charlie observed his companion, feeling drawn to his melancholy countenance.

"Where you from Chuck?" said Charlie in an attempt to bring the boy out of his silence.

"New Orleans," said Chuck in a deep baritone.

"Got any relatives there?"

"Just my mother."

"You see her much?"

"No, haven't seen her in three years." Chuck lowered his eyes.

The two continued their search in silence, heading northeast. They crossed a series of dry stream beds filled with fallen leaves, the first signs of an early autumn. A crow flew overhead, calling out a warning, and nearby a pair of quarreling squirrels scampered up a tree.

"How long are we gonna stay camping here?" said Chuck softly.

"Three or four weeks I guess. Then we'll be moving out to our permanent campsite."

"They have any TV out there? I sure do miss having a TV."

"No, I'm afraid they don't. At this point there's nothing out there but trees, animals, and a lot of imagination." Charlie smiled.

"You mean there's no 'lectricity?"

"Not only no electricity, but at this point no water, toilet, or place to sleep or eat other than under a tree."

"Don't sound like much fun to me." Chuck shook his head as he kicked a stone from his path.

"Oh it'll be great. You guys don't even have to go to school. And when we get settled we're gonna take some trips, wherever we decide to go."

"You mean we can go anywhere we want?"

"That's right." Charlie detected a note of enthusiasm in Chuck's voice.

"You think maybe we could go to New Orleans and see my mama?" Chuck looked up at Charlie.

"Well, you never know Chuck, you just never know."

Charlie checked the watch he had borrowed from Keith. It was time to rendezvous back at camp. The pair had had no luck finding Russ, nor had they encountered anyone else on their long walk. Mr. Johnson did know how to pick isolated spots, Charlie mused, as he and Chuck walked back to camp.

Charlie and Chuck were the last pair to return to camp. Russ had been found. He sat next to Bud on the picnic bench, his head hanging down blonde curls defining his face. His hands were clutched tightly between his knees and his eyes were fixed on the tabletop.

Bud quietly studied Russ, his features expressing a desire to reach out and help the boy.

"So you found him huh? Where was he?" said Charlie, gazing at Russ.

"They found him up in a tree, Vince and Keith did. Seems like Vince is quite the tracker. Didn't take him anytime to find him."

"What were you doing up in a tree Russ?" said Charlie, surprising himself with the irritable tone he detected in his voice.

"Just sittin," Russ muttered, his eyes still glued to the tabletop.

"Well we were warned about you, thought maybe you'd run away."

"Would have if I'd known where to go."

Charlie turned to Bud. "Did you ask him about the break in at the campsite?" Charlie felt a tension in his chest.

"No, not yet, haven't had much luck getting him to talk. Took us a while to talk him down out of the tree. He must have been sitting up there for hours."

Russ maintained his study of the table top, his self-defiance heightened by Charlie's growing irascibility.

The two counselors eyed Russ curiously.

"You didn't happen to be around anybody else's campsite today, did you Russ?" said Charlie, attempting to control his virulence.

Russ removed his eyes from the tabletop for the first time since Charlie's arrival and raised them to meet Charlie's. "No, I haven't," he said gruffly.

"Good, I'm glad to hear that," said Charlie. "And now that we are on the subject, I want to make one point perfectly clear. As long as I'm your counselor, I'm going to believe what you tell me. I'm going to assume that you're telling me the truth. But if I find out that you've lied to me, then neither you nor I are going to be very happy." Charlie's earnestness was not to be doubted. "You all understand that? I want the truth, no matter what. You tell me the truth and I'll tell you the truth. OK?"

The boys nodded reluctantly and gathered around Bud and Charlie.

"Once we get to know each other and understand the rules, I think we're going to have a lot of fun. At least we're going to try," said Charlie. He moved his gaze over the circle of faces and his heart pained at the vacant, distrustful looks.

CHAPTER VI

Dusk cast its long shadows far into the surrounding woods. The last breezes of the day swept through the willows down by the lake.

Bud and Charlie prepared the evening meal. The smell of frying hamburgers drifted into the waiting nostrils of the boys scattered aimlessly about the camp. Keith, Vince, and Roy lounged in the bus, absorbed in the comic adventures of The Hulk, Spiderman, and Captain America.

Chuck, Sherman, Russ, and Jerry stationed themselves at the table, where they debated the exchange value of a ready-roll versus a roll-your-own smoke. The boys lined up their painstakingly acquired caches of Winstons and Marlboros in front of them. The less desirable stimulants, the Bugler and Kite loose tobaccos, were kept off to one side. These brands were still cherished, but not held in as high a regard as the Marlboros and Winstons. Money changed hands, cigarettes changed hands, and the boys smiled at their about-to-be-appeased nicotine hankerings.

David and Danny lingered at the edge of the campsite, drawn to the activity of the two counselors. Dinner consisted of hamburgers on a bun, potato chips, corn, and Kool-Aid to wash it down. The boys' applause of smacking lips rewarded the chefs' efforts as the meal disappeared in only a fraction of the time it had taken to prepare.

Charlie watched the clan huddled around the table. The boys stuffed, shoved, prodded, and cajoled food into their mouths. Grunts and burps announced their satisfaction. Bits of food flew from their mouths as they tore off large chunks of bread and meat. Shirt sleeves were used to wipe faces and hands. David and Sherman seemed to be the only ones who displayed some degree of civilized manners.

Charlie's eyes strayed from the feast to the school bus which stood waiting to accommodate. It was a 1964 Ford school bus, the twelve passenger model. In its present position it served multiple functions, as game room, private consulting office, bunkhouse, library, and the group's sole means of interaction with the outside world. The interior consisted of six equally spaced, two-passenger, green-vinyl-covered, straight-backed seats. Personal items ranging from cigarette lighters to safari hats lay scattered throughout the interior.

As he scrutinized its weather-beaten exterior, Charlie hoped the bus was reliable.

An anguished cry broke the air. Charlie spun around. Bud was racing towards the campfire, where two boys stood framed against the leaping flames. One boy lay rolling on the ground while the other, who looked to be Russ, hovered over him. The erect figure gripped a metal bow saw used for cutting fire wood, holding it high above his head with both hands.

Charlie bolted from the table close on Bud's heels. Bud grabbed the saw from Russ' hands as Charlie restrained the raving boy from behind. Keith convulsed in agony on the ground. His free hand sought to comfort the searing pain at his shoulder. Bud, loosening his hold on the assailant, went to the aid of the suffering victim.

Bud removed Keith's hand from his shoulder. A burn some eight inches long sizzled with the odor of seared flesh.

"What the hell happened?" Bud shouted, looking from Keith to Russ.

"The fucker called me a fag!" said Russ. "He said I was a fucking queer and I'd like to taste what he had to offer, so I burned him. Took that saw, heated it up real nice and hot, and burned that ass."

The two men remained speechless, realizing for the first time the true potential for violence that lay within the boys.

Bud broke the silence and began to doctor Keith's wound with the contents from the first-aid kit. He bandaged the injured shoulder and administered painkillers to make the night easier.

Russ was warned that any further outbursts were going to bring Bud and Charlie's combined wrath down on his head. Charlie sent him to the bus for the night. Russ resisted, but finally conceded after an exchange of virulent gestures and dialogue.

Charlie's head throbbed as he tromped toward Bud's tent, which was set up on the far end of the campsite, at the point farthest away from the road. He groped in the dark for the entrance to the tent.

Charlie entered the tent, ducking his head. He rested his eyes on Bud, who was seated alongside Keith. Keith lay on an army cot against the back wall of the tent, moaning softly.

"How is he? Is it bad?" said Charlie, studying the prone boy while keeping his voice low.

"Well, he'll be around for a few more years, but for the next few days anyway he's gonna have one hell of a sore shoulder," Bud said in a calm voice. "What did you do with Russ?"

"I didn't know what to do exactly. I did try to let him know that as long as we're counselors that crap isn't gonna fly around here. I wanted to kick his ass from here to Dallas though, I will confess that."

Feet shuffled outside. Roy and Danny eased inside the tent. They nervously eyed Charlie, then Bud, then their injured friend.

"We thought Keith might like a couple of cigarettes, might help the pain a little," Roy said with a solemn expression.

"Yeah, we thought they might help some," said Danny in a more cheerful tone.

"Thank you guys," said Keith, attempting to smile.

Charlie and the boys filed out of Bud's tent, all wishing desperately that they could alleviate Keith's agony. They marched quietly in the knowledge of their helplessness. Each felt guilt at having been fortunate enough to have escaped the pain that Keith felt.

Roy lumbered off toward his nesting spot and said goodnight to the others. Danny continued to silently tag along behind Charlie, who was anxious to reach his tent. The long, difficult day had made him yearn for peace and quiet.

"Charlie," said Danny softly.

Charlie looked at Danny.

"I was wondering if you could help me do something, that is if you aren't going to bed right now, that is," continued Danny.

"Well, I guess that depends on what it is sport," said Charlie mechanically.

"I was just wondering if you could help me write a letter to my brother? I can't write too good, and I sure would like to write him!"

Danny's plea overcame Charlie's resistance. "I suppose that could be arranged. You get the paper and pencil and I'll do the writing. Is that a deal?"

"That's great, I'll be right back," Danny blurted out joyously. He made his way toward the bus and bounded inside, waking several of the sleeping boys. Danny rifled through his belongings and found a pencil and paper.

The excited boy flopped down on the picnic table beside Charlie. The surface of the table was illuminated by a Coleman Lantern.

"Partner, you just tell me what you want to say and I'll put pen to paper for you," said Charlie. "Fire away."

"Dear Dave. My brother's name is Dave and he's in the Navy. He used to take me everywhere with him. Dear Dave, I miss you and mom, especially you though. Do you think the Navy would let you come and see me? I live in the woods now and boy is it fun. I've already seen a raccoon and a opossum, and Russ, one of the boys here, found a nest of baby flying squirrels right in our campsite, they are so cute. Maybe I could come see you too. I love you. Signed, Danny Boy."

Danny smiled with love for his brother. "Danny boy, that's what he always called me."

"How long has it been since you've seen your brother Danny?" said Charlie.

"When I was twelve. I'm fourteen now. I wish he was here now though. I think you would really like him. He's a real neat guy. He's a lot like you but he's better looking and stronger."

"Sounds like quite a brother," said Charlie, trying to suppress a chuckle. "How about your mom Danny, where's she at?"

"I don't know exactly. But her boyfriend is a millionaire and when they get married me and my brother are gonna live with them.

She writes me every once in a while, but she never sends an address most of the time, so I can't write back." Danny's eyes filled with tears. He wiped them away with his shirt sleeve. "But Dave and I are gonna go live with her when she gets married. She said we were."

Charlie put his arm around the boy's trembling back and rested his hand on his shoulder. Danny put his face into Charlie's shirt and cried.

Charlie crawled into his pup tent even more exhausted than the night before. His nerves were shattered and he needed someone to talk to. He wished with his whole being that he could pour forth his doubts to Bud, but his stubborn independence wouldn't permit him to confide in anyone. He knew Bud would listen with an attentive ear, but he preferred keeping his feelings of vulnerability and frustration to himself. He often felt that by admitting these feelings the weakness they represented would take control of his life.

Charlie undressed and prepared his sleeping bag. This was his favorite hour, a time for reflection and introspection. A time to learn from those who had established themselves as truth-seekers. He reached for his books, deciding between "How to Survive in the Woods" and "Thus Spoke Zarathustra." He chose the latter as being the most appropriate for his current situation and settled into the warmth of his sleeping bag.

CHAPTER VII

Dawn broke with a quarter moon still hanging low in the morning sky.

Charlie emerged sluggishly from his tent, desiring to postpone the day's duties as long as possible.

Bud had been up for hours. In solitary contentment he had started a fire and brewed his coffee. He was gazing dreamily into his second cup of coffee when Charlie approached.

"Morning, how's the patient today?" said Charlie.

"Fine. I think, it scared the kid as much as anything else. Although that was one nasty burn," said Bud quickly, as if to shake off the lingering vision of violence.

"What's on the agenda today?" said Charlie. "I'd like to try again to get a shower and into some clean clothes. I know all the boys could use a little scrubbing too. I feel pretty grimy." Charlie groaned.

"Sounds good to me too. Let's say after breakfast we head for Daingerfield, get some showers, and spend the afternoon swimming. Maybe we can catch Mark, Hooper, and Lamar and see what the word is on the arrival of their group."

Bud and Charlie were interrupted by the sound of Mr. Johnson's truck pulling into camp.

"Looks like the boss is checking up on us. I hope we didn't lose anybody during the night," said Charlie. He chuckled half-heartedly. "Well, maybe a couple wouldn't hurt one way or the other."

"Got anybody in particular in mind for eliminating?" said Bud.

The two counselors smiled in mutual understanding.

"Well, I haven't gotten quite that far yet, but I have arrived at one conclusion." Charlie paused, sustaining the suspense.

"What's that?" said Bud, nibbling at the bait.

"I have decided that you can stay." Charlie broke into a belly laugh which was soon shared by Bud.

Johnson approached the counselors. "Sounds like you two are having quite a good time. Seems like I have nothing to worry about after all." Johnson pumped first Bud's then Charlie's hand enthusiastically. "How's everything going? Any major problems? Got everybody accounted for I hope."

"Everything's fine. A few rough spots here and there, but nothing to get worried about," said Bud. "We had a bit of an accident last night, but everything's under control now."

"Yeah, that's cause they're all sleeping," said Charlie.

Bud and Johnson laughed.

"By the way, I thought we were supposed to get ten little rug burners. I only counted nine," Charlie wondered aloud, directing a curious gaze at Johnson.

"You're quite right Charlie. Sorry I couldn't explain the other night, but with taking Duane to the bus depot and everything else going on it just slipped my mind. The ranch tells me our missing boy, Jerome is his name, ran away the morning the bus left. I just got a call from the ranch saying that the sheriff had found him hitchhiking east and that they were going to get him back today. That means we should have him up here by the middle of the week. The second group of boys will also be arriving this Friday."

"What are the plans for getting out to the acreage and starting to build some shelters?" said Charlie. "Feels like fall already."

"Within two weeks I'd like to see a total move out there by both groups and some structures starting to go up." Johnson glanced from one counselor to the other, seeking affirmation from both.

Before either could reply, Johnson was surrounded by five half-clad boys. They pulled and tugged at him, demanding answers and firing a series of requests, complaints, and pleas.

Johnson freed himself from the boys and turned his attention once more to Bud and Charlie. "The way we will work the money is simple. Each group will be given two hundred dollars per week, on which you will purchase everything you require until the following week. The exceptions are for clothing, which will be supplied by me at various intervals, and gasoline, which you will charge using these cards." Johnson passed out gas cards to Bud and Charlie. "You can use the money any way you see fit. All details are left to you and the group to work out, just as long as everyone is fed properly of course."

The basic idea, as Bud and Charlie later agreed, was that a predetermined and unchanging budget would support the group regardless of where they were or what they were doing—whether they were backpacking, canoeing, or merely joy riding. Both men, upon mutual consultation, agreed that the system was workable and that the established budget appeared adequate.

The morning passed swiftly after Johnson's departure. Hooper, Lamar, and Mark arrived in Lamar's pampered '62 VW pop-top minibus. Despite the early hour, all three appeared to be under the influence of some mind-expanding substance. They had ventured from Daingerfield lake to see just what awaited them on Monday, when they would meet their own group of boys.

Hooper and Lamar managed to pull Charlie off to the side for a report on exactly what they could expect. Although Lamar offered a joint, Charlie fought the urge and reluctantly refused, knowing the value of keeping his mind sharp at all times.

Hooper and Lamar brushed off any information about the boys that was less than cheerful.

"Alright Hooper. I guess what you really have to do is see for yourself. Your day's drawing near. Maybe I'm just too shell-shocked to be objective about the situation," said Charlie.

"I'd have to agree with that," said Lamar. "You seem a bit paranoid to me. You sure you haven't already taken a few tokes this morning?" Lamar grinned slyly.

Charlie laughed. "Let's have this same discussion again on Wednesday. I think it'll be more relevant then."

Hooper, Lamar, and Mark departed and promised to meet the others later at Daingerfield.

After Bud and Charlie made the announcement that the day was going to be spent swimming, the boys displayed exemplary self-discipline. David, Roy, and Keith appointed themselves leaders and dictated chores to the others.

The bus rolled into Daingerfield State Park. The group located the showers and the swimming area. Charlie and Bud established the ground rules and released the boys onto the campgrounds.

A few hours later, Charlie noticed David lying alone on a sandy hillside.

"Hey Dave, how's it goin? How come you're not out swimming with the rest of the group?" said Charlie as he lowered himself down on the hill.

"Just checkin out the girls. I don't really feel like getting my hair wet," said David reluctantly, obviously not used to explaining himself.

"Where'd Bud go? I saw him heading back towards the campground." Charlie propped himself up on his elbows and stretched his legs out.

"Danny told him that he saw Keith and Sherman down by the toilets. Guess it was in back of the toilets in the bushes." David hesitated, building suspense. "He said they were taking turns humping some broad. I guess he thought Bud better check it out."

"You must be kiddin!" said Charlie. "We've only been here a couple hours."

Chuck came barreling toward David and Charlie from the direction of the campgrounds. "Charlie Charlie, you better come quick! It's Vince, he fucked up something good!" Chuck fought to catch his breath. He pointed toward the campgrounds. The urgency in his tone made Charlie take a deep breath.

"What the fuck happened!" said Charlie.

"You better come and see for yourself. I think we better run. There's a whole lot of people seem to be pretty mad at him right now."

Charlie and Chuck raced toward the campgrounds. They passed the concession stand and rocketed down the grassy knoll leading to the campsites. Each site was on a secluded section of the lake shore and was fronted by the camp road. The distance to Charlie and Chuck's destination was almost a mile, allowing Charlie sufficient time to imagine various cataclysmic scenarios, all of which involved violence, blood, the police, and jail.

Charlie's stride broke and slowed as he neared the scene. Fifteen to twenty people were gathered around a large RV with the words "Executive Coach" emblazoned on the front.

Vince's voice rose above the crowd that surrounded him. Charlie spotted Bud in the middle. He was attempting to extract Vince from the grip of a park ranger and at least one camper, a beefy, ruddy-faced gentleman intent on administering retribution.

Charlie pushed through the group, gaining a clear view of Vince. He immediately became aware of the boy's forearms. From fingertips to elbows they were covered with what looked very much like cake frosting. Charlie looked to Vince's side. The remains of a large, double-layered birthday cake lay scattered and dismembered near an overturned table.

'What's going on here?" said Charlie, trying to slide into the situation as peacefully as possible.

"It seems as if Vince went and put first one fist and then another through these folk's birthday cake," said Bud, endeavoring to gain control of the moment. "I'm not sure how it happened, but the evidence is pretty damaging." He held up Vince's cake-laden arms.

Charlie detected a sudden flash of amusement beneath Bud's angry features.

"The boy looks guilty to me," said Charlie. A wave of assenting grunts issued from the injured parties. "I think we should reimburse these people for the damages and I think it would appropriate for Vince to make a public apology."

The crowd murmured in consideration.

"I don't know what kind of kid you got here mister, but I think he belongs in reform school, not in the park," said the ranger. He scrutinized first Bud then Charlie then Chuck. "I watched you guys drive up in that old bus and I smelled trouble coming. I'm serving official notice on you right now, that you are banned from the park for one month, and when you do return it will be on probation. Now get the rest of your group together and get out. First though, I want that apology from this kid here."

"Fuck you Smokey the Bear. What do you mean, saying I belong in a reform school?" said Vince.

"Cool it Vince," said Bud, squeezing Vince's arm tightly.

"These people deserve an apology Vince, and I want it now," said Charlie.

"Alright, screw it man. I'm sorry alright, but nobody's gonna tell me about no reform school." Vince cast a look at the ranger.

Vince, Chuck, and the two counselors extricated themselves from the crowd.

"What got into you, doing a foolish thing like that? I mean that makes absolutely no sense at all," said Charlie as they headed back for the beach.

"It was Chuck, man. He bet me two ready rolls that I wouldn't do it. We was just walking by these people, the cake was sitting there nice and pretty like, and Chuck just blurts it out."

"I didn't say you *had* to do it Vince. I just said that if you did…" said Chuck, playing his cards carefully.

"Yeah, well, you called me a chicken shit. What'd you think I was gonna do?"

Vince's motives began to unfold to the counselors. A dare had been made and according to an intricate code it could not be ignored. It was an instance of maintaining reputation and upholding one's position in a bizarre brotherhood. The rules the boys adhered to bore little resemblance to standards recognized by the rest of society.

Charlie wondered during the bus trip back if the boys had always been outcasts, unwanted, with no place to go and no one who cared. He speculated that he was witnessing the inevitable result of a life full of rejection. Or perhaps they were just misfits, beyond help, banished to the woods for the good of society.

The excitement of Sunday afternoon drifted into the monotony of a Monday.

The group made the trip to the Longview K-Mart, thirty miles south of headquarters, to buy food. Chuck and Danny had drawn shopping honors for the week. Charlie accompanied the two boys into the supermarket while the remainder of the gang warmed the bench outside, amusing themselves between the covers of comic books.

Charlie noticed that Chuck had disappeared from the shopping party. Charlie carefully and efficiently searched the aisles, leaving Danny in charge of gathering food.

Rounding the far end of the "spices and canned goods" aisle, Charlie caught sight of Chuck. He stood with his back to Charlie, at the rear of a ravishing brunette. Her shapely form was bent over the soups. Her finely sculptured legs were well-exposed above the knee and were obviously the attraction for the little voyeur. Chuck was standing in an odd position, with his right foot extended towards the woman from behind. Charlie closed upon Chuck and noticed a shiny object fastened to the toe of his boot. It was a mirror, neatly taped in such a way as to allow a revealing perspective of any object positioned directly above it.

Charlie grabbed the boy and yanked him out of his daze.

The gang brought their first mundane chore to a close and started on the second goal of their expedition. On their way out of the campsite they had noticed a secluded Washateria nestled by the roadside. Charlie and Bud entered in the wake of their ragged crew and noticed a dried-up little man leaning forward out of the darkness in a far corner of the room. His features were set in a scowl.

The little man scanned the group carefully. He suddenly burst from the darkness as Chuck and Sherman entered the front door.

"You all can't wash in here," the man screeched.

"What do you mean, we can't wash in here? The sign says Washateria, doesn't it?" said Charlie.

"Yeah, but you didn't read the other sign, that one over there to the right of the door."

The two counselors walked casually to the door and peeked around the corner. They shared a moment of disbelief as they read the bold type.

"No Coloreds Allowed."

"You all," said the man, pointing in the direction away from Chuck and Sherman, "can stay in here, but those two are gonna have to wait outside. And if you give me any trouble I'll call the sheriff."

"What's he mean we can't come inside?" said Sherman.

"He means, Sherman, that you and Chuck, because you're black, can't wash your clothes in here," said Charlie.

Sherman glared at his persecutor in the corner.

Meanwhile, Bud noticed more movement in the opposite corner. He turned to face a young, attractive raspberry blonde, who confidently approached the group.

"Excuse me, but I think it would be better if your group left. This guy can be real trouble," the blonde said with the demure twang of a Texas flower. She drew close to Charlie. "I know another place you can go where you won't have any trouble. I know where you guys are camped, saw your bus out at the lake. Heard the rumors first though."

After the young woman had given her directions, Bud gathered the group and herded them out, retrieving their clothes and hurling insults towards the man in the corner.

"If they can't come in, none of us want to come in," said Bud, echoing the thoughts of everyone else.

The young woman called to Charlie on his way out. "By the way, my name's Rhonda. I'm really sorry this had to happen. These people around here aren't all like that."

"Thanks for your help anyway," said Charlie, his attention fixed on the smiling girl, who exuded an alluring country freshness. "If you're ever out our way, stop in and see us," he called out as he boarded the bus.

The group carefully followed the girl's directions. They led to a secluded gravel road which snaked through the center of an East Texas colored town. All the faces were black and all the houses were rundown, clapboard structures laboring under the weight of one hundred years of having sheltered the poorest families of the region. The largest structure was the Laundromat. Almost equal in size and just a short distance away was the pool hall. The greeting the group received was warm and even the white members were allowed inside to wash clothes and shoot pool.

CHAPTER VIII

Momma's Boy

The bodies lay motionless in the heat of the late afternoon. The room smelled of sex, sweat and elaborate lies. A cool breeze moved the thin translucent curtains in rhythmic undulations of pleasure. The woman's clothes were neatly folded on the bedside chair. Her high heels were placed carefully under the bed and her jewelry lay out on her dressing table. It had been this way for a year now. This afternoon interlude of carnal games secretly carried on while school children made their way home hoping they would be there in time to see their favorite television program. The children's day had been full of the noise and commotion which accompanied elementary school children's frenetic activity like a cart follows the oxen. The woman rolled over and studied her partner. She had trained him well. He had been a fast learner an eager student of the intricacies of her body of the wonders of his own.

The relationship did not blossom until after her husband had died suddenly from a stroke. He was in the office on the phone and one minute was closing some deal on vacation land in Florida, more swamp than land, and the next minute he lay crumpled on the floor dead his chair overturned on top of him his customer still talking to him on the abandoned handset.

She had tried many men after his death in fact she had several affairs during the marriage but by then he had ceased to care. He had other cares more important financial deals that needed some fixing. But this one was her favorite so giving so loving everything she desired from her man. She caressed his body so smooth and soft so willing and then he turned over and with voice, more man than child, he said. "Are you alright mom, is everything ok did I do better this time?" He looked at her through his pale blue eyes with only the adoration that a twelve year old has for a mother. "You did just fine sweetheart, don't worry you did fine. Momma loves you".

She studied his face so eager to please her and once again she thought how much he looked like his father more every day. The sloping forehead drifting into a large nose buttressed by a distinct bowed rib giving the impression of a boomerang. His hair reminded her of randomly scattered pieces of straw stiff and unruly. He was not a handsome boy but he had a quick mind and a sharp tongue, one getting him into trouble and the other getting him out of it. She loved him. She needed him. He was her shield against the bleak wail of reality which clamored incessantly inside her head. She was his best friend and he was hers. He understood her. Somewhere inside a small but incessant voice barely audible warned her that this could not end in anything good. But how could anything which was filled with so much love be wrong. How could the compassion which she felt for her son which motivated her to reach out and help him anyway she could not be right.

That is what she told herself at those times when she suffered nagging pangs of conscience that all the Gin in the world could not drown out the pain the ugliness of all that she was. Those days seemed so long ago but it had only been weeks now. She missed him so much and worried about the detention facility where they placed him after the incident with that girl. She knew that the little tramp had led her boy on had promised him something which she was not willing to deliver. She knew that this eleven year old girl had the mind of a twenty year old and she was after her son. She could tell the way she looked at him when she came to the house and they studied together. The voice of conscience told her she was just jealous but her heart told her she was protecting her son.

It wasn't until they came and took him away from her when they asked her rude questions and looked at her like she was a criminal. Didn't they know how much he meant to her how close they were how much he depended on her to comfort him when he needed her most? It was so humiliating to be taken to the police station and be interrogated like she was a common criminal. It reminded her of the time when the police had questioned her about what "games" her father had played with her. It had been dumb of her to tell her best friend at school about her father about what he made her do but those were the kinds of things you told your best friend. She promised to keep it a secret but by noon that day everyone in her class seemed to know and then it was the principal's office and then the police station. All that came back to her and tears welled up in her eyes and cascaded down her cheeks like sheet rain over a rock cliff face, alone, desperate, broken. It was all so long ago but now it seemed like only yesterday. Her father really did love her.

He sat in the dark office with the social worker behind his desk studying him much as he had been studied by his mother who it seemed was always watching him even before he started hurting the girls. She had always been there for him when he wanted something and his father would say how she was spoiling him making him a "momma's boy". He owed her everything. She loved him without limit and protected him from those who sought to take him from her. The teachers, police, social workers all viewed him as a problem child, no more than a sexual pervert who required counseling and medication to control his urges. Every time he was "bad" with some girl or another he could see the disappointment in her eyes the anguish it caused her. The social worker was silently waiting patiently observing him. He knew he wanted to hear more about what his mother made him do but with all his questions he would truly never understand the love that he and his mother had. That was the same love he tried to find in the other random skirts that he approached and then took to some quiet corner where he could be alone with them.

He preferred this dark dank office to the holding cells the juvenile hall the boy's ranch. Those places were filled with cruel boys who had no understanding of what love was and whenever he tried to explain to tell them he was ridiculed, mocked, beaten, raped. He saw the social worker studying the yellowing remains of a shiner which he earned by talking trash to a scrappy black kid who had no patience for no "momma's boy". The boy was frightened now living in a constant fog of pain and assault. It seemed that those afternoons with his mother were no longer clear memories and he often wondered if they were only a dream. The life in "juvie" was no dream it was his worst nightmare."What are you thinking about?" the social worker asked peering through bifocals into the boy's very soul. "I don't think I can take this anymore. If you make me stay with those boys any longer I don't know what I am going to do. I am going to just die." A muffled wail escaped from the boiling cauldron of his pain. He bolted out of the chair and threw himself out the second floor window before the social worker could even blink. When the boy recovered from his cuts and bruises and broken arm he was returned to the juvenile facility where his rapists waited and smiled cruelly as he tried to reenter the crocodile infested swamp which was "juvie" without alerting the reptiles. He had to find a way out he could not survive here. All he could think about was ending this in any way he could. He missed his mother. He missed the sound of children passing on the street their innocence carried on the soft Spring breezes announced in squeals of delight as they played their children's games reveled in their perfect freedom from all cares.

CHAPTER IX

Charlie left the group behind on Tuesday and went for a solitary hike along the lake's edge, seeking to sooth his frayed nerves amid nature's beauty. He returned to camp around noon, when the day had begun to cool, with the wind coming off the water from he north, and was greeted by Bud and David.

"Hey Charlie, somebody was here looking for you," Bud cooed.

"Yeah, that girl down at the Laundromat. You know, the one you were mooning over," David cut in.

"I told her we were going swimming this afternoon down at the beach and you'd be there. She seemed like a real nice girl, pretty too," Bud continued.

"She was kind of cute, from what I remember, probably about nineteen I'd say," said Charlie. "Is everyone ready to go swimming?"

"I think we should eat first, don't you? She'll wait for you Romeo. Don't worry about that," said Bud, casting a smiling glance at David.

"I don't know Bud, don't you think it's a little cool to go swimming today?" said David, wetting his finger and holding it up to the wind.

"Well, maybe you're right. Now that you mention it, it does feel a bit chilly."

Bud and David laughed and slapped each other on the back. They watched Charlie blush and shift uneasily.

The group ate lunch and the counselors organized the boys for the trek to the beach in a fraction of the time usually required.

Charlie spotted Rhonda first. She was seated on a picnic table, her feet on the bench, her hands thrown back behind her on the table top for support. She turned and smiled and the pack of sex-starved boys descended. A feminine softness embraced them all and smiles appeared on even the hardest of faces.

Before long, Jerry, Charlie, and Rhonda became involved in a game of water tag. In the excitement of the chase, Charlie came up with a pair of small swimming trunks, much to Jerry's delight. Jerry headed for the buoy, squealing with laughter. He ascended onto the buoy and belly flopped back into the water.

"That looks like fun," Rhonda called gleefully to Charlie, who was quick to take his cue and add his trunks to the pair already hanging on the buoy.

Charlie and Rhonda suddenly found themselves alone. Rhonda hung her swimsuit up with the others. Charlie's passion grew and Rhonda melted into his arms.

Charlie was to see her only one more time before the gang moved from the lake. He borrowed Bud's car and met up with her. They repeated their relations, this time in the backseat, though the fire had dimmed substantially since their last meeting.

Bud herded the boys back to the bus. "Alright you guys, this is the last time I'm gonna say it, get your things together and your asses on the bus."

"We don't wanna go man. We like it right here. None of us guys want to go live out in the woods. At least there's a few girls around here, but there's fucking nothing out there," said Keith.

"Yeah, why can't we just stay right here? or even go back to the ranch. This is fucked man, I ain't going nowhere," said Chuck.

"If that asshole Johnson wants to live in the woods, then let him live in the woods," said David.

"I don't mind going if there's raccoons and possums out there," Danny chirped in. "I'm gonna get a trap and catch some of those critters."

"Fuck you Danny. Nobody cares what a wimp like you thinks," said Vince.

"And right now gentlemen, I don't give a fuck what you think. I want you on the bus in one minute and that means everything you own with you. Everything else gets left," said Bud.

Bud aided Vince on board the bus with a kick in the backside.

The other group of counselors had arrived at the Lake the previous evening. They had already lost one boy, who had decided to take off on his first night. Bud and Charlie expected to spend at least another week at Lake of the Pines, but Johnson arrived at camp shortly after they returned from swimming to shorten their stay, due to the bad news.

"The other group had a rough time of it last night and I think it would be better if you moved these boys out today. We don't need an epidemic at this point," said Johnson.

Charlie and Bud nodded.

"It will be best if we get them started right away on building some shelters," continued Johnson. "Fall will be here soon and it can get cold in the country. I'll arrange to get the tools you'll need tomorrow and bring them out. The other group won't be out there for another week, so that will give you boys a chance to get acclimated. You will need to get a pit for the outhouse dug first, another pit for garbage, and as for water, we'll have to porter it in. I plan to have a water line put in next month, but for awhile you'll have to use fifty gallon canvas water bags."

Bud and Charlie listened attentively.

"The arrangement of your camp is up to you and what you feel will work best for you and for the boys. The idea is to let them accomplish something. Something they can be proud of and look back on, saying, "Yeah, I really did that. That was me and it was a good thing I did, it was hard too, but I did it." Cutting through all the other mumbo jumbo you've heard about what we're doing here, that's what we're really after." Johnson smiled. "Make them feel good about themselves and you have done something."

Johnson breathed deep.

"So with that, I'll let you go. I'll be in tomorrow to see how things are going and to bring the tools."

The group took Highway 59 southwest to the acreage that was to become their permanent home. Five miles out of Gilmer they turned down Farm Road 1080 and the bus snaked through low, rolling hills of productive farmland.

At homebase, Danny was the first out of the bus and Vince the last. Danny explored every rock, evergreen, and sassafras root within reach while Vince explored his reasons for staying.

The howling of wolves nearby kept the campers awake most of the night and frightened all but the adults into the safety of the bus. The boys locked the doors and shut the windows against the night.

In the morning, Vince was nowhere to be found.

"I'm going after him," Charlie called to Bud as the boys gathered around.

"I want to go. I could help you find him," said Danny. "I've read a lot on tracking in the boy scout manual. I know I could help."

"Me too," Chuck and Sherman blurted out in unison.

"You might need some help bringing him back," said Chuck. He smiled and punched his palm.

"Yeah, that goes for me too. I could help you bring him back with Chuck," said Sherman, mimicking Chuck's punch.

"Alright. You three come with me. Let's see if we can pick up his tracks on the road out," said Charlie.

Charlie led the expedition back down the dirt road leading into camp. The boys quickly located a pair of tennis shoe tracks. The group stayed on the trail until the tracks suddenly disappeared around a bend.

"What do you think Charlie? I don't see anymore tracks. He must have taken off through the woods," said Danny while Chuck and Sherman scoured the road, looking for signs of trespass. The pursuers' vision was limited by the second growth pine which lined both sides of the road.

"Did you hear something?" said Charlie. He raised his head slowly and scanned the periphery of the woods.

"There he is. I see him in there!" said Chuck, pointing to the dense foliage just as a figure burst from the brush and ran into the denser thicket.

Vince heard his four trackers before he saw them. He cursed to himself as he barreled through a blackberry thicket, the vines tearing at his face and bare arms.

Charlie ran headlong into the wall of blackberry vines. He thrashed through the thorny entanglement, bleeding and swearing more fervently with each step. Chuck and Sherman raced at Charlie's back, against the painful barbs, leaving Danny behind in the rush.

.Vince turned. Chuck leaped forward and knocked him to the ground. Sherman jumped on top of the combatants and helped Chuck wrestle Vince to the ground.

"All right you guys, get up. Let him go!" said Charlie, yanking first Chuck then Sherman off of Vince.

"Motherfuckers, you're gonna pay for this. Fucking niggers!" said Vince.

"Cool it Vince. They were just doing what had to be done," said Charlie.

"Yeah asshole, you fuck with me and you got trouble. You want some right now, then you come and get it," said Chuck.

"You too Chuck. I said that was enough. If you guys want to fight someone maybe Bud will take you on. I'm too tired," said Charlie, drawing defiance first from Chuck then Vince before the two cooled down.

"Come on Vince, let's go back. You should've known we weren't gonna let you go very far," said Charlie. "I want you guys to know," he continued, directing a determined look at each of the four boys, "that no matter how far you run, Bud and I are coming after you and bringing you back. I want you to do me a favor and pass that on to the others. If you think I'm kiddin, just try us."

Vince hung his head and kicked up dirt.

"The other thing I want you guys to know and pass on," Charlie continued as the group walked back to camp, "is that as long as people are running away we are not going to do anything or go anywhere. That means no swimming, no movies, no allowance, nothing!"

The ragged crew returned to camp sporting erratic patterns of bleeding scratches. Vince claimed a walnut-sized lump on his forehead where Chuck's fist had made its mark. Danny circulated Charlie's ultimatums among the boys.

During the group's first ten days at their home site, following Vince's initially unsuccessful attempt, there were three more efforts to escape, all of which ended as Charlie had predicted. Each attempt carried the counselors further in their pursuit. Russ set the record when he was finally apprehended outside of Diana, some seven miles away, thumbing a ride to anywhere. After that last futile effort there was a sudden absence of runaways. Not even a likely candidate could be found. It was as if a cycle had run its course.

Bud and Charlie waited patiently for the next unscheduled departure, but it never came. The boys seemed to have finally grasped Charlie's warning—if you run away, they are going to come after you and bring you back. They couldn't seem to understand why the counselors put so much effort into making sure all of them were accounted for at camp. The only answer which they consistently returned to was that maybe, just maybe, Charlie and Bud really liked them and wanted them there—just maybe that was it.

Things were not so well for the other group of campers. Lamar had resigned, contending the situation was impossible to cope with. One boy had run away, stolen first a car and then a gun, and when cornered by police, shot himself with a 45. caliber Smith and Wesson.

Charlie, Bud, and the boys thus began building a life in the woods. The foremost thought in the counselor's minds was the approaching winter.

The first structural effort was to be the bunkhouse. A scant footpath ran into the woods, threading between a small rise on the right, atop which would be the outhouse pit, and a slightly diminished mound to the left, which was to be the future site of the cookhouse and dining room. The bunkhouse was to be built in a clearing which branched off the main trail.

The bunkhouse plans called for a structure which would house twelve individuals, with adequate space for personal belongings and a common area with a pot-bellied stove. The structure was to be laid out on an east-west axis, with the main entrance facing east. The total length was calculated at forty feet with a width of twenty. The proposal called for six bunk beds. Each side of the structure would accommodate three pairs of berths at equidistant intervals, their twins positioned directly across on the other side of the room. Like all shelters to be built at camp, the frame would be from indigenous pine while the skin would be canvas.

The morning the decision to build the bunkhouse had been made clear to the boys, Stymie, a frequent visitor from the other camp, had wandered over to see if he could procure his morning repast. He was a likeable youth and his requests were never denied. His hair was bushy and Medusa-like and his entire body seemed to twitch in rhythm with the flow of words that issued from his toothy, grinning mouth.

"We get to have a party almost every night over at our camp," said Stymie, Cocoa Puffs spilling from his mouth. "We even get to have beer and some of the guys said that they even smoked some marijuana, but I'm not sure about that. We all got it pretty cool over there. Nobody got to do nothin if we don't want to and each one of us gets food money every week."

"You lying nigger," said Sherman. "Ya'll ain't got no beer or marijuana and most of all you ain't got no money."

"Screw you man, I'll show you what I ain't got." Stymie pulled a wadded sheaf of cash from his dirty pocket and layed a five on the picnic table.

The other boys stared enviously at the gloating youngster.

"That Mark and Hooper, man they cool. They give us our money every week for groceries, but we can buy anything we want with it."

"Is that why you're always over here looking for something to eat?" said Bud.

"Maybe, but it's kinda nice getting to have three meals a day. I like having the money, but I like the way you guys eat too." Stymie flashed a smile.

"Hey Stymie, what are you guys gonna do about some place to sleep? I didn't see anything going on over there," said Roy, weighing the possibilities of having to supply a dry spot for the little beggar to bed down.

"Oh, that's no problem. They said we could build our own places or a couple of us could build one together. They just going to let us decide."

"You're probably gonna dig a hole and live in it, right Stymie?" Like the hole at the shelter?" said Chuck.

"Fuck you Chuck. Me and Jimmy gonna build a real neat place. You wait and see."

"That's what we wanted to do over here, but that fucking Charlie said no way. The prick thinks he's hot stuff sometimes," said Roy. "Pushin us around all the time."

"Come on Roy," said Bud, "once we have the bunkhouse finished, you guys will be free to build whatever you want, but first of all we're going to need a shelter for this winter." Bud eyed his accused partner, who sat quietly on the perimeter of the group.

"I thought we already talked about that Roy. I'm sorry you're not pleased with the plan, but I have a feeling this winter will change your perspective a little," said Charlie, trying to stay cool.

"Well, I don't know about no perspective, but I sure as hell don't like the plan or this group too much. Too many shitty rules." Roy threw a stick in the cook fire, hoisted himself up, and walked dejected toward the bus.

The bunkhouse had not been a unanimous decision, but Bud and Charlie had decided that it would be for the best. The arrangements which the other group had adopted were much more laissez faire. To Charlie it sounded as if there was some organization lacking, but it was too early to judge. Time would tell which system would be most effective. As for the beer and pot parties, that was another matter. Both he and Bud had heard rumors that they were going on but they had been so busy with planning the shelter that they hadn't had an opportunity to venture to the other camp to confirm them.

Bud glanced at Charlie. "Don't let him get you down. You know it's best for them, and sometimes they need to be led, let's face it.

"I know, I know. I guess it's just that we're outnumbered. I wonder sometimes if maybe the other group knows something we don't. I mean you don't hear their guys saying they want to join our group. Granted, they eat here, but I want these guys to want to be here too," said Charlie, seeking reassurance from the older man who embodied maturity and experience. Bud was the one Charlie used as a barometer; Charlie trusted the veteran's superior judgment almost implicitly.

"Just be patient Charlie. We're just beginning and things sometimes look different in the beginning than in the middle or even at the end."

The two men sat blinking away the smoke which the breeze carried away from the dying fire.

"Did I ever tell you the story about the rancher?" said Bud.

"No, I don't think you ever did," said Charlie morosely.

"Well, there was this rancher in Wyoming, owned a big horse ranch and he had one son helping him around the place. Well, one day his son caught a wild stallion and brought it back to the pen to train. The neighbors came around all exclaiming what good fortune it was. The rancher just said, "We'll see." Next day, the boy, while trying to break the horse, was thrown and he broke his arm. The neighbors were back again, this time all saying what bad luck it was. The rancher, in his own inspired manner, replied "We'll see." Next day, the army came around conscripting young, able-bodied men for immediate service. The man's son was passed over because of his broken arm. The neighbors were back again, this time chanting in unison that the rancher must indeed be a very lucky man. The old rancher just looked at them without the slightest blink of an eyelash and proclaimed, "We'll see.'"

Bud cast a look in Charlie's direction. "That's what we have here Charlie—a 'we'll see' situation."

"I never thought about it that way, but that story does make things a lot clearer. I'll remember that and I owe you one," said Charlie.

Charlie remembered reading the same story in a Zen training manual, but the immediate relevance of Bud's version cast new light on his dilemma.

CHAPTER X

By October the threat of an early fall had passed and the group basked in the soft, warm breezes of an Indian summer. Water maple shimmered and the oak trees began to shed the first of their leaves. The skeleton of the bunk house stood completed, looming as a tribute to what the group was capable of achieving.

The nature of boys being physical, they enjoyed employing their hands to build and grew especially fond of felling trees and putting the actual structure together. They worked well together when they needed to. Charlie could sense the boys' satisfaction at each stage of completion of the project. They liked admiring their own work and the sweat and effort they expended reflected itself in the pride on their faces.

Once the bunkhouse was completed, beds were constructed and the woodsy dormitory was almost ready to house the tenants. The last task of measuring for canvas was completed and Mr. Johnson delivered the measurements to a sailmaker. The group had even decided on skylights in the roof, three heavy plastic panels which were to be sewn into the canvas.

The kitchen was erected next, a much more modest structure, but one big enough to house a table for twelve and a four burner wood stove. The cook tent also furnished shelter for the camp ice chest, which had acquired a padlock after several midnight raids by large raccoons.

Mid-October arrived and the campers settled in for the winter. The canvas for the kitchen and bunk house was finished and put into place. The outhouse sat at the top of the hill, where it waited, coverless.

One evening Keith approached Charlie on his way to the toilet.

"Charlie, I've got a little problem and I need some help," said Keith, lowering his voice.

"Sure Keith. What is it?"

"Well, I was just up at the john and when I came back I couldn't find my wallet. I know I had it when I went up and I always carry it in my back pocket." Keith paused. "I was just thinking that maybe it fell in the shitter."

Charlie laughed. He put his hand on Keith's shoulder. "Well there's only one way to find out, but I think we're gonna need a flashlight and at least one other person to help out."

"OK, But why don't we get Bud and then nobody else will have to know."

"What happened Keith? Lost your wallet in the shitter huh? Why don't you go down and get it," said Chuck as he came out from behind the canvas, laughing and slapping his thighs. "Hey you guys, Keith's going down in the shitter. Let's go watch."

"Fuck you nigger, who asked you. You're always sticking your ugly puss in everybody's business!"

"Come on Keith, let's get this over with," said Charlie. He turned to Bud. "I think we're gonna need your help. I'll get the flashlight."

Charlie headed for the bunkhouse while Keith and Bud led the parade towards the toilet.

A quick look down the hole confirmed Keith's fears, much to the delight of rest of the boys. The top was removed and Keith was lowered head first, hands outstretched, amid complaints from Chuck seconded by Vince and Roy that they couldn't hold it in a second longer and they just had to use the toilet.

Keith retrieved his wallet and Chuck bestowed on him the title of manager of lost and found within the department of the shitter.

The group had worked hard and achieved their goal of providing shelter for the winter ahead. The work done and nothing left to unite them, the boys became more anxious than normal, fights became increasingly frequent, and flaring tempers and desultory moods became commonplace.

Charlie lay propped up on one elbow in the bunkhouse, a discarded comic book at his side. Bud eyed his partner from across the room.

"Charlie, what say we take the group on a little trip? It looks like the weather's gonna hold out and I think we might be able to sneak in a short one, kind of a celebration."

"I think we could all use a little vacation. Where do you want to go?" An image of the seashore came to Charlie's mind.

"I don't really care as long as it's warm."

"My vote's the beach, somewhere around Corpus Christi. There's some beautiful spots down there. We could make the round trip in a couple of weeks, and if the weather holds out it would be great."

"Sounds good. Why don't we leave tomorrow? We'll let Johnson know when he comes out today."

Charlie considered Bud's proposition. Those endless details which beset the average vacationers were non-existent in the group's case. There was no boss to check up with, no house to lock up, no reservations to be made, no money to be saved, and no school to worry about. In fact, there was absolutely nothing aside from inertia which kept the group from going.

The route which the travelers decided on would cover four-hundred-and-twenty-four miles and pass through Dallas, Waco, Austin, San Antonio, and finally Corpus Christi. The return journey would hug the Gulf Coast shoreline, carrying them back through Houston, Nacogdoches, Henderson, and home again.

The boys rejoiced at the news. It was to be the first trip for either group and those being left behind felt the agony of a rejected lover. The veil of boredom that hung over the camp quickly lifted.

Charlie lay awake the night before the trip, listening to the boys' banter. Their adolescent chatter had become a nightly ritual since the group had come together in a common sleeping area. Stories were told, lies exposed, secrets revealed. The din of excited conversation inevitably fell off, replaced by rustling sheets and muffled groans.

"Roy, quit jerking off," said David.

"Screw you David, I'll do what I want," Roy growled as his bunk shook harder.

"Roy's always beating off," said Keith from across the room.

"Well at least I didn't screw my mother," said Roy.

"I told you not to say anything about that. You said you wouldn't tell nobody."

"Everybody knows anyway. The guys at the ranch told everybody. That Ricky guy, he said your mother use to make you do it. Is that true Keith?" said Roy.

"None of your business you bastard, at least my father wasn't a drunk who beat the hell out of my mother."

"At least I knew who my father was, even if he was a drunk."

Charlie took it all in. He pieced together the few fragments that were available from the boys' pasts. The common denominator, with the exception of Danny, was an endless procession of foster homes, institutions, and faceless, nameless adults informing the boys that they simply weren't wanted.

Charlie's ruminations on the boys' pasts were slowly pushed aside by more personal and selfish concerns related to the imminent trip. He knew they were going to be camping outside of Austin and he had already arranged with Bud to borrow the bus for the night to see Linda. It had been seven weeks since he had heard from her. Although he had mixed feelings about the reunion, he was anxious to see her. The second item on his personal agenda was a visit to his parents in Tomball, Texas, a small town forty miles northeast of Houston. He planned to take the boys by and let them have a great big helping of farm life with mashed potatoes and gravy on the side.

Charlie's thoughts ran tirelessly until the early hours of the morning. He tossed and turned in unison with the others. At four a.m., Sherman, David, and Roy yanked him out of bed. The boys quickly scattered and Charlie lay groaning in a contorted heap in his sleeping bag.

The group completed their chores post haste. They loaded the bus and settled in comfortably. Charlie pulled the door closed and said farewell to the camp as all eyes peered forward, willing the trip to be a good one.

Charlie sat behind the wheel and started the bus up, singing at the top of his lungs, "He's got the Whole World in His Hands." Bud and the boys started a sing-a-along. Bud added each boy's name at the end of the refrain, as the refrain was all they knew.

A cluster of boys huddled in the door well, singing crude melodies in each other's faces. Charlie approached a two way stop. The school bus eased across two southbound lanes. Charlie proceeded past the island. The nose of the bus crawled forward into the fast lane of northbound traffic, hidden from Charlie's view by the singing boys. Charlie glimpsed a dark shadow out of the corner of his eye. He hit the brakes, sending the contents of the bus, bodies and all, flying forward. A semi-truck and trailer loaded with oil field pipe zoomed within inches of the front of the coach.

Charlie took the lucky miss as a good omen, a sign of a fruitful venture. He glanced at Bud and the two exchanged silent recognition. The group resumed their singing and the stunned truck driver shook his head as the melody drifted through his window. Another rule was established after that—absolutely no standing in the door well. None of the boys objected to this command.

The first day, the small band covered one-hundred-and-sixty-three miles, retracing Charlie's initial route to Daingerfield. They passed through Dallas at midday and headed on 35 east to Hillsboro, then took Highway 22 to Lake Whitney, the first stop on the trip.

The group set up camp on an isolated shore of Lake Whitney State Park, bare except for the prairie grass caressing the water's edge and spreading its tawny carpet in all directions.

"Did you hear something?" said Danny to no one in particular. He stared, his senses alert, off towards the shore. "Wait, there it is again. I saw something moving over there. See, right there."

"Yeah, I see it too!" said Vince. "It's a skunk. Wait. What's that over there? To the right, there's another one."

A string of confirming hoots and hollers accompanied each new sighting.

"Let's catch one!" said Russ as he jumped from the bus, armed with a cardboard box.

The rest of the boys joined the chase close on Russ' heels.

An observer coming upon the scene would have witnessed a strange sight, as nine teenage boys, slightly resembling renegade Indians, and two adult men, acting like children, gave chase to a platoon of wily skunks.

Russ threw the box over a bounding skunk.

The box overturned and Russ and Roy stared down the barrel of a fully loaded skunk atomizer.

The boys discovered two important facts about skunk scent that night. First, that it clings to clothes and emits a phosphorescence and Second, that the nose gradually becomes accustomed to the odor, especially if everyone present is saturated with it.

Camp broke late the next morning. The bleary-eyed group ate a breakfast of cold cereal and boarded the bus. They made a brief stop in Waco, at Baylor University, to see the University mascots lumbering about in the famous bear pits. The bears were a modest sensation; the coeds, however, received the majority of the boys' attention. The youths received an inordinate amount of stares from passersby.

Back in civilized society, Charlie noted that a gradual transformation in appearance had overcome the boys since establishing their home in the woods. Their hair was considerably longer and the habit had been formed, at least among Vince and Roy, of wearing bandanas. They had also accumulated an odd assortment of hats, from Dino's Sam Snead cap to Roy's safari hat. A considerable amount of grime had accumulated under fingernails, on clothes, and in every nook and cranny of the bus.

The boys' personal grooming habits varied to a considerable degree, with David always appearing neat and well-groomed and Russ and Vince consistently barefoot, bare-breasted, and unwashed. The only deterrent to their slovenliness was the presence of girls. At those times, preening rituals were taken more seriously. Personal attire was also handled differently depending on the boy. There were those who could almost always locate their own shoes and pants to put on in the morning and those who went from the extremes of concealing their personal items in locked boxes to discarding their clothes wherever they might land, usually in the main aisle of the bus. This latter group could always be identified by footprints walking up the backs of their shirts.

All things considered, it was a colorful collection of individuals that proceeded toward their next stop, outside of Austin.

Bud and Charlie chose Mckinny Falls State Park as the logical stopping point, six miles south of the home of the Texas longhorns. Once the group was settled, Charlie borrowed the bus, leaving Bud to fend for himself, and headed toward Linda's apartment.

Austin was a quiet University town of two-hundred-and-fifty-thousand inhabitants. The university tower, made famous by a mad sniper in the 1960's, loomed over the town as freshmen scurried by. The University of Texas set itself the task of educating forty-five-thousand students annually. As in most University towns, students sought off-campus housing in the neighborhoods surrounding the campus.

It was in this labyrinth of alleyways, one-way streets, and converted garages that Linda lived. She occupied the second story of a private residence, the bottom being inhabited by the landlord, a grizzly-haired, toothless old woman who delighted in cursing her tenants on a regular basis. In the rear was a converted garage apartment housing another student. His fondness for hot air balloon piloting was made clear by the gondola parked in the backyard, next to Linda's motorcycle.

"If man was meant to fly, it wouldn't have been in a basket!" the old landlady would repeat regularly as she maneuvered her push mower around the gondola.

Charlie parked the school bus in front of the two story residence. He bounded up the stairs, toward Linda's. Her front door was closed and the blinds were drawn. Charlie recognized a familiar scent escaping from inside. He opened the door quietly and stepped in.

Charlie approached the bathroom door.

"Who is it?" said a muffled voice from behind the door.

"It's me, Charlie. Let me in."

The door creaked open and Charlie was asked in. He adjusted his eyes to the smoke-filled room while the door closed and locked behind him.

"Hi Charlie. Where you been? I expected you here a couple of hours ago," Linda crooned from her seat on the toilet. Everybody, this is Charlie. Charlie, this is everybody. I think you know Dierdre, Betty Jo, and Eric."

Charlie recognized the three students gathered in the bathroom. Dierdre was an Irish graduate student, a linguistics major, whom Linda had found wandering on campus, lost, in the middle of summer, wearing a full-length wool coat and carrying all her belongings. Then there was Betty Joe, an unnaturally quiet, shy, but keenly intelligent pre-med student, whose lack of femininity created a male vacuum in her life. Finally there was Eric, the physics teaching assistant who over the years had gone from conscientious, outstanding student to conscientious objector. Commode, the stray black cat that Linda had picked up out of a trash can, was also present.

"Still gettin the cat stoned, huh Linda?" said Charlie as Linda blew smoke into Commode's face.

"Yeah, and he still loves it."

Smoking marijuana in Texas was a felony, so the formality of smoking in the bathroom, behind closed doors, had been adopted to enable quick destruction of evidence.

The only two other personalities in the room belonged to an older, early-forties black man named Edward, and John, a young student whose chief characteristic was his flaming-red mop of hair.

Most of Linda's gatherings developed along the same lines: she inevitably held forth, sometimes for hours, chain smoking and elucidating her theories on whatever topic held interest at the time.

The discussion was becoming animated as Charlie caught Linda's eye. She quietly left her seat and followed Charlie out the door and into the bedroom. Linda quickly closed the door and the drum of debate was soon mixed with the sounds of Charlie and Linda's passion. Sex was a mutual attraction which had brought and still held them together. Linda's appetite for books and other cerebral nourishment was equally matched by her carnal appetite. Charlie was the willing victim, enjoying each moment regardless of where or when Linda's urges possessed her. In the park, in an alley way—be prepared wherever and whenever seemed to be the only rule.

As Charlie and Linda lay entangled, Charlie's memory began to turn to the events of the first day they had met, following the scuffle he had just avoided in attempting to come to her aid.

*　　*　　*

Linda was leaning against the signpost where Charlie had left her in attempting to defend her honor, blowing smoke.

"What went on over there? It looked like you got yourself into quite a spot," said Linda, still flustered by her own run in with the unruly group.

"No, just thought I could straighten things out a little. Just makes me mad to see a girl treated that way."

"Well screw them, I appreciate your trying. By the way, what did you say your name was?" Linda coolly sized up her new Lancelot.

"Charlie. I work at your dorm. I've seen you there before." Charlie felt the first flushes of embarrassment in front of this brash young woman.

"Where do you live? Maybe I can walk you home. By the way, you don't have a light do you?" Linda watched the color rise in Charlie's cheeks.

"No, I'm afraid I don't smoke."

"No, you don't look like the type that would. Let me see then, you're definitely the clean cut type. Polo shirt, cords, loafers. Oh yes." Linda smirked. "Probably a good Catholic boy and virgin to boot."

Linda continued her acute character analysis while Charlie tried to keep the blood from rushing quickly to his face in order to not look any more virginal than he already did. Her estimate of his sexual experiences was accurate, yet Charlie would be the last to admit it. In his entire sheltered life he had never encountered any woman quite like Linda and he was completely unaware of how to deal with her. His fall back position in difficult social situations had always been to listen attentively and that was exactly what he did for the next several hours.

Charlie and Linda meandered through the quaint, tree-lined neighborhoods of Austin, filled with the sounds of rustling leaves and barking dogs and the thousand indistinct noises of suburbia. They talked about their majors at the University and the classes they were taking. She was in Psychology, a freshman, and he was a sophomore in Biology. Charlie felt drawn to Linda, this girl so different from any other he had known—and certainly not someone to bring home to mother. She was full of different ideas, independent, and there seemed to be no end to the books she had read.

Linda led Charlie into a run-down, unkempt neighborhood studded with a number of abandoned houses, and suddenly suggested that they explore one. They approached a two-story white clapboard house, obviously neglected and abandoned for sometime. The yard was overgrown and the discarded bottles of Thunderbird and Boone's Farm scattered across the lawn showed evidence of night visitations by local winos.

Inside proved to be devoid of any furniture and was filled instead with the miscellaneous debris often piled up in old, abandoned houses: an old bicycle tire, shoe boxes, a pile of indistinguishable clothing and, upstairs, the item that proved to be Charlie's downfall: an old stained and worn mattress, abandoned and left to die after the hundreds of pleasure-filled nights that it had provided. It was upon that sad, defeated bed that Charlie laid down his boyhood and felt for the first time the joy of manhood. It wasn't like he thought it would be. Of course, at the time, he didn't really know what to think. He was so concerned that someone might walk in unannounced and interrupt his initial foray into sex that he had a difficult time concentrating on his duties, whatever they might be.

Charlie was lying face up on the tattered mattress while Linda lay prone across his chest. She studied him closely a minute and then with a calculated sweep of her hand brushed the hair away from his forehead. She quickly noticed the anxious look which crossed his face and read his thoughts.

Linda laughed quietly to herself. "My, but you're unattractive with your hair like that. Don't ever wear it that way whatever you do."

Charlie's heart sank; his ego was crushed. Linda knew then that she had an innocent young man under her control. The sensation of pulling the leash was one she was to grow to like. As for Charlie, he was hooked. His well-guarded inferiority complex had suddenly been brought to the surface. It had come out of the darkness as a frail and sickly creature with an overwhelming need to be accepted and had fallen solidly into the grasp of someone who had every intention of working it to her advantage.

Evening came, and Charlie and Linda made their way back to the dormitory through the dimly lit parking area. The only other person in sight was hunched intently over the bicycle racks lining the front of the dorm, securing his bike for the night. The moon was nearly full and the sky glistened under the clear, cool starlight.

Linda and Charlie heard footsteps approaching from behind. Two young black men quickly skirted around them and came to an abrupt a halt in front of them, blocking their path to the dorms. Taken by surprise, Charlie instinctively moved to shield Linda. The closer of the two men was dressed in a faded navy blue sweatshirt, black slacks, and black tennis shoes. He studied Charlie's features.

"Hey whitey, aren't you the motherfucker that started the trouble downtown today? Who you think you are anyway, fuckin' with us that way."

Before Charlie could even begin to formulate either a reply or a plan for extracting himself and Linda from the immediate threat, the second black man stepped forward. His breath washed against Charlie's face. Beads of sweat worked their way from his forehead down his nose and around his eyes.

"I'm gonna cut your heart out, you honky motherfucker," the man said in a deep voice.

Charlie glanced down and discerned the outline of a ten inch butcher knife in the man's hand. The pale glint of steel promised to fulfill his threat. Charlie quivered with a mixture of fear, anger, and adrenaline.

A young longhaired man suddenly approached cautiously between the two men. The Hippie turned toward them.

"Hey brothers, what's going on here? This racist pig giving you dudes a bad time? Well, just fuck him, don't waste your time on trash like that. White trash, that's what you're dealing with. Ain't worth no kind of trouble."

The men's attentions were suddenly captivated by the newcomer.

"He ain't worth it. Come on, let's get out of here," continued the hippie.

The two men exchanged questioning glances and the second eased his grip on the knife, as if his rage had been subdued by the white boy calling him brother and sounding cool enough to pull it off. Both men turned on their heels and fell in stride with the miracle worker, casting a final barrage of curses in Charlie's direction as he and Linda marched off into the dark.

*   *   *

Dierdre's voice from the bathroom calling for the two lovers brought Charlie back to reality.

"I guess we better get back to our guests," said Linda. She got out of bed and began pulling on her jeans.

Charlie was reclining on the bed. "You're right. I can only stay a couple more hours, then I have to get back."

"Maybe we can drive Dierdre and Betty Jo back to their places, then we can have some time to talk."

CHAPTER XI

The party disbanded and Charlie, Linda, Dierdre, and Betty Jo gathered in the school bus. Charlie dropped the two women off and parked the bus in a deserted area behind the Geology building.

The conversation shifted from what Linda had been doing to what Linda was going to do. She announced her plans to attend graduate school in Arizona in February. She had already been accepted in the experimental psychology department.

"That sounds great," Charlie said with forbearance. "But I'm not sure when I'll get to see you again."

"Don't you ever get a vacation from that place?" said Linda, an edge forming in her voice.

"I'll get a month vacation probably in November, but not until then."

"That's just great." Linda shook her head. "Well, at least I'll get to see you on the way back from Corpus Christi."

"I guess I didn't tell you, but I'm taking the kids by my parents' place on the way back. Thought they might like a home cooked meal."

Linda took a prolonged drag on her cigarette. "You mean to tell me you're goin to see your mother instead of me?" she accused, her voice rising in unison with her anger.

"I thought the boys—"

"Screw the boys!" said Linda. "How about me? That mother of yours hates my guts, she won't even let me in the house."

Charlie turned and saw a campus policeman peering into the bus.

"Open up. This is the police. What's going on in there?" said the officer.

A second and third patrol car entered the previously empty lot.

"Nothing's going on," said Charlie, opening the door from inside.

"What in the hell does he want?" said Linda.

"Just be cool. Let me talk to the man," Charlie stated firmly, his arms outstretched, palms down, in an effort to calm Linda down. He turned to the officer. "We were just having a discussion. You know, just wanted a quiet place to talk."

"Whose bus is this?" said the officer.

Charlie persuaded the officers through a lengthy explanation that the bus wasn't stolen and that Linda wasn't kidnapping him.

The ride back to Linda's apartment was subdued. Charlie drove and Linda fumed in the back, looking lost and forlorn.

"Look, don't go away mad. I said I'll come down in November, and if you want I'll take you home and help you get some of your stuff before you move," said Charlie.

"If that's the best you can do, I guess it'll have to do. See you in November then," Linda spit back, jumping from the bus. "And say hello to your mother for me. Give her my love and tell her I'll be screwing the pants off her little boy, OK?"

"Sure, take care and I'll see you in about a month," Charlie yelled after Linda's retreating figure.

Charlie felt miserable on his way back to camp. He took things from Linda that he wouldn't take from anyone else and he couldn't figure out why. More often than not she was harsh and rude to strangers as well as friends; however, she was helping him to know himself and that made it all worthwhile. Besides, he loved her.

Back at camp, Charlie sat in the bus, watching the group gather around the picnic table for dinner. Those young faces that were so new to him only a short time ago were beginning to feel like family. The thought struck him that the boys and Bud could also be used as tools to help him in his quest for self knowledge. He simply and honestly wanted to mine the mysteries of his burgeoning self by whatever means possible.

The next morning at sunrise the group headed south. Bud drove while Charlie sat motionless in the back, hanging his feet over the seat in front, deep in conversation with Keith, David, and Chuck.

"You went to college, didn't you Charlie?" said Keith.

"Yeah, I went to school back in Austin, the campus we passed yesterday."

"Was it hard?"

"Parts of it were. I mean, it took some time, the academic part, you know, the studying. The hardest part was probably just making the money to stay in." Charlie puzzled over Keith's interrogation, searching for a hidden agenda.

"Well, do you think that somebody like me could ever go to college?"

"I don't see why not. You're certainly smart enough. It's just a matter of applying yourself."

"You know, I did real good at the ranch school until I had trouble with the teacher there. I do like school though and I know I'd like to go to college." Keith turned Charlie's words over in his mind.

"Keith, you're too stupid to even get into high school, much less college," said Chuck.

"College is only for punks," said David. "Look what it did for Charlie. Look where he is."

"If you mean here with you guys, David," Charlie said calmly, "that's exactly where I want to be right now. What college or anything else does that you have learned is simply give you more alternatives."

"What's an alternative?" said Chuck, furrowing his brow.

"It's just a choice. For instance, take you guys. There aren't many alternatives or choices that you have other than what you're doing right now. Someone else has put you here and running away is not particularly attractive. That's what I mean by alternatives."

Keith, Chuck, and David attempted to follow Charlie's reasoning.

"You know," Charlie mumbled half to himself, "there was once a Roman Emperor by the name of Marcus Aurelius, who lived a long time ago, almost two thousand years ago. He was quite a big guy in his time. He wrote a small book to tell people how he thought life should be lived and the important things to remember as you go through life. One of the things he said in that book is what we were just saying. He said that everybody, whether it's Chuck, Keith or whoever, is given the ability to get exactly what they want out of life. Now, not everybody is willing to do what is necessary to get what they want, but they do all have the ability."

"So that means that I could go to college, doesn't it?" Keith pressed.

"That's exactly what it means," said Charlie.

Keith fell back in his seat. He stared out the window, absorbed in the cows and telephone poles moving rapidly into the past. Chuck too sat daydreaming. David moved to the front of the bus and found a seat directly behind Bud.

Over the last few weeks, Charlie had noticed Bud and David growing increasingly close. Bud had taken a paternalistic interest in David's well-being.

Charlie shifted his vision to Russ, who sat slumped in his seat, absorbed in a Spiderman comic. All of the boys except for Russ had grown close with one or the other of the two counselors. Charlie knew that so far he had failed abysmally with the boy. Each encounter he had had been violent.

Charlie knew that he wasn't approaching Russ the right way, but he didn't know how else to go about it. All his good intentions disappeared when he met with the erratic emotions lurking behind the boy's cherubic countenance. There were times when Russ could be as appealing and fun-loving as the rest of the boys. The problem was his erratic mood swings and seemingly incomprehensible bursts of malevolence. Bud had also noticed the same issues with the boy.

The other boy who was hard to reach, or at least establish a connection with, was Vince. He possessed traits common to all the others; fiery independence, rebelliousness, moroseness, disregard for authority, a powerful physical presence, and animal ferociousness, existed in him to a greater degree than in the others. Although the rest of the boys would often appropriate one or two of these traits and attempt to use them to their gain in particular situations, Vince was the embodiment of all of them at any moment.

Charlie found himself drawn, in terms of personalities, closest to Chuck, Roy, and Danny. He perceived an innate intelligence in Chuck. The boy's propensity for practical jokes and derogatory satire was not enjoyed by all, but it added freshness to the group. Though both Chuck and Roy were withdrawn, Roy was the more pronounced of the two. He very seldom used his physical dominance of the group, which he shared only with Sherman, viciously. Once a certain cohesiveness had begun forming in the group, Roy had found his natural niche as both protector and enforcer. He often found himself taking sides with Jerry and Danny, the two smallest boys, who could be easily intimidated and coerced into participating in certain activities they would rather not be a part to. Roy had developed his role as enforcer to a level where blows were not always necessary.

Danny's appeal to Charlie was the boy's love of nature. He had an insatiable appetite for knowledge of the living world. His residence in camp so far had been one continuous nature hike. He would tramp about in the woods by himself for hours, always bringing back odd animals and plants.

The remaining three boys also added distinct personal touches to the group's character. Sherman was dubbed the simplest of the clan. He acquired the role not through lack of mental capacity, but by sheer absence of education. Charlie had discerned, in his talks with Sherman and some of the other boys who had known him while jointly spending time in Chicago institutions, that he had never attended school. He couldn't read or write and was unable to recite the alphabet. His education had been totally neglected and at fifteen the world was leaving him behind. He had never known his parents and had been passed from one temporary home to another for the entirety of his young life. As a result of his alienated upbringing, he had acquired a keen ability to sympathize with others. His unpretentious, simple, and friendly manner invited the same from those who recognized it in him.

While Sherman was the easiest to understand, little Jerry, or "Dino," aside from Russ, was the most difficult. His anxiety and agitation acted as a barrier through which it was difficult to penetrate. Because of the his high strung nature, his moments of joy were intense. His raptures animated his small frame, and his laughter, clear and bright, told of a hidden place within him where happiness reigned, untouched by the shroud of fear which characteristically enveloped him.

Fear was also an important factor for Keith. Although he was the tallest and heaviest of the group, he possessed limited physical strength and was easily intimidated by most of the other boys. His weapons were of the mind, not the flesh. He could employ his quick wit and incisive intelligence just as quick to get himself into trouble as he could to get himself out. His propensity for fast talk, interweaving fact and fiction without hesitation, was unmatched by the others.

The tenth member was due to arrive after the group's return from their trip. Charlie was anxious to see exactly how the new boy would fit in.

CHAPTER XII

The Gulf Coast of Texas boasted hundreds of miles of sandy, windswept beaches which seldom saw the presence of man. A series of three narrow islands cushioned the instep of the Texas coast from Brownsville, which rested on the Mexican border, to Freeport, the haven of Texas surfing to the North. Matagorda was the northernmost of these thin sand spots encroaching on the sea, and was trailed in a southerly direction by San Jose Island and Padre Island, the largest of the three islands. The waters of the gulf coast were gentle for most of the year, except for late summer and early fall, when hurricanes were often born deep in the womb of the Gulf Coast.

The bus rolled onto the sands of Mustang Island, the northern-most portion of Padre Island, late in the afternoon. The crew came to a halt on a relatively isolated portion of the beach, about one-and-a-half miles from the nearest tourist attractions. The group established camp and the counselors set the boys free to explore the sand and sea at their leisure. The boys and the counselors erected tents in the sand dunes to protect against the surge of onshore breezes.

Bud and Charlie hovered over the inside rear wheel of the bus, which had gone flat.

"I thought it felt a little funny these last few miles," said Bud.

"There's nothing we can do about it except get some help," said Charlie, eyeing the useless wheel. "I'll walk back to that last spot we passed. I saw a phone booth there. I'll try to find someone who can come out and fix it or at least take it to be fixed."

"Sounds good. I'll stay here with the guys. We'll have some dinner cooking by the time you get back." Bud sat down against a sand dune and watched Charlie go. He stretched out his feet and took a drag on his cigarette.

Charlie located a phone booth on the outskirts of the isolated beach town the group had passed through. He noticed a girl watching him closely from the opposite side of the street. She shot him an inviting smile, which he eagerly returned. Fifteen minutes and six calls later he had located a gas station that could do the work in the morning if the bus was brought in early.

Charlie stepped from the booth and approached the girl across the street.

"Hi," the girl cooed.

"Hi," said Charlie, his eyes scanning her body.

"You're not from around here," the girl purred.

"No, I'm not." Charlie took the girl's hand and pulled her toward him. He searched for signs of resistance and found none.

Charlie put his hand inside her blouse and explored her breasts. She pressed her body against his and they kissed. Her hand explored the contours of his faded blue jeans.

"Where are you staying?" said the girl, drawing back gently.

"We're camped down the beach about a mile and a half."

"There's gonna be a dance tonight here on the beach. Maybe you could meet me there."

Their mouths came together again.

"I'll certainly try," said Charlie before parting from her.

Charlie arrived back at camp at night, thoughts of buxom young ladies filling his head. The group lounged in the heat into the night while the sea breezes kicked against their bodies and the water rushed against the shore. They crawled into their sleeping bags tired and burned.

Morning arrived with the tide bringing the sun in all its splendor. Charlie crawled head first from his tent. He rested his eyes on Bud, sitting in his ritualistic coffee and tobacco trance.

"Morning Bud," said Charlie.

"Oh, mornin Charlie. I didn't even hear you get up. I must have been daydreamin. Thought I better get up early and take that bus in."

"I gave you the name of the station and address, didn't I?"

"Yeah, you did. It shouldn't take too long. I think we better shove off later today. This sand is pretty bad."

Charlie turned toward the sand dunes where the tents had been pitched. He was unable to distinguish the boys' tents until he noticed their dark green roofs slightly visible above the sand.

"It looks like a couple tents got buried along with their inhabitants," said Charlie with a laugh.

Muffled curses issued from the nearest of the tents.

"Seems like the think the captives have finally realized their condition," said Bud.

"I guess we better let them out. It would probably be too suspicious looking if we just left them there," said Charlie. He casually made his way toward the trapped boys, who had begun to pound on the sides of their tents.

"We're coming!" said Charlie.

Bud and Charlie uncovered the tents

"I'd better get that bus in," said Bud after the boys had been freed.

Bud started the bus up and the roar broke the silence of the morning. The bus jolted forward, heading toward town as Charlie and the boys looked on.

Charlie looked around at the boys. He panicked. "Where's Sherman?"

Suddenly Chuck pointed toward the top of the bus. He screamed with delight. The others turned their heads and followed his finger.

Sherman rose from his sleeping bag on top of the bus.

"Bud, Bud, stop!" shouted Charlie and the boys.

The group raced down the beach after the bus. Bud, unaware of the commotion, continued to motor down the beach. Sherman watched his sleeping bag leap into the air. He started to pound on the top of the bus, lifting Bud from his trance.

When Bud returned with the bus the boys had already eaten breakfast and explored the shoreline numerous times. Much to their delight, especially Danny's, there were hundreds of small nurse sharks ranging in size from six inches to two feet washed up on the shore. Danny spent the entire morning holding, inspecting, and dissecting one after another of the sharks.

The group boarded for departure around noon. Charlie glanced back at the phone booth on the deserted corner as the bus passed by. For an instant he thought he saw the young girl, receiver to her ear, watching him. He blinked once to clear his vision then sought the booth again, only to find it empty.

The group took Highway 35 back to Texas and their next stop, Charlie's parent's house. The highway winded along the Gulf Coast and passed through Corpus Christi, Bay City, Old Ocean, Sugar Valley, Alvin, and Houston.

The group stopped for a short time on the outskirts of Corpus Christi to join a gathering of locals who had waded into the shallow waters to raid an oyster bed. The boys too had to taste the marine delicacy. They waded in knee deep and with bent backs stuck their hands into the shellfish habitat below the waves. There seemed to be no greater delight for oyster connoisseurs than to pull one directly from the sea and pop it from shell to mouth. There were also those more sophisticated partakers who required a touch of catsup with their meal. Bud and most of the group also partook while Charlie and those members whose weak stomachs resisted watched from the sidelines.

The crew made their way to the sparsely populated countryside forty miles northeast of Houston. They passed through Cut N' Shoot, Tomball, and onto the back-roads of Magnolia.

Charlie and Bud chose a location on the outskirts of Tomball to make camp. Spring Creek Park was a well-hidden recreation area studded with live oak and pine. It offered the main attributes of a good camp, lots of room and isolation.

The crew erected their tents and the boys headed in various directions to check out the terrain for signs of interest.

Charlie walked to the park phone to call his parents in order to find out what time he and the boys should come for dinner. On his walk back he considered how these two elements, the boys and his parents, one which raised him and the other which he was having some hand in raising, would relate to each other.

Charlie thought of his parents as products of the depression and World War II, both of which their generation religiously deferred to when questions of ethics, morals, or economics were raised. They were those men and women who had fought in Europe and the South Pacific: real American farm boys, and girls who had stayed behind to work in factories, assemble airplanes, tanks, and other paraphernalia of war, waiting for their men to come home. The men that had returned had been filled with a desire to procreate against the death they had seen and wanted to forget. The baby boom had begun and millions of Americans had bought their memberships to the American working class.

Charlie wouldn't really call his parents middle-class or lower-class, but working-class. Generally they could be described as against welfare, for religion, and as unshakeable advocates of the American way.

Charlie came within view of the camp and heard the screech of tires immediately accompanied by a horn blaring behind him. He turned in time to see his younger brother Joe's familiar 1949 Jeep Wagoneer outfitted with chrome wheels, extra-wide rear tires, and dual glass packs pull up beside him.

"How you doin, Charlie? Ma told me you were down here. Thought I'd come and take a look. See how my big brother's doin," said Joe, hanging out the window of his Jeep, a broad smile on his face.

"Didn't take you long to get here little brother. I'm surprised that thing's still runnin," said Charlie. He grinned and took a playful swipe at Joe's head.

"Come on, I want you to meet the guys," said Charlie. He jumped in the passenger seat and pointed toward the camp.

Joe was treated like all initiates into the group. He quickly ran out of cigarettes, did mock battle with Sherman and Roy, and turned down six requests to drive his car. The boys took to him quickly.

A '66 Impala pulled up on the roadside near Charlie, Joe, Bud, and the boys. Charlie noticed two young toughs sitting in the front seat.

"Hey Joe, I want to talk to you," demanded the driver of the Chevy.

Joe hesitated.

"I said I wanted to see you Joe. Now get over here." The driver's cockiness ignited Charlie's anger.

Joe strolled good-naturedly to the car and entered into a lengthy debate with the driver, accentuated by threats and challenging looks in Charlie's direction. The boys looked on in their own leisurely manner, sizing up the situation.

Joe walked back to Charlie from the parked car, the skin drawn tight around his eyes.

"These guys are real troublemakers," said Joe. He motioned to the driver. "He's always giving me a bad time. One of the local punks. Says he and his buddy are gonna kick my ass. He said you'd get the same if you interfered. He's always starting fights with someone."

Before Joe could finish, Charlie began moving toward the car.

Charlie leaned into the driver's window.

"I hear you've been threatening my little brother," said Charlie softly, attempting to hold back his anger. He moved his gaze slowly from the driver to the passenger, measuring the amount of fear present.

"That's right," said the drive, his cockiness catching slightly in his throat.

Charlie reached through the window and grabbed the driver by his coat, lifting him slightly out of his seat and pulling him close.

"I don't want to ever hear that you're threatening my brother or me," said Charlie, tightening his grip. "And I don't want to see your ugly face around here while I'm here. So put your foot on the gas and beat it." Charlie lowered the boy back into his seat.

Charlie turned and slowly walked back to the group as the Impala screeched out of the park.

Charlie exchanged a sly grin with Joe.

"I sure do feel hungry. Let's say we load up and meet you at the apartment," said Joe.

The reception of the boys at the small apartment occupied by Charlie's parents and his little brother was more than Charlie had hoped for. His mother had the unique gift of making everyone feel welcome and wanted. Her experiences in raising four boys, breaking up fights, consoling losers, and feeding mouths that never seemed to get full, were all applicable to this group of young hellions that her son had brought to her door.

Charlie couldn't remember when he had seen the boys so restrained and courteous. Not that profanity was lacking, but if Charlie's mother heard it, she reprimanded the offender with maternal effectiveness. The boys loved being mothered, having someone to tell them to wash their hands and comb their hair, and savored every moment of it. Roy got Charlie's mom to sew a patch on his hat and other mending jobs soon followed, all of which were studiously supervised by the owner of the garment.

Charlie's father, a shy, quiet man who had spent his adult life following construction jobs halfway around the world, warmed to the boys, especially Vince. The two seemed inexplicably drawn to one another and an unspoken understanding formed between them. Charlie couldn't have been happier, for these were people he cared for and now he could see that they too could care for each other.

Enormous quantities of ice tea, fried chicken, mashed potatoes, and corn on the cob were consumed. Bud was not neglected. His plate was kept full and his smile was exercised as stories were swapped, each member of the group attempting to better his predecessor.

"How's my son treat you boys anyway?" said Charlie's mother as the group cleared the supper dishes.

"Oh, he treats us pretty bad," Keith spoke up quickly. "He's always beatin us up and pushing us around."

"Yeah, Keith's right. He's real mean to us, always pickin on us," said Roy.

"Is that right Charlie? Are you mean to these boys?" said Charlie's mother, her hands on her hips and her chin thrust forward. "I better not hear that you're beating these kids up, or else."

"Oh sure, of course. I have to beat these guys up all the time. It's the only way I can get them to behave, isn't that right?" Charlie looked to Bud for confirmation.

"Don't drag me into this. I'm innocent," said Bud, leaning back in his chair and patting his bloated stomach.

"Maybe we should give him a taste of his own medicine," said Charlie's mother, moving behind Charlie's chair and grabbing his arms. "What do you think boys?"

The boys swamped Charlie and his mother and knocked Charlie to the ground. A mass of bodies rolled on the living room floor. Laughter and shouts issued from the pile. The damage to the apartment consisted of only one broken dish, a record considering the countless pieces of furniture that had been broken over the years.

Charlie, Bud, and the boys departed after a large dose of television and an invitation from Charlie's mother to return for Christmas.

The bus bumped back down the sandy road outside of Gilmer. The surface showed signs of recent rains. The beautiful, warm days and mild nights the group had experienced during their departure, had, during their trip, slowly drifted into chilly nights and threats of rain.

The two counselors had decided to return on Saturday afternoon. Bud was due for a vacation starting the next day and Duane was to be there when they arrived in order to facilitate a smooth transition. Charlie was nervous about saying goodbye to Bud and hello to Duane, as Bud had been a stabilizing influence. The two had become good working partners, each having complete trust in the other's ability to handle any situation which might arise.

Charlie felt an added burden on his shoulders as he stepped from the bus and moved slowly towards Duane, whom the boys totally ignored.

"Hello Charlie. How'd it go? You look a little sunburned," said Duane. His manner was enthusiastic and he seemed ready to go.

"It was great weather most of the way and it was especially nice to get away from here for awhile," said Charlie tiredly, sitting on the fender of Duane's '62 Plymouth Valiant.

"The group sure has done a lot of work since Lake of the Pines. The camp looks great," said Duane. "I didn't know where to put my stuff, so I just picked a bunk in there. How's it going with the kids anyway?"

"Hello Duane!" said Bud.

Charlie sensed a slight mocking sarcasm in Bud's tone.

"No need to rub it in buddy," said Charlie.

"Oh, come on Charlie, lighten up," said Bud. "I'll be thinking of you guys every minute while I'm snuggled up with my sweater in front of a warm fire, chugging beer and telling the tales." Bud grinned and consoled Charlie with a slap on the back. "By the way, I thought you might want to know I'll be gone about four weeks, so if you two decide to take a trip before I get back, that's fine. I'll just fill in at the other camp until you get back. Then maybe we'll let Charlie have a vacation. Well, if there's anything left to send on vacation." Bud laughed and vigorously pounded Charlie on the back.

"If you keep enjoying yourself at my expense so much, there won't be anything left of me before you go on vacation," said Charlie, feigning a bad back.

Duane stood to the side, closely following the antics of the two veterans. His well-groomed appearance and reserved manner offered a stark contrast to the unkempt and free flowing style of the two tested counselors.

Despite his lack of confidence regarding Duane's ability in some areas, Charlie could discern a sense of fairness and a desire to help in the new counselor which would possibly be enough to see him through.

"One more thing I wanted to clear with the two of you before I leave tonight," said Bud.

"You're leaving tonight?" said Charlie.

"I don't see any reason not to now that Duane is here. In fact, as soon as I can get my gear loaded up I'm on my way. I'm also gonna ask Johnson if I can take David with me for a week. I hope that'll be alright with you two." Bud fixed his gaze on Charlie.

"Sure, that's fine," Charlie said in a subdued tone as he contemplated the implications of Bud's favoritism of David on the boys, as they had already begun to quarrel over it. "I hope you have a good vacation." Charlie wished he were the one leaving, the emotional demands of the last two months pressing on his body.

"Me too," said Duane. "I mean, I hope you enjoy your vacation too, and don't worry about us, we'll be fine," he continued, brimming with the confidence of the uniformed.

Bud packed his gear and departed shortly. Charlie felt more alone than he had in a long time as he watched Bud drive off out of sight.

Duane met Jerry and Danny, the only two boys who had remained in the vicinity of the camp. The others had headed quietly for the other camp, not bothering to even unpack their belongings from the bus, hurried on by the impulse to share the news of the new counselor.

CHAPTER XIII

Wild Man

He knew he shouldn't do it. He knew deep down in his soul that this was the last thing he should be doing and it would be the end of him of this life, shabby as it was, it was his. But he was not strong enough to resist. It had always been that way. The feelings came over him building from a smoldering disquiet to a roaring rage blind to all else but release, violent and brutal action which always left someone brutalized beaten and bloody. It was the only way to quell his obsessive waves of madness. It wasn't until the victim lay helpless and immobile beneath the labored breathing of the tortured beast that he could rest. Once unleashed the cauldron of hate, fueled by deep seated fear and the need to hurt to kill to sow destruction, would only subside make a retreat when it was exhausted spent its foulness smothering the latest victim with a blind fury.

He put the muzzle of the gun squarely between the man's eyes as the sweat flowed freely from his forehead down his face erratically around the barrel of the gun. He could feel the man's panic his rush towards insanity as he pulled the trigger once again and only the echo of hammer against empty chamber could be heard. "I didn't mean it, I take it back," the victim struggled to get the words out to make it right but it was already too late. It felt like only yesterday but he knew it was an eternity that he played this game tortured his torturer caught up in the feverish insanity of his life at that moment.

The constant roar of prisoners above and below him, five stories of caged animals driven mad by their solitary lives lived out in four by ten cells, was maddening. It carried the evil, hopelessness, psychosis, bottomless despair, and group insanity which whirled about him like a dust devil dancing over barren desert terrain. He could still see the fear in the man's eyes, smell the content of his bowels as he pulled the trigger a final time and the man's head disappeared into a spray of blood and bone and bottomless fear drowning in the abysmal darkness of death. Why wouldn't they shut up? As he sat in his cell staring at the metal door and its single one foot square Cyclop's eye of a window he could not shake the man's face as it exploded, the blowback of brain and bone and blood as it splattered against his face. "Shut the fuck up you mother fuckin bastards" he screamed through the eye into the concrete jungle of tortured souls drowning in the hell that possessed them. He grabbed his knees with his arms and drew them to his chest softly rocking back and forth back and forth. He sobbed uncontrollably as the world collapsed around him pinned him to the concrete floor stained with the ill spent years of thousands of other discarded and broken minds discarded hearts.

"I am sorry" he would begin almost inaudibly and then gradually it would increase in tempo and grow in volume until they could all hear. "I am so sorry Lord, I am so so sorry". The cacophony of terror and insatiable regret rumbled through the tiers of death row setting it ablaze with an echo of madness spoken in a hundred different tongues but all saying the same thing. "I am so sorry, I am so sorry. Lord please forgive me". He reached for the picture carefully secreted in the threadbare pillowcase. It was the same ritual every day. The picture was the only thing that remained for him the only memory which could dispel the self hatred the interminable loathing which lived in him which fed on his very life source until he could not breathe. It was the only memory of love which remained from the nightmare which was his life.

He was in the center of the picture. He was young just a teenager, a seasoned survivor at 16. He sat on the man's lap with strong arms wrapped around him from behind and big smiles on his face and on the face of Charlie's dad. Of course the other guys were in the picture too but all he could see was him and his dad for he had convinced himself after many years alone in this cement casket that this man was his real dad. Somehow somewhere he knew and so did Charlie's dad that they shared some history, perhaps not in this lifetime but before this life in a better time a happier time when he knew who his mother and father were when he knew what they looked like and sounded like when they laughed when they put their faces to his and told him they loved him. He would look at the picture each and every day until the tears were exhausted and he fell into a coma-like sleep awakened only by his victim's terrified eyes pleading begging until it exploded into the farthest reaches of the universe.

It was from this interminable cycle of guilt, remorse and regret that he sought release. The picture, the fantasy of family, love, caring, was the palliative which sustained him. It was all he had. There was no one for him now, no one to visit him in his lonely cell to write him call him think about him. He was a no body, a no one, a non-person known only to him, loved by no one including himself. He clutched the picture willing it into existence forcing the frozen smiles and unseen love into the present into the cell. He knew he was loved that year that one year of the long string of thirty one years that chronicled his life and he guarded and nurtured that oasis of love. He recalled the camp in the woods, the river trips, the runaways but above all he learned in that year what a family was what it meant to live with people who were tied together by fate and whose survival and well-being was a collective responsibility. The dried and mal-nourished seed of hisown forgotten ability to love flourished in those woods. He cherished those days kept them secreted in the deepest recesses of his mind where they could not escape not be forgotten.

He never tired of telling others of that story which they often dismissed as fabricated or worse yet sought to demean to discredit. But in the end he had the picture and it was proof. That was him sitting in that chair a fatherly embrace of love and a light which shone from both his and his father's face as they sat there alone unto themselves while surrounded by the gaggle of boys and counselors all chattering and joking. That man with the exploding head wouldn't listen and even after seeing the picture denied its truth. He ridiculed him laughed at the sadness of his efforts to kindle a spark of love from an old fading photograph.

"The old guy is probably already dead and you are just some second rate stick up artist" he taunted while relishing the obvious pain he was causing. He wouldn't let it go wouldn't let it rest. In the end it was both of their misfortunes that his tormentor was oblivious to the rage which he was unleashing the fires of anguish and self hatred which he was fanning. The lead projectile was the only means of stopping him of quieting his lies. He saw the picture. Why couldn't he have just let it go let him have his peace his escape his only untarnished, priceless talisman of normality, of love, of family?

"I am sorry dad I am so so sorry please don't hate me dad. I couldn't stop it I couldn't let him talk about you like that about us like that. He didn't have the right. He didn't know. I love you dad please don't abandon me. I am so so sorry." He pleaded with the ghosts of his life to pardon him to just let him have his moment of love of hope. "Shut the fuck up you stupid mother fucker. Quit whining about your daddy," came the response from lost souls floundering in the painful recollections of their own fathers, mothers, lovers, ghosts. He held the photo tightly and pressed it against his face trying hopelessly to resurrect that moment in time which would for him would be the last thought he held in this life.

On the day they executed him his last wish was to have the picture placed where he could see it with the last breath of life that he took. In that moment on that day he was at peace with his own demons his soul slipped quietly out of his body and flew into the night in search of his father.

CHAPTER XIV

harlie heaved himself up on his bunk, taking his recently purchased copy of "The Last Days of Socrates" with him. He felt an urge to lose himself in philosophic thought, which often served as an antidote to boredom and depression. He tried to become involved in the opening pages, but his mind continually wandered back to the boys and an uneasy premonition he had had earlier that morning on the return trip.

Charlie had begun to feel the mood of the group swing. The good natured camaraderie, evident during the trip, seemed to have vanished, and been replaced by a more sullen and angry, almost black mood. A few fights had broken out on the bus. Even Keith was abnormally quiet and restrained. Duane's arrival, Bud's leaving, David's being asked to go with Bud, and the imminent arrival of the tenth boy, Jerome, at the end of the week—too many changes too fast, Charlie thought, were likely to upset the precarious balance which had taken so long to establish.

"Oh there you are Charlie. I've been looking for you," said Duane, sauntering into the bunkhouse. "You know, Jerry and Danny seem like real nice kids. I'm looking forward to meeting the others."

"You'll meet them soon enough," said Charlie quickly, trying to decide if a warning was called for. "I think you should know, the group is a little edgy right now. You know, not wanting to come back to camp and all."

"They seemed fine to me, at least those two. Maybe you're just a little tired yourself."

Charlie reflected on his own initiation. Duane would just have to find out about the boys for himself—it would really be the only way.

"Maybe you're right. I guess I'm just ready for a vacation myself," said Charlie, exchanging searching glances with the neatly-pressed counselor.

Roy, Chuck, and Keith pushed past Duane and toward their bunks.

"Whose crap is this?" shouted Roy, picking up Duane's backpack from his bunk.

"That's mine," said Duane, unaware of the undercurrent of anger in Roy's voice.

"Well get it the hell off my bunk."

Roy threw Duane's things onto the middle of the dirt floor.

"Wait a minute there," said Duane, "you can't do that."

"We'll just see if I can't."

Roy rifled through Duane's personal belongings, ignoring the bewildered newcomer.

Duane looked questioningly at Charlie, who sat high on his bunk, passively observing the scene below. Duane, finding himself alone, marched over to Roy.

Chuck and Keith had joined in to scatter the counselor's belongings.

"Excuse me, but I think you should pick up my things and apologize," said Duane.

"I said fuck off doofus!" said Roy in Duane's face, shoving him backward.

Duane stumbled over his belongings and fell beside them on the floor. His mouth hung open and his hair draped into his face. His legs lay tangled in his backpack and bedroll. He directed a baffled stare at Roy, then at Charlie's reclining figure and stern face.

"OK Roy, that's enough. I think you owe Duane an apology and some help picking his stuff up," said Charlie.

"I knew the little fucker had been in my stuff. I just knew he was lying about that rolling machine," said Roy. He turned and headed for the door.

"Roy, get back here!" said Charlie, hopping down from the bed.

"What the fuck do you want? I don't have time for you now."

Roy continued toward the door.

Charlie caught up with Roy at the door and pulled him around. Chuck and Keith ceased their activities and Duane remained immobilized on the floor, his face contorted in an effort to understand what was going on.

"Well Mr. tough guy, I think you better make time for me. I said I wanted you to first help Duane with his things and then apologize to him, and if you decide you don't want to do that then you and I are going to have to have a little discussion," said Charlie.

Roy could sense Charlie's anger. He had learned that when the counselor said something he meant it. He also knew from previous experience that Charlie could not only kick his ass but wouldn't hesitate to do it if the situation called for it.

"That goddamned Stymie stole my rolling machine. I saw it in his trunk when I was over there. Chuck and Keith saw it too. He said he bought it at K-Mart," said Roy.

"We'll take care of Stymie in due time," said Charlie. "Right now we have a little business of our own to take care of. Now, what's it going to be, you and Duane or you and me? The choice is yours."

Roy looked down, avoiding Charlie's stare. He reluctantly moved around Charlie and toward Duane, who had picked himself up and was brushing the dirt off his shirt.

"You better take Bud's bunk Roy. I think that would be best," said Charlie, closely watching Roy's progress.

Roy stooped over and picked up Duane's dusty backpack. He trudged to Bud's vacant bunk and tossed the pack on the bed. Grumbling to himself, Roy once again moved toward the door.

"I think you forgot something, didn't you Roy," said Charlie.

Roy stopped. He slowly turned around and approached Duane.

"I'm sorry," Roy muttered in a subdued tone.

"That's alright," said Duane, extending his hand in an effort at reconciliation. Roy studied Duane's outstretched hand then looked into his nervous eyes. He hesitated, then quickly took one step toward Duane and clasped his hand.

"That's better. Now what's this about Stymie?" said Charlie.

"Those guys came over here and went through our stuff while we were gone. They took my comic and Keith's cigarette lighter too," said Chuck, his usually calm manner giving way to agitation.

"Chuck, I want you to go to the other camp and get the rest of our guys. Bring them back here and we'll get to the bottom of this. You two guys just stay right here until we get everyone together," said Charlie as he decided on the best course of action.

"I'll go get Jerry and Danny and bring them in," said Duane, seemingly recovered from his recent setback.

Once the facts were sorted out it became evident that the other group had indeed made a series of raids on the vacationers things, carrying off whatever they thought they could conceal without difficulty. Charlie, Duane, and the boys made a list of the items missing while Duane got acquainted with the rest of the group. Charlie, Roy, and Keith led a delegation to the other camp, demanding that all items be returned within twenty-four hours.

Hooper and John, a newly hired counselor, replacing Lamar, claimed not to know anything about the theft, but guaranteed that if the boys' things were in their camp the boys' would get them back. The counselors remained true to their word and returned all the boys' items the following day, but the incident elevated the tension already present between the two camps.

The other group's larceny had not been confined only to the vacant camp. According to reports Charlie and Duane received from Stymie, the boys had managed to obtain a large quantity of goods from the local K-Mart during their last shopping spree. As Stymie related the story, Bobby, one of the more daring boys, had led a group of four thieves and they had emerged from the store with a duffel bag overflowing with merchandise. Stymie thought the rival group should also be warned about the pair of BB guns that were now in Bobby's possession.

Duane's initial encounter with Roy set a precedent upon which all his future relationships with the boys were to be based. His first experience was followed by a series of harassments, any of which would have been more than enough to stop a less determined spirit.

Duane, however, appeared inured to the constant ridicule and physical abuse he received. The boys nicknamed him Doofus, accepting Roy's spontaneous assessment. When they felt more benevolent toward him it became Goofy Duane.

Duane's second incident with the boys came quickly after the first.

The first thing Charlie saw was Chuck and Duane stomping down the path toward the bus. Chuck, in the lead, appeared sullen and unhappy, not at all typical, while Duane, following behind, attempted unsuccessfully to halt the boy. Duane set his hand on Chuck's back in a futile effort to appease him. The argument which ensued led Charlie to believe that Duane was caught in the predicament of trying to enforce rules, a role he was not at all well suited for. Chuck's idea for settling the dispute was to take it into a clearing and slug it out.

Duane saw the idea as a way to possibly regain his lost respect. He miscalculated Chuck's power with bare knuckles and emerged with a pair of broken glasses, a bloody nose, and what was to become a reputable black eye.

Charlie was concerned about the situation and was at a loss in terms of how to assist the struggling counselor. He knew for certain he couldn't turn into his personal body guard. He came to the conclusion that Duane would have to establish his own position in the egregious brotherhood, whatever that might be. He did realize he had an inherent responsibility to keep his well-intentioned partner from serious harm until the group had learned to accept him for who he was.

Charlie fully realized his responsibility to Duane the night he went to the other camp to visit Hooper, leaving Duane alone with an apparently subdued camp. As Charlie returned less than an hour later, Jerry came rushing into camp breathless and wide-eyed.

"You better come quick, Duane's in trouble!" Jerry pleaded anxiously.

Charlie set off on a swift flight along the narrow path winding through the pines.

In the dense woods, Charlie heard a cacophony of laughter and jeering, accompanied by a chant of "Kill him, Kill him" cutting through the night.

Charlie exploded onto the scene of Duane and the boys, stopping abruptly to let his mind register what he saw.

Duane was perched some ten feet up in a pine tree. He clung to a few spindly branches. The back of his sweater was smoking and he was desperately trying to extinguish the remaining flames with his free hand. His legs were tightly wrapped around the trunk of the tree in a strained effort to support the weight the branches couldn't hold.

The boys had formed a circle around the base of the tree. Russ was armed with an axe, with which he had taken several chunks out of the tree, only inches below Duane's dangling feet. Vince and Keith were armed with crude torches and were trying in vain to set the rest of the tree on fire.

The boys spotted Charlie and those fast enough bolted into the woods. The rest were sent slinking back to camp with kicks and shoves.

Charlie looked up at Duane. "Come on down Duane. Are you alright?" Charlie stepped back and watched Duane's descent.

Duane made a final jump out of the tree.

"What in the hell happened?" said Charlie.

"I really don't know myself," said Duane, shaking and still smoldering.

"You better take that sweater off. I think it's ruined anyway." Charlie helped Duane remove the smoking garment.

"It just happened so quick," said Duane to no one in particular. "Kind of a game they said. I was in with Danny and they started calling for me. I thought maybe something was wrong, so I went to see. They were all standing around the campfire. You saw how they looked, no shirts, hair looking wild. All their talk stopped suddenly when I came out of the bunkhouse."

Duane observed Charlie's worried countenance. "I'm not really hurt. I don't think they really meant any harm. Anyway, before I knew it my sweater was on fire. I didn't know what had happened.

They were all being so nice to me just before that. I tried putting out the fire, but before I could finish Russ was after me with that axe and I didn't like the look in his eyes. It was crazy."

"You had me worried there for a minute." Charlie observed his partner, who appeared to have regained some of his composure. "One way or the other, we're going to have to put an end to this. We can't have them setting you on fire every time I'm not around."

Charlie watched Duane arrange himself as best as possible. The two counselors strode solemnly towards the bunkhouse, where the boys waited anxiously for their arrival.

Charlie entered the tent first, Duane directly behind him.

Jerry and Keith cast surreptitious glances in the counselors' direction, while the other boys, hoping they would go away, tried to ignore the moment of judgment.

"Does anybody have anything to say?" said Charlie. He searched the boys' faces, waiting for an explanation. Duane stood behind and to the side, looking more composed, yet still somewhat anxious.

Chuck spoke first, in a barely perceptible tone, and again when told to speak up, in a deep, slow baritone. "We was just having fun, we didn't mean nothing. It was that crazy fucking Russ. He starts yelling, setting Doofus on fire and chasin him with that axe."

"And you guys were just all innocent bystanders? That what you're saying Chuck?" said Charlie.

"Well, no not exactly," said Chuck, his voice trailing to an incoherent mumbling.

"Don't blame it all on me Chuck!" said Russ. "You guys were the ones that told me to do it."

"I see. So now the story becomes a little clearer." Charlie paused. "I want you guys to try to remember real hard what I told you in the first few days of camp about telling the truth. Who can tell me what I said?"

"I remember, Charlie" said Sherman, proud to be able to be helpful. "You said that we better always tell you the truth no matter how bad somethin was that we done. You always want us to tell you."

"The second part to that is, if I ever find out you lied to me, I'm going to kick your ass so far and so hard you'll wish you never heard of me. The quickest possible way for any of you to get on my bad side is to lie to me. Now, I'm going to ask one more time, what happened tonight?"

The boys avoided Charlie's gaze. They shifted nervously while Charlie stood in the center of the floor, feet planted firmly and arms crossed, waiting.

Roy cleared his throat. "It was me and Keith's idea. It was just gonna be a joke, then we got carried away. We talked Russ into putting the lighter fluid on him and setting it on fire."

"That's better," said Charlie. "Now, I want you guys to decide on a punishment for yourselves. Something that will even things out. When you've come up with something, let Duane know and he'll decide if it's adequate or not. Does that sound fair?"

The boys nodded their acquiescence in unison.

"I'm also going to tell you one last time—no bullying each other. That includes counselors."

The boys huddled together. The courtroom tension in the room was transformed into the studied decision making atmosphere of a board meeting. The group decided that a week without going to the movies, their special treat, was adequate punishment. Duane readily agreed.

The conflict resolved, the group dispersed and went to bed for the night.

Chuck lay awake, unable to sleep. "Charlie?" he called into the darkness of the bunkhouse.

"What Chuck?"

"Do you think you could teach me to tell time?"

The wolves howled in the woods.

"I didn't know you couldn't tell time. But sure, we'll do it tomorrow alright? First thing after breakfast."

"You guys pipe down over there," Vince grumbled, tossing in his bunk.

"Charlie?" said Sherman.

"What is it Sherman?"

"Why are you always talking about telling the truth? I mean, like why is it so important." Sherman was unsure if he was treading on dangerous ground with such a question.

"Let me put it like this." Charlie lay in the dark, wondering how to begin.

"You hear those wolves out there?" Charlie waited patiently for Sherman to answer.

"Yeah, I hear em."

"And you know how dark it gets in the woods at night and how easy it is to get lost?"

"Yeah, I know. It's scary out there too." The wolves' cries punctuated Sherman's words.

"Well, life is like the woods at night with wolves prowling around. And the truth is like this bunkhouse and how you're not scared in the bunkhouse." Charlie paused. "In other words, the truth makes you strong. It's like lifting weights—the more weights you lift, the stronger you get. Well, the more you tell the truth the stronger you get too, until the truth makes you so strong that it's the best weapon you have."

Charlie lay staring at the canvas roof. He slowly turned on his side. He closed his eyes and remembered the first lesson he had learned about telling the truth, and just what a humiliating lesson it had been.

The instruction had taken place in the fourth grade. He knew the exact year because that was the year his mother and father had gotten back together again. It was been a silly thing, really, telling a lie because he hadn't done his homework. It was an overly elaborately lie for an artless boy who wasn't yet equipped to tell competent ones. The lie had involved an overnight trip to visit his uncle some three hundred miles away. He had reported to his teacher in a sad tone how his uncle had suffered a heart attack. The situation had been under control until the teacher had called his mother expressing condolences for such a serious and sudden illness in the family.

It was the punishment which his mother and teacher had collaborated on that had shattered Charlie's mendacity. The next day at school, during a play rehearsal, his mother had appeared unexpectedly, a stern and uncompromising look crossing her face. Charlie never forgot the humiliation of having to apologize to his teacher in front of the entire class after his mother paraded him upon the stage.

The morning dawned crisp and cool. Duane had promised to make the boys hot biscuits and he rose early to prepare them. He had arrived at camp with an odd assortment of camping paraphernalia, including a cast iron cooker, a bivalve contraption with six hollows arranged linearly, three to a side. Duane prepared the dough and built a campfire in order to have a good supply of hot coals. He buried the cast iron mold deep in coals, then packed it tightly with sand. He heaped a finishing portion of coals on the lid.

Duane, Keith, and David watched the lid intensely.

"Time's up," said Keith. He jumped from his seat and headed directly for the buried oven.

"Wait a minute Keith. You'll need some sort of hot pad for that," said Duane, following behind Keith.

Keith unveiled the finished product. The boys tasted the biscuits. Their wide eyes and open mouths indicated that Duane had finally earned a little respect.

"Hey Doofus, these are pretty good biscuits," said David. A succession of grunts confirmed his opinion.

"I think the next thing we'll try is a ham in the whole," Duane stated cautiously.

"What's that?" said Jerry. "Sounds nasty to me."

"That's only because you're nasty," said David.

"Screw you, David. I'm not nasty." Jerry frantically chewed his nails.

"What about that time at the ranch when you let those girls put that cork up your ass," said Roy. "How bout that, Dino?"

"I didn't let them Roy. They ganged up on me and pulled my pants down and did it. I didn't let them Roy."

"You may not have let them, but that didn't stop you from liking it," said Roy.

"I don't care what you say. I think ham in the hole sounds good, whatever it is," Sherman interjected.

Duane felt relieved from the boys' first act of acceptance toward him as he sat in the middle of the group, eyeing the remains of his biscuits. He had already begun to calculate the necessary ingredients and preparations for a second dish to impress the boys. His instincts told him that the sooner he earned a second victory the better his chances would be to gain the acceptance he sought.

Only the previous night Duane had felt as if all hope was gone. He had been unable to find common ground on which to relate to the boys. They seemed to be just like all the other ruffians and tough guys he had encountered over the years. His entire life, it seemed, had been filled with insults and ridicule from such bullies.

Duane recalled the sleepless nights he had endured even as a young boy, asking himself Why me? What is it about me that attracts such viciousness? His first four days in camp, until this very morning, had been one relentless attack, both physical and mental. During those years of derision which he had waded through in solace, he had, as a means of survival, developed a center deep within himself that was unreachable by the outside world. This sanctuary was where he had retreated so frequently in the last few days, gaining renewed strength from each visit.

"Yes," Duane repeated quietly to himself as he sat lost in thought, the boys still scrambling for verbal advantage around him, "I will come out of this alright. They will learn to need me and respect me."

Duane knew the boys would come around, for other people had before, in other times and other places. It was like his father advised him—hang in there Duane, don't let them get you down and they will come around.

"Hey Doofus, when can we have that ham in the whole?" said Sherman, shaking Duane by the shoulder in an attempt to bring him out of his reverie.

"Huh? What did you say?" said Duane, scratching his head and returning to reality.

"Look at old goofy Duane. Boy is he weird," Chuck said just to harass.

After breakfast, Duane and Danny, who were fast becoming friends, completed the cleanup chores. Meanwhile, Charlie began to impart to Chuck the knowledge of time locked away in the big hand and the little hand.

CHAPTER XV

Chuck's lesson was Charlie's first attempt at transmitting mechanical knowledge to any of the boys. Chuck proved to be a bright pupil with a quick mind, which prevented the instructor from possibly placing the blame of potential failure on his student.

Charlie had assumed that a watch was the best tool for learning how to tell time, but after a half hour of futile attempts to teach Chuck with the timepiece, he changed to paper and pencil. With the new technique, Chuck immediately grasped the subject. Charlie felt joy at successfully teaching the boy and Chuck was delighted with his newly acquired skill. He recited the correct time every fifteen minutes for the rest of the day.

Following the morning chores, Duane suggested a lengthy hike for the group. The boys eagerly accepted the suggestion as a welcome diversion from the daily monotony. With a minimum of preparation the group tramped off northwest through the woods.

As the group trudged back along the sandy road to camp, the school bus bore down on them from behind, jolting and jarring its way down the road. There was no attempt by the driver, the new counselor of the other group, Charlie recognized, to slow the speeding coach. The counselor smirked as he spurred the bus on into the straggling line of boys. The boys leaped into the protection of the brush on either side of the road. As he crashed into the brush, Duane spotted two shiny black barrels protruding from the windows.

"They got BB guns!" said Duane.

The bus rolled past and left the ground as it hit a bump in the road. At thirty miles an hour, the accuracy of the five guns protruding from the windows was hindered, leaving only Keith with a trifle of blood down his arm. He proudly declared it a gunshot wound.

The group hauled themselves out of the bushes and made their way back to camp, the boys cursing and firing middle fingers back at the retreating bus.

The group slowly rounded the last turn in the road, where they were greeted by Mr. Johnson and the new boy, a black youth. Mr. Johnson was desperately trying to assert his authority, while the boy, his arms waving wildly, was attempting to land a blow on his captor. His fury was inhibited by Johnson's bony hand gripping the back of his shirt collar.

"Now Jerome, Jerome. I said settle down. You have no choice, you have to stay here," said Johnson, staying calm amid the whirlwind he was attempting to restrain.

"Looks like you've got a problem on your hands there," said Charlie. He approached Mr. Johnson and the new boy cautiously.

The second Mr. Johnson's attention was distracted, Jerome managed to yank himself free. Charlie grabbed the boy before he could escape.

"Whoa, just a minute there," said Charlie, gripping Jerome's shirt collar.

Jerome kicked and cursed.

"I said cut it out!" said Charlie. He tugged hard on Jerome's sweatshirt and lifted the boy off the ground.

Jerome received the message this time. His body went limp and his anger withdrew into his eyes. Charlie lowered him to the ground, keeping a grip on his collar. Jerome sized up his new tormentor.

The veteran boys stood around in a semicircle, looking on in amusement.

"What happened Jerome, not so tough anymore. Why don't you try runnin again?" said Chuck.

"OK you guys, get lost. We don't need a peanut gallery," said Duane over his shoulder, intently studying the new arrival.

Jerome was small, about four foot ten, maybe one-hundred-and-twenty pounds. His tiny frame was covered with sagging garments that swallowed his limbs. His ill-fitting clothes caused him to fidget first one way then the other. He would hike up the sleeves of his sweatshirt in an attempt to free his hands, then grab his pants by the waist and yank them up. Charlie thought that perhaps a belt would help to control his pants. The remnants of a jagged scar remained visible on his forehead.

As Charlie scrutinized Jerome, Jerome too studied his jailer.

Jerome could gauge from thirteen years of experience of the hand of authority on his backside, with a good deal of accuracy, just how far he could push any particular adult. The stern look that he received from the grown up coupled with the rough, powerful grip warned him that he shouldn't push too far. Just how far he wasn't quite sure yet, but in time he would find out. After his three runaway attempts at the ranch, those white bastards had sent him out to this godforsaken place in the middle of nowhere. Not that the ranch was that great, but this was unbearable.

He already knew all the boys in this backwoods prison. He had spent time at the ranch with them. They weren't too bad, except for that little faggot Dino, but he knew he could take care of him alright. As for the others, he was well aware of which ones to avoid. Chuck and Sherman were there, so at least he wouldn't be the only black. He was surprised to see Chuck looking so content. He remembered from the ranch that Chuck had been almost as adamant as he had been about not leaving, but now, well, he looked different. He knew his first step would be to check things out as quickly as possible. Chuck would tell him what he wanted to know about this counselor who had his grimy hands on him.

"Uh uh uh, I'd like to go now," said Jerome, announcing a stutter to the two counselors.

"You think you can behave yourself well enough for me to let you go?" said Charlie, determined to hold the boy all night if that would be what it took to break him.

"Sh sh sure I can," said Jerome, kicking up dirt and refusing to meet Charlie's eyes.

Charlie let Jerome go and the boy ran off toward the woods. Mr. Johnson and the two counselors watched him until he was lost among the trees.

"No one seems to know what do with him," said Mr. Johnson. "He's caused nothing but trouble wherever he's been. He doesn't seem to make friends. The only person he's ever been friendly with is Chuck. He doesn't seem to like whites at all, that much we do know."

The three men exchanged questioning looks. Mr. Johnson felt relief at being rid of the boy. His new guardians wondered what new crises would arise with his arrival.

Mr. Johnson inquired about the group's plans for their next trip. He mentioned casually that Bud would be coming for David next week. Despite his close surveillance, Charlie failed to detect any signs of hesitation on Johnson's part concerning David's preferred standing. Charlie thought it was peculiar, however, that there was a push for the group to plan a trip as soon as possible.

"Maybe even a short trip would be appropriate," said Mr. Johnson, fishing for a bite from either of his employees.

"I for one would really like to go," said Duane. His exuberance sent his eyelids into a flutter. He adjusted his glasses and attempted to smooth down his cowlick. "What do you think Charlie? Why don't we go somewhere next week, at least for a few days. It feels to me like the time's right."

Charlie realized that Duane was at least partially right. With David going there would be a good deal of bad humor. Charlie had already noticed the difference in David's attitude and the group's attitude toward David. Bud's blatant favoritism toward the boy was a source of envy for the others. They were well aware that he received extra money and cigarettes, albeit discreetly. Resentment was slowly being cultivated by those less fortunate. It was Bud's good-nature and the obvious respect the majority of the group had for him that had thus far kept the situation manageable.

David's natural sense of superiority and ascendancy over the others was only magnified and reinforced under the special attention he received. As a result, Charlie's relationship with him had become one of mistrust and animosity. Charlie contemplated the problem frequently. He hated to see anyone picked out for special favors. It simply wasn't fair.

"I think you're right actually," said Charlie after a protracted silence. "I think the state fair grounds in Dallas would be a good place to take them next week. It's close and it may offer some educational attractions."

"That sounds great to me. I know they have a neat aquarium and several museums," said Duane.

"Now that we're talking about it, I think we should take an extended trip through the south before Bud returns." Charlie looked directly at Mr. Johnson, his mind already made up.

"Sure Charlie. I don't see why not, with winter coming on and everything, you might as well go where its warm. How far were you planning to go?" said Johnson.

"I would say all the way to Florida would be about right."

Duane was taken aback. He fixed his eyes on his colleague and his mouth hung open. All the way to Florida just like that—on the spur of the moment. Charlie certainly didn't hesitate. He may not have been the friendliest person or the most helpful for that matter, but he did get things moving.

"Well, if everything's agreed on then I guess it's Dallas next week and off to Florida the week after. We'll let the kids draw up the actual itinerary. How does that sound Duane?" said Charlie.

"Great," said Duane, smiling at Charlie and hoping that he was successfully transmitting his desire to be friends.

Charlie, too, for the first time in a while, actually noticed Duane. He wasn't so bad after all—likeable really. Though he couldn't be relied on for discipline, he did seem to be able to communicate with at least some of the boys, Danny and Sherman especially, in a way that Charlie had been unable to.

The familiar sounds of a fight in progress came up the path from the direction of the bunkhouse. Charlie was off at a sprint with Duane following close behind.

Mr. Johnson remained behind, motionless, a thin smile on his pallid lips as he watched the counselors racing away. He sighed deeply and walked back to his pick up truck. Johnson lowered his skeletal hand to the gear shift and drove away without looking back.

Charlie and Duane came on the scene. Vince and Jerome were embroiled in a collision on the dirt floor of the bunkhouse. The other boys casually reclined in their bunks while shouting encouragements. From volume alone it was discernible that the audience's support was in Vince's favor.

Charlie stepped into the center of the fighters. He reached down and yanked Vince up and away as Duane collared Jerome. Vince's fury waned rapidly. Jerome hissed and spit, his face covered with a combination of tears, dirt, and blood. Charlie ordered Vince to his bunk and went to the assistance of Duane with an impatient tread. The two men pinned Jerome between them as he cussed and fumed.

"It was that nigger started it!" said Vince. "Wasn't my fault Charlie. He came in here acting tough, pushin Dino and Danny around, telling them he was gonna beat their asses if they didn't do what he told them to. I swear it Charlie. Ask Chuck, he'll tell you."

"How about it Chuck?" said Charlie, grappling with Jerome, whose energy seemed boundless.

"That's right, it was Jerome's fault," said Chuck. "He came in here talking big, sayin how he was gonna do whatever he wants to here. He said he didn't care what the counselors did to him, he wasn't afraid of no white trash."

Charlie studied Jerome's disheveled features. "I guess I'll have to sit on him for a while." Charlie maneuvered Jerome to the ground and lowered his back onto the boy in such a way that Jerome's frantic efforts were quelled. "OK, why don't you guys go find something else to do while Duane and I have a little chat with the new member of our group."

The boys shuffled out, casting sidelong glances at a prostrate Jerome, whose face was contorted in a mixture of anger and humiliation.

Jerome fumed and looked out of teary eyes. The faces mocked him as they passed.

"Settle down Jerome. We're going to stay just like this until you calm down enough to talk to us, then we'll let you go," said Charlie in a soothing tone.

Duane reached down to wipe the mess off Jerome's face. Jerome whipped his dusty head from side to side to avoid the contact and Duane withdrew his hand.

"Keep your white motherfuckin hands off me!" said Jerome.

Jerome's limbs began to ache from the weight of the body on top of him. A familiar feeling of helplessness came over him. His tears washed away his hatred and left loneliness and fear in its absence. He knew what would come next. That overwhelming sense of desperation which drew him into himself, sometimes for days, not talking to anyone, hardly eating, just going through the motions of being alive. His stutter always got worse then, it seemed. He couldn't make people understand him.

"You alright Jerome?" said Charlie. "You ready for me to let you up now?"

Jerome lay still, his head on the dirt, lost in thought.

"I said, you alright Jerome?"

"Yeah." Jerome had a powerful urge to lay down in the comfort of solitude. He wanted everybody to leave him alone. He wanted to die.

Charlie and Duane slowly withdrew from the tent. They turned back at the entrance to study Jerome's back. He lay curled up on the bunk, motionless and silent.

"Vince, I told you I didn't want you starting any fights around here. If you got a problem, you come see me," said Charlie, emerging from the tent and running head on into the group of boys huddled outside the door.

"Damn, it was his fault. I didn't do nothing," said Vince.

"You just remember what I said."

"You think we'll be alright on the road with this new kid?" said Duane.

"We'll be fine. In fact, we better get everyone together tonight after dinner and let them know what we're planning. We should also ask for some volunteers who'd like to help plan the trip south. I think Chuck would probably like to help with that."

"That would be great. I'll get some of the guys together. We'll break out the atlas and do it."

"By the way Duane, thanks for your help with Jerome in there. I appreciate it." Charlie squeezed Duane's hand.

Duane and Charlie parted and Charlie wandered through the camp and into the woods. The scene with Jerome had troubled him. He couldn't shake the feeling of desperation which the boy had transmitted to him. Something about this one was different.

The sound of excited boys came from behind Charlie. Duane had obviously broken the news of the impending trips to the group. Charlie wished he had been the one to tell them. It was better that Duane had done it though, for in a small way it would help to bolster his image. Charlie did miss seeing the excitement on their faces— these boys so different from the millions of others their same age who ate hot lunches in school cafeterias around the country, their conversations revolving around who likes who and the upcoming school dance. Happy faces with homes and parents to return to. A far cry from what these kids were experiencing.

Charlie stopped at a small clearing beside the stream that the boys had named "Wolf Creek," in honor of the wild creatures that roamed its banks at night searching for sustenance. Charlie solemnly lowered himself onto the bank, against a thick carpet of fallen oak leaves. He rested his back on a fallen cypress.

He knew what it was about Jerome that troubled him. It was that same feeling of impotence that he experienced when trying to deal with Russ. What was he really accomplishing out here in the middle of nowhere besides keeping the boys from killing each other? He wasn't sure there was anything else. He knew the boys respected him, but that seemed to be merely on a physical level, the respect that those lower in the pecking order reserve for those above.

The sounds of rustling leaves and snapping twigs brought Charlie out of his reflection. He glanced up and saw a figure approaching at a run from the depth of the woods.

The wolf hadn't become aware of Charlie, the counselor's lowered position hiding him from the animal's searching eyes, until the two were almost on top of each other. The creature seemed more occupied with something behind it, although Charlie saw no signs nor heard no indication of a pursuer. The animal was large, what Charlie in his limited personal experience with wolves would declare a superior specimen, its strength and vigor apparent in its long, loping stride and thick, healthy coat. The wolf's tail and ears were cocked in the traditional pose of leadership and although there appeared to be a sense of flight about the animal there was no evidence of fear.

For a short period, Charlie's eyes met the wolf's. Communication seemed impossible across the gorge between nature and man; Charlie recognized the feeling of complete powerlessness which had driven him to seek solace by the stream.

The wolf quickly disappeared into the thickness of brush and trees, its steps still barely audible above the gurgling of the stream.

David soon left with Bud and a noticeable bite developed in the group's personality after his departure. The knowledge of the upcoming trip seemed to be the only remedy for the rejection some of the boys felt.

The departure for the trip went smoothly. Jerome's retreat into his own private world had lasted only a day, after which he had returned to his state of creating constant upheaval wherever he went.

The bus motored along, heading due west, basking in the weakened rays of the fall sun.

"Alright Jerome, this is the last time I'm going to tell you," said Charlie as he watched Duane unsuccessfully attempting to bring the growing pandemonium in the back of the bus under control.

"You come right back here and sit down with me," said Duane, lurching down the aisle in pursuit of Jerome.

"Screw you Doofus!" said Jerome, losing his balance and almost falling head over heels as the bus quickly swerved to the shoulder and came to a grinding halt.

"Enough is enough," said Charlie. "I can't drive and discipline you at the same time. Duane can't drive all the time, so let's trying something new." Charlie scanned the boy's faces, waiting until he had their attention. "How many of you guys would like to learn how to drive?"

Six hands flew up immediately.

"I already know how to drive. I've stole lots of cars," said Keith.

Jerome and Russ joined Keith in claiming careers in auto theft. Charlie could sense their defiance. They weren't going to be drawn into any kids game just to shut them up.

"OK then. You guys that raised your hands can take turns driving the bus. I'll sit behind you and tell you what to do, but it's all yours. About fifteen minutes apiece should do the trick."

The six boys jockeyed for seats closest to the driver's, hoping to be the first to try. The dissenters, Keith, Jerome, and Russ, began to have second thoughts.

"I wouldn't mind practicing a little more though," said Keith, "I'm probably a little rusty."

Jerome and Russ, not ready to give in, grumbled and walked to the back of the bus.

"Well, if we have enough time you can be last Keith," said Charlie. "We'll start with the littlest guys first and go on up from there."

The words were barely out of Charlie's mouth when Dino appeared before him, biting his fingernails and acting as if he needed to go to the bathroom rather than drive.

The driving lessons proved to be an effective sedative. The smaller boys required the extra height of a duffle bag to enable them to see out of the window. Their stubby legs were barely capable of reaching the gas pedal.

The group arrived in Dallas in late afternoon. They stopped first at Safeway to procure those items necessary for meals for the next few days, the last cans of baked beans having been wolfed down at lunch. Charlie and Danny assumed the shopping duties while Duane remained behind with the rest of the boys.

As Danny and Charlie neared the coach, their arms full of groceries, the bus suddenly exploded with activity. Boys jumped out of the doors and the windows. Duane came flying out of the emergency exit, his hand covering his mouth and nose, followed closely by Sherman and Roy, both gagging.

Charlie and Danny stood mesmerized by the sudden flight. Within seconds the bus was empty, or so it appeared until Charlie caught sight of a lone figure reclining in the back, seemingly immune to the dreaded malignancy that had sent the others fleeing.

The group staggered back and forth, clutching their throats and gasping for air.

"What in the hell's going on here?" said Charlie. He pounded Duane soundly on the back in hopes that it would revive his color, which had changed to a dark shade of blue.

"It's Jerome," said Chuck, "he cut one."

"You mean that Jerome farting brought all you guys flying out of the bus, like it was on fire? One person passing gas couldn't be bad enough to cause this kind of commotion."

"You'll see," said Roy before Charlie disappeared into the interior of the bus. Seconds later he reappeared, holding his hand over his mouth and nose, disgust on his face.

Jerome meanwhile enjoyed the fanfare. He had discovered a potent weapon to add to his arsenal of insults and badgering. He repeated his feat several times after that, knowing full well that no one dared return until the air had cleared. The air did clear some forty minutes later, after Jerome reluctantly opened all the windows and doors, a task which he performed with little enthusiasm. He earned himself a certain amount of respect that afternoon, as he was from then on recognized as being in possession of a singular talent, unpleasant as it may have been.

The group established camp at Lake Lavon, five miles north of Dallas. After a hot dinner of hamburgers and corn on the cob they settled in for a peaceful night on the shore. A Halloween moon hung low in the sky. The waves lapped at the shore, herded in by a chilly northeastern wind.

Charlie crawled into his tent. He felt the nearly sixty days of straight time that he had served at camp weigh on his body. He sat up, bumping his head against the roof. Charlie removed his shoes and socks then his jeans and pulled his T-shirt free of his head. He rolled his jeans and shirt into a neat bundle and carefully deposited it in the bottom of his sleeping bag, a strategy which guaranteed a warm set of clothes in the morning cold. Charlie shut his eyes. The sound of an argument came in through the screen mesh.

"Shut up out there. If I hear one more word from anyone I'm gonna come out and personally kick your butts across the lake!" said Charlie.

Charlie's threat pierced the hull of the bus and froze Jerome and Vince in mid-sentence. They traded glares and turned away from each other, each promising to himself to continue the argument at a more opportune time.

"You always startin some kind of trouble, you know that Jerome," said Roy. "You gonna get your ass kicked good and proper one of these days nigger."

"I ain't afraid of you or anybody else. That includes that asshole Charlie. He ain't nothing but a big mouth," said Jerome in a muffled tone.

"Yeah, that's why you shut up so quick while ago, cause you ain't scared of Charlie," said Chuck.

"Naw, I just didn't want to fight with Vince. He's too dumb."

"You think you're so smart?" said Chuck just above a whisper. "You can't even read."

"Who says you have to read to be smart anyway?"

"Hey Chuck, who was you writin that letter to today, you and Duane?" Sherman interjected.

"My mother."

"What you writin her for anyway?" said Jerome, his curiosity aroused by the far away look in his friend's eyes and the sudden sadness in his voice.

"We're goin to New Orleans and I'm gonna see her."

"Who says? Nobody told me nuthin about goin to New Orleans. Nobody ever tells me nothing," Jerome thought aloud.

"That's cause you're always causing trouble. Nobody wants to have anything to do with you," said Roy.

Silence descended and eliminated all further conversation. Chuck, anxious about seeing his mother after so long, wondered how she was. He hadn't heard from her in three years and didn't even have her address. He had to get it from Mr. Johnson. Still, as he curled up in his sleeping bag on the backseat of the bus, he missed his mama and wanted to see her.

Jerome too was troubled and restless. He respected Chuck and wanted to be his friend. So why did he have to be so mean to him? He often found himself saying and doing things he knew he would regret. He wanted friends. Like Russ and Vince, they were good friends, they talked and shared tobacco and comic books. At least Chuck had a mama to write to. Someone who cared.

Jerome tossed and turned into the night. He dreamt of monsters trying to grab him. His legs were heavy as he tried to run away and call for help. He awoke just when he was about to be devoured. It was those monsters in his dreams that made him do bad things— he knew that. But he couldn't get away from them no matter how hard he tried.

The group was up and on the road early the next morning after a quick breakfast of cereal and fruit. The group decided, at Charlie's suggestion, to visit the zoo first and try to learn something about the animals.

At the zoo, Charlie and Sherman had fallen behind the main group and when reunited discovered the others at the chimp cage, deeply engaged in learning. The chimp, although outnumbered, was holding his own. He would swing to the far end of the cage, away from the boys gathered in front of the bars, then, in a frontal assault, throw himself at the bars, spitting at whomever was closest. The boys returned spittle for spittle as they dodged the liquid projectiles.

"All right all you monkeys," said Charlie, "I think you've mastered your zoology lesson for the day. Let's go before they put you all in a cage."

Charlie's voice distracted the boys long enough for the chimp to swing toward them. A baffled expression came over Duane's face. He felt the wetness on his shirt and made the connection. The boys backed away from the cage, convulsing with laughter.

The group ate a lunch of Peanut butter and jelly sandwiches and Kool-Aid aboard the bus. Visions of T-bone steaks and baked potatoes filled Charlie's mind as he lowered himself into the driver's seat and headed for the fairgrounds. He felt the grunginess of his dirty hair and unwashed clothes. A hot shower wouldn't be bad either.

One of the worst hardships for Charlie was the absence of cleanliness—the sheer inability to experience the luxury of a hot shower and clean clothes on a daily basis. He had neglected through oversight to have his hair cut before he came for the job. It had been close to three months since his last haircut. At camp he had taken to wearing a headband, something he had picked up from the boys. Surprisingly enough, it was an efficient means of keeping his unruly mop of hair out of his face.

The boys entered the fairgrounds in high spirits, their adrenalin pumping after their confrontation with the chimpanzees.

Vince and Sherman took the lead. Charlie knew this was because it gave them the advantage of not only spotting, but making initial contact with eligible females. Charlie positioned himself in the middle of the group. He called out directions and kept a cautious eye open for any signs of trouble. Duane and Danny brought up the rear, their heads thrown back, eyes staring up in wonder at Tall Tex. His two story bulk decked out in cowboy hat and boots welcomed visitors to the fairgrounds in a deep voice.

Charlie wondered if he looked as tired as Duane.

"How are you doing Duane? Did you get any sleep last night?" said Charlie.

"Oh, a little bit, guess I'm not used to sleeping on the hard ground yet."

"You'll have plenty of time to get used to that."

"I guess I will." Duane sounded only half-convinced.

Duane considered the still evident spot on his shirt from the chimp. It was another in an endless series of events which seemed to conspire to make him the fool. He knew better though. They must have been some kind of tests—somebody or something out there was simply testing him. Duane felt his confidence rise as he entered the aquarium in the wake of the others.

The boys raced from exhibit to exhibit. They fired question after question at the counselors, who tried to the best of their abilities to produce reasonably accurate answers.

The boys crisscrossed the fairgrounds repeatedly and insisted on investigating every inch. Near sunset, the group made their way back to the bus, parked on a back road alongside the railroad tracks.

Vince and Sherman, the two self-appointed scouts, lengthened their lead on the group and ducked into the gymnasium on the edge of the fairgrounds. They reappeared a few minutes later, just as the main body of the group swung by the gym. Neither of the boys gave anything away by the expressions on their faces. Charlie soon found himself curiously in the lead of the group, the two scouts having disappeared again. When he turned to look for the two boys he observed a group of black teenagers bursting out of the gym door. Vince and Sherman kept guard as the group increased. The second time Charlie turned to monitor the situation the crowd from the gym had tripled in size.

"Come here Vince," Charlie called.

Vince approached Charlie.

"What's goin on here?" said Charlie.

"I don't know man."

"What do you mean you don't know? You go in the gym one minute, next minute you come out and you got twenty guys dogging us, lookin like they mean business."

"I didn't do nothin man."

"OK you guys, let's stay together now. Come on Duane, get those guys going." Charlie fell to the rear as he issued the orders. The bus stood twenty yards away. Charlie was desperately trying to decide how to keep the lingering menace, now numbering some two dozen, and beginning to pick up rocks, bottles, and sticks, from cracking up the vehicle.

A fist-sized rock slammed into the railroad tracks ten feet to Charlie's left, sending up a gathering of smaller rocks. Several other projectiles followed, all coming in close range. If there was one thing Charlie simply could not tolerate, it was bullies. His blood simmered as he turned and faced the advancing threat. He focused his mind on the center of the attacking line.

The teenagers halted twenty yards from Charlie. He stood across from the crew, his feet spread and his arms folded over his chest. The teenagers spread out. Rocks and bottles smashed against the pavement, inching closer to Charlie's unwavering figure. Charlie bent over slowly and picked up a rock in each hand. An enemy projectile whipped within inches of his ear.

The next thing Duane saw, huddled within the group some five yards in front of Charlie, was the counselor charging directly for the center of the angry wall of teenagers. Duane's mouth dropped open and disbelief came over the group, immobilizing them. Vince let out a war whoop, Charlie having set the tone. Before Duane could command his legs to move, he saw the attackers break and run back toward the gym. The sight of the fleeing enemy got the boys' adrenalin flowing. They let out one collective yell and ran after the broken ranks. The boys launched bottles and rocks at the bullies and chased them into back alleys and side streets.

The threat had been contained and the bus saved. Charlie, Duane, and the boys returned to the coach unable to contain their emotions. They hugged each other and filled the bus with catcalls, bursting finally into song. The group spent the journey back to camp telling the tale of their triumph, which grew more daring with each repetition.

Within minutes of the group's arrival back at camp, the boys rushed to the other camp to sing their own praises. The stand was a long awaited victory, a solidification of the group's unity, which Charlie knew would be essential as they attempted more daring outings demanding total cooperation. Duane, too, although not as familiar with the life cycle of the group thus far, could sense the change, not only in the boys, but in him.

The only member who was immune to the metamorphosis was Jerome. His attention grabbing antics became more frequent. The other boys, bound closer than ever together, took less notice of his abrasive behavior. As a result, his disruptive influence was somewhat reduced.

The bunkhouse remained a center of animated conversation until past midnight. The pot belly stove was continually stoked with pitch pine to ward off the near freezing temperatures.

"Hey Jerome, what you sulking about?" said Vince jokingly as he approached Jerome, who lay in the darkness of his bunk.

"Leave me alone, I ain't done nothing to you."

"I was just trying to be friendly. "

"Well fuck you. I don't want to be your friend."

The insult sparked Vince's anger. He reached down and punched the back of Jerome's hidden torso.

Jerome exploded from his bunk and hurled himself at Vince. The two boys slammed into the pot-belly stove, knocking it ajar. Jerome had not awakened not only Vince's desire for revenge, but the entire group's. The residue of their good mood had all but been destroyed by Jerome's attitude. His disdain for his peers, as well as for the counselors, was clear on his face. Roy and Keith's locked up resentment forced them into the scuffle. They were intent on teaching Jerome a lesson he wouldn't forget. By the time Duane reacted, his powers to stop the beating were inconsequential.

Charlie was up at the kitchen helping Danny write a letter to his brother about the day's activities and the impending trip to Florida, where Danny's brother lived, when he heard the commotion of the fight.

Charlie burst into the tent. Vince and Roy were so involved in pummeling Jerome that they failed to notice Charlie's presence until he threw them off Jerome one by one. The assailants fled to their bunks. Jerome lay on the dirt floor, cursing wildly, his face smeared with snot, saliva, and blood. He lashed out at Charlie's extended hand.

"What happened Duane?" said Charlie, temporarily removing his attention from Jerome.

"It was Jerome with his smart mouth again," said Duane as the rest of the group added their confirming testimony.

"How come when I came in here it was three against one?" said Charlie. "Is Jerome that tough?"

"He was asking for it, like always," said Vince.

"We was just going to teach him a lesson Charlie," said Roy.

"I told you guys about fighting. I don't care if Jerome did start it, that's no call for all of you to gang up on him like that. Look at him, do you think your lesson did him any good?"

Jerome writhed on the ground and cried out.

"I guess this means no movies again this week," said Charlie.

A storm of objections arose from the boys and drowned out Jerome's lament.

"It was him that did it!" said Chuck.

"Yeah, it was Jerome. I don't see why we have to be punished for what Jerome does," said Russ.

The group continued their protests, their animosity toward Jerome increasing.

"I guess he beat himself up then. Is that what you're trying to tell me, that when I came in here I didn't see three guys piled on top of him?" said Charlie.

The boys were silent. Charlie scrutinized their faces, waiting for an answer.

"He started it Charlie. It's always Jerome. I wish he'd never come here. He's nothing but trouble," said Roy.

"Let them go to the movies," said Jerome in a trembling voice, from the floor behind Charlie.

All attention turned to Jerome

"What did you say?" said Charlie.

"I said, let them go."

The group gazed in disbelief at Jerome. Charlie didn't know what to make of the situation.

"Well how bout it?" said Chuck anxiously.

"You mean that nobody should be punished for this?" said Charlie, seeking guidance from the group as he tried to decide on the best course of action.

"It was Jerome's fault. I know the others were right in the middle of it, but Jerome's the one that really started it," said Duane soberly.

"You mean, Jerome should be punished. The rest of you should go to the movies and Jerome should stay here. Is that what I hear?" said Charlie.

"Sure, why not," said Jerry.

A long moment passed within which hope flourished and anxiety built.

"Alright, Jerome and I will stay here, the rest of you can go," Charlie heard himself say before he realized he had made a decision. "Now I want everyone in bed and the lights out."

Those not already in their bunks went silently about the process of getting in them. Charlie, too, made directly for his bunk. He stopped first at Jerome's side.

"Are you alright?" said Charlie.

Jerome nodded slowly.

"You better get yourself cleaned up and into bed. Do you need any help?"

"No," said Jerome softly.

Charlie was exhausted from the emotional drain of the day. He longed to curl up in his sleeping bag, close his eyes, and let the darkness wash away his weariness.

Charlie extinguished the Coleman lanterns.

Jerome lay motionless where he had so recently taken his bruises. His labored breathing filled the whole bunkhouse.

"Jerome, I'm sorry I got mad at you like that. I didn't mean what I said about not wanting you in the group," said Vince.

"Me too Jerome," said Roy. "I'm sorry about beatin up on you, and thanks for saying that about the movies."

Jerome rustled and lifted himself from the floor. He shuffled to his bunk by the light of the pot belly stove and threw himself on top of his sleeping bag.

"Goodnight everybody," said Charlie.

"Goodnight you guys," said Duane.

The boys woke in good spirits the next morning. The day promised a trip to Longview, where hot showers would erase their grime and the Laundromat would yield them clean clothes. There was something about the prospect of Saturday night at the movies in Daingerfield that made each boy pay particular attention to how he looked and smelled, considerations that at any other time were frivolous.

There was no single event which held more importance to the boys than Saturday night at the movies. The Daingerfield movie theatre was a center of social activity for the teenagers of the small east Texas community. It was a place that promised kissing, holding hands, and the myriad other activities associated with budding sexuality. The majority of the boys had no idea what movie was showing.

They spent their time proceeding up and down the aisles, watching others and enjoying being watched. This was their opportunity to be a part of the real world, to make friends, talk about girls, and just have a good time. The boys would pass Charlie and Duane, strategically located on either side of the theatre in the back, and flash smiles when they had some local girl in tow or hopeful grins when they had promising prospects, which always seemed to be the case.

Saturdays were also a time of especially good behavior, as no one dared to jeopardize this most important night. Mr. Johnson frequently made appearances on Saturdays, sensing that the odds of being caught up in one of the boys' frequent battles were greatly diminished.

This particular Saturday, Charlie found out from Johnson that Hooper was quitting, along with Mark, although Johnson was too wily to come out and say directly that he had sensed some peculiar goings on at the other camp.

Charlie deduced that Mr. Johnson was intent on seeing things change at the other camp. Charlie knew full well from his own observations, as well as from the almost daily reports from Stymie, that conditions were out of control. The few shelters that had been built by the more industrious boys were incapable of retaining heat or repelling water. The sudden cold snap had finally brought the group to their senses, however, and plans were being made for a communal bunkhouse. The lack of discipline continued to be a problem.

Mr. Johnson indicated that Bud would probably have to serve extended periods of time over at the other camp until the situation was under control. Johnson announced his intention to put newly hired counselors into Duane and Charlie's group in order to help acclimate the fresh recruits. Charlie's reaction was slight, for he knew none of this would come to pass for him anyway until he returned from his vacation, much too far in the future to warrant a great deal of concern. Duane, on the other hand, was visibly concerned, as the changes would most certainly fall on him.

Charlie and Duane walked slowly back down the trail to camp after saying their farewells to the boss.

"Don't worry Duane, everything will be alright. Let's just wait and see what's going to happen," said Charlie.

"I sure hope so. It seems like everything's just starting to run smoother and now this. By the way, you sure everything will be alright tonight at the show with just one of us?"

"I think you'll be able to handle it. I have a feeling they're gonna be on their good behavior after what happened last night. I sure can't figure that Jerome out though. You never know what he's gonna do or say. That is, besides causing trouble. I have a feeling he's gonna come around though. I think last night was a real turning point for him. I hope so anyway."

Duane and the boys left for the movies soon after, leaving Jerome and Charlie alone in the bunkhouse.

The previous night had been emotionally turbulent for Jerome. First came the beating and the insults, then the flurry of apologies, and finally the feeling that a crack was beginning to appear in the wall—that group resistance to acceptance that no one but he felt, for he was the only one on the outside of that imposing barrier. He was the newcomer, the outsider, there was no place for him here. He hadn't participated in building the bunkhouse nor had he been present in the early stage of the group at Lake of the Pines. His arrival had simply been untimely, for a partial retarding of the emerging group identity was necessary in order to make room for one more personality previously not considered.

Jerome sat on his bunk, peering up at the prone figure of Charlie on the bunk above him. Despite the resistance from the group that he still felt, that barrier to acceptance seemed to have widened enough since last night for him to step through if he was careful. He had had his dream again and even that had changed somewhat. The frightening monster that threatened him and his inability to move were the same, only this time when he yelled for help someone came and the monster vanished at his arrival.

"How's it going Jerome? You feeling alright?" said Charlie, contemplating the lonely boy sprawled on his bunk. He looked particularly vulnerable in the emptiness of the bunkhouse.

"Yeah, I'm alright," said Jerome as he stared at the floor. Jerome had never really known a white man before. He had been acquainted with many, not all bad, but none who had taken any real interest in him.

"You took a pretty good beating last night partner. Three against one, those are pretty mean odds. Seems like you did alright for yourself though," said Charlie.

"Yeah, I guess," said Jerome sullenly. He glanced at Charlie, only to meet his gaze head on.

"You know Jerome, we really want you to be a member of our group. I mean, a real member, so that you feel like you belong."

Charlie's words resounded in Jerome's ears. Jerome felt a longing inside of him awaken. The force of his long repressed need for love wracked his small frame and brought tears to his eyes.

"How about some hot chocolate?" said Charlie. "Just because those guys are out having a good time doesn't mean we can't have a good time too." Charlie felt a lump form in his throat as he lowered himself to the floor and approached Jerome. "How about it Jerome? What say we go have ourselves a treat."

Jerome nodded. He wiped a tear from his cheek. His sleeves fell over his knuckles as he stood up. He hung his head low, not trusting his vulnerable state to the steady gaze he knew was waiting. The weight of an arm fell gently on his shoulder. His head raced with joy. He would have given anything to have been able to throw his arm around his new friend's shoulder as he had seen men do before.

Charlie and Jerome proceeded solemnly to the kitchen. Jerome seated himself at the table while Charlie started a fire in the stove. Charlie filled the tea kettle with water and rummaged around until he found the Nestle Instant cocoa.

"Did I ever tell you about that time we caught all them skunks?" said Charlie.

"No."

"Well, it was like this…"

Charlie embroidered the story at every opportunity. Jerome's face became more radiant with each exaggeration. Although Chuck and Danny had previously told him the real story, Jerome realized the new version was for his benefit alone and that brought a light to his eyes and a smile to his face.

Jerome rode horseback on Charlie down the dark path to the bunkhouse.

"I think you and I just might wind up liking each other. What do you think partner?" said Charlie.

Jerome kicked Charlie's sides and let go a laugh as he urged his steed onward at a faster pace.

CHAPTER XVI

The group spent the following week preparing for the coming trip. Johnson arrived with two new sets of clothing for each of the boys, much to their delight. Although each boy received a pre-designated parcel, they all traded in order to get the style and color they preferred.

Duane, with his committee of three, consisting of Chuck, Keith, and Roy, with periodic consultations from the remainder of the group, finally completed the itinerary. The trip was scheduled for a two to three week period and would take the group through Baton Rouge, New Orleans, Biloxi, Mobile, Everglades National Park, Miami, Daytona Beach, and Jacksonville. Personal visits were scheduled for New Orleans, where Chuck would see his mother, and Jacksonville, where Danny's brother was stationed in the Navy.

Charlie and Duane checked the bus' tires, changed its oil, and gave it a lube job. Both counselors harbored misgivings about the vehicle. They were jointly concerned about its age and general overall condition. Mr. Johnson assured the two that between the gas credit card and the telephone any emergencies could be easily taken care of.

The counselors bought new Coleman lanterns along with a three week supply of Coleman fuel. They obtained a two burner Coleman camp stove as an additional luxury item. Duane suggested the stove because of the ease with which it could be used, even in the rain, and the others agreed on its usefulness. The veteran campers had not yet had the opportunity to start a campfire in the rain or with wet kindling and wood. As the problem had never presented itself, it had never been considered. A supply of fresh water was taken on board along with the irreplaceable ice chest, which received a long overdue washing.

Each boy was required to bring a tent, whether they planned to use it or not, as no one knew exactly what conditions would be met with on the trip. Pots and pans were organized, and plates, silverware, cups, and bowls were all neatly packed for easy access.

The group subjected the interior of the bus to an intense purge. The sweep unearthed precious treasures which had been assumed lost or stolen long ago. Reuniting these wayward articles with their rightful owners proved to be a difficult task. In one instance, a quarter package of Kite tobacco found wadded up and crumpled in a corner, still containing an unrecognizable mass of molded leaf, was claimed by no less than six nicotine addicts. At the other extreme, a pair of jockey shorts in desperate need of laundering were claimed by no one.

The enthusiasm and sense of unity in the group were balanced by the turmoil that was coming to a head in the other camp. Their bunkhouse was still yet to be completed and the new counselors continued to struggle to manage the group and build unity.

Charlie frequently speculated on the reasons for the differences between the two groups. He found life at his camp preferable in all ways: the physical setting of camp, the boys themselves, and the counselors he worked with. It appeared at times as if his group had been granted more than their share of good fortune while the other camp had engendered the majority of misfortune.

Both Chuck and Danny received correspondence from their family members and arranged for reunions along the way.

Bud returned David to camp one late afternoon. The boys gathered around to admire a new watch and shirt which David gallantly displayed. David was more reluctant to share a carton of Winstons which he held tightly under his arm.

Regret came over David's face when the group revealed their escapades in Dallas. He was angry at having missed the excitement of the fight.

Later that evening, Duane and Charlie sat in the kitchen making final plans for the trip.

"You mind if I join you guys?" said David as he strode into the tent and slid in next to Charlie.

"Not at all," said Charlie, finding himself suddenly on guard.

"How did your vacation go David? Did you and Bud do anything special?" Duane inquired, not knowing how to best approach the youth who now held him in a contemptuous stare. David ignored the question with an aristocratic air.

"I heard you guys had a run in with a gang in Dallas," David said coolly, directing the statement to Charlie.

"We had a little trouble, nothing much," said Charlie

"Anybody have any zip guns?"

"I don't think so, but to tell the truth I wouldn't know one if I saw it," said Charlie.

"You never seen a zip gun?" David relished Charlie's ignorance.

"No, just heard about them is all."

"I killed a guy with a zip gun once."

"You did what!" said Duane, almost choking.

"I said I killed a guy once with one. I put three nails in him before he knew what happened."

Charlie appraised David. He wasn't lying—too matter of fact for that.

"How, why? I mean, who did you kill? Why did you kill him?" said Duane.

"I was coming home from a friend's house late one night when this guy grabbed me and pulled me into this alley. He threw me up against the wall and pulled a knife. He wanted all the money I had. It was really simple enough. I just reached inside my coat as if to get my money and zapped the guy before he knew what happened. I was halfway down the street. I didn't hear until the next day on the radio that they had found this guy in the alley. I guess he bled to death." David kept his eyes on Charlie while relating the incident, attempting to gauge the counselor's reaction.

"I guess those guns can be pretty deadly. What are they made out of anyway?" said Charlie, not intimidated by David's confession.

"Oh, just bits and pieces of junk really. I'll show you how to make one sometime. You never know when they may come in handy."

David swung his leg over the bench and stood up in one fluid motion, displaying a keen sense of dramatic timing. "Well, I'll leave you two alone now." He sauntered towards the bunkhouse entrance. "I am sorry I wasn't with you in Dallas though. It could have been fun."

David disappeared down the dark pathway. The strength of his personality left a prolonged silence in his wake.

"He sure is one cocky kid," said Duane before plunging back into the lists and maps he had spread out before him.

"Well he's certainly different, so grown up," Charlie said quietly, filled with unvoiced thoughts about David. "Whatever he may be, I think Bud has pretty much taken him under his wing. I don't think you and I are going to have a lot to do with him. He doesn't really consider himself like the others, a real integral part of the group, and neither does Bud."

Duane looked up and adjusted his glasses. "Do you think we'll have any trouble with him because of that?"

"I'm sure we will."

The group departed at eleven the next morning after a frantic three hours of checking and double checking the lists Duane had prepared. Mr. Johnson and Bud, along with a few boys from the other camp, came to say their goodbyes. This time the group had taken the added precaution of leaving nothing of value behind.

The bus rumbled on the dusty road out of camp, headed for Highway 20 East and the first stop of any importance, New Orleans.

Duane reclined among the baggage in the back seat, looking more peaceful than Charlie could remember since the first day they met at Daingerfield Lake. It was so long ago.

The bus roared through Marshall. The entrance into yet unexplored territory brought all heads forward, noses stuck to the windows. Silence pervaded the bus. Each boy was lost in his private world—wondering, hoping, dreaming of adventures yet to unfold, people to be loved, and deeds to be done.

The bus passed the Louisiana border. Charlie surveyed the boys through the rearview mirror. Jerome sat immediately behind him. Since the night they were left alone, Jerome had displayed a new personality. His temper was still fierce, but in place of his unapproach-able mean-spiritedness there was now an inviting openness.

Vince sat directly behind Jerome, his eyes intently focused on the passing scenery. The boy's gutsy fearlessness was impressive. He was stubbornly willful and possessed the raw power so necessary for achievement. His problem, like many of the others, was in harness-ing that power.

Danny winked at Charlie from across the aisle. His eyes ran over his recently received pamphlet on small animal traps. Charlie reserved an added measure of nurturing for the baby of the group. He was the most in need of a powerful guardian angel. His vulner-ability to physical and psychological acts of violence worked as an attractive lure for sadistic tendencies. Thus far however, he had dis-played an indomitable presence when protecting himself.

Sherman lounged directly behind Danny, his creased forehead visible over the small boy's shoulder. The whites of his eyes shim-mered against his dark skin. Sherman's innate affability and good cheer had been a bonus to the group. His optimistic attitude helped balance the black moods that occasionally strangled the group. He more than compensated for his lack of quick wits with his strength of character and willingness to help.

"Hey Charlie, what you gawking at?" said Keith.

Charlie shifted his gaze to Keith, seated at the back of the bus, across from Duane.

"You oughta keep your eyes on the road. Remember, that's what you told us when you let us drive," Keith continued.

"Yeah, but I'm a better driver than you all, so I don't have to keep my eyes on the road all the time. Besides, in this case the danger is in the bus and not on the road, so I'm doubly justified."

Charlie and Keith's playful banter was of no interest to anyone but themselves. Keith's shock of unruly hair stood straight up as he eyed Charlie in the mirror.

"Can I drive now? What do you say?" said Keith.

"Not now Keith, just relax. It's too rainy. Don't worry, you'll get plenty of chances to drive."

Charlie caught David studying and searching him for weaknesses. David cultivated the reserve of an introvert. In contrast to Keith's extroverted nature, he disguised his feelings and talked of only impersonal matters. His silence was the hush of the cougar—watching, waiting, stalking.

"Jerry, quit picking your nose for Christ's sake. You're making me sick," said David.

Jerry lowered his bare torso further into his seat, attempting to withdraw deeper into himself. He began to bite his nails. His attention darted in David's direction and back to Charlie. A faint mumbling escaped his gritted teeth.

"Get your feet off my seat you little rat," Russ barked at Jerry, who was becoming jittery under the pressure of the ill-will around him.

Russ hunkered down and cast threatening glances at Jerry. It had become evident that Jerry's perpetual chicken little act attracted a large share of abuse. He too possessed at least an average intelligence, yet his emotional state was a shambles. His reactions were more befitting a war zone. Despite the continuous harassment he endured, he was one of the most popular boys in the group, perhaps because he was so consistently singled out for ragging.

It was Russ, Charlie realized as he studied the boy's worried countenance, who was his greatest challenge. Charlie judged his overall progress with the group by his ability or inability to get through to the boy. There were times when he felt optimistic about the group's progress only for his excitement and hopes of progress to be shattered by a violent confrontation with Russ. The encounters always ended with Russ screaming profanities and vowing his hatred while Charlie stood groping for a means of reaching out to help. So far Charlie felt as if no progress had been made and it appeared that neither Bud nor Duane were having any better luck. The boy's own internal emotional cycles were apparently in charge, carrying him one minute to the heights of joy only to drag him screaming into the depths of despair the next. His emotional state was the least stable of the group, yet in some ways it personified the drastic emotional ups and downs that each boy experienced. It was those emotions that each boy would have to bring under control before they could give any direction to their lives.

Roy's safari hat, decorated with a half-dozen miscellaneous patches, was pulled down over his eyes. His head rested against the window. His erratic snores drifted lazily toward the front of the bus. Roy was much like Sherman. Although from the city, he seemed the caricature of the farm boy, slow willed but well-intentioned. His temper carried a long fuse, but once it exploded his anger was blindly destructive. He was easily led and he gladly followed. His relationship with David, it seemed, was based on that premise.

Charlie realized, as he moved his gaze over the bobbing passengers, that he too had a distinct place in the family and that he enjoyed being be a part of it more than anything else in the world. A tingle raced up his spine and made the hair on the back of his neck stand up.

The group established camp outside of Bossier City, Louisiana, at Lake Bistineau. Due to their late departure and frequent stretching stops along the way, it was dark by the time they rolled into the campgrounds. The rain had since passed and left a chilly, drenched countryside in its wake. The only objects visible in the headlights were a picnic table and fire pit.

Sherman and Russ, in an attempt to avoid the unpleasant task of making a fire and preparing a hot dinner for the group, proposed peanut butter and jelly sandwiches.

"But it's too cold and wet to get out there and build a fire," Russ whined. "There won't be any dry kindling."

"You look hard enough and you'll find some," said Charlie.

"I'll help you Russ. Come on Sherman, get your flashlight and let's see what we can find," said Duane. He followed the two reluctant boys out of the bus and into the soggy night.

"God, it's cold," Keith moaned from the backseat of the bus, where he sat curled up in his sleeping bag. The other boys reclined in similar positions, glassy-eyed, tired, and hungry.

"You're not gonna set up your tent tonight, are you Charlie?" said Danny.

"You bet I am," said Charlie as he stepped into the darkness, his tent under his arm, his flashlight illuminating his way.

Duane, Russ, and, Sherman soon returned with kindling and started a fire. The first sparks flared up, sputtered, then caught hold and blazed forth as Charlie knelt in deep concentration over his tent. The inviting warmth and light of the fire beckoned to the boys aboard the bus.

The group huddled around the crackling flames.

"You know," said Charlie as he stood over the fire, "I read in my survival handbook that the Indians used to put rocks in their campfires on cold nights, letting them heat up, and then before going to bed they would take them out and put them in their teepees to provide heat for the night." Charlie scrutinized a ball-sized rock sitting on the edge of the light.

"Sounds like you just made that up," said Chuck, his dark eyes reflecting the campfire. His hood was pulled over his head, giving the impression of a sorcerer calling demons forth from the night.

"All I can say is what I read," said Charlie. "But I think I'm gonna give it a try." He broke from the circle, walked stiff-legged to where the rock lay, picked it up in one swift movement, and rolled it into the center of the fire.

After dinner, Sherman and Russ heated water for washing dishes while the other boys dragged themselves back to the bus. A drizzle soon fell over the coach. The Coleman lantern illuminated the interior of the bus with an eerie light, which combined with the surrounding darkness to cast macabre shadows over the campground.

Charlie placed the Coleman lantern in the far back corner of his tent, along with two heated stones, and closed himself in for the night. He immediately felt the heat radiating throughout his small enclosure. Fifteen minutes later he lay uncovered, naked on top of his sleeping bag. Perspiration ran down his back. He dozed off to sleep while visions of sweating cavemen huddled around heating stones passed through his mind.

The group passed through Alexandria, Bunkie, Ville Platte, and Opelousas on their way to New Orleans. They made a short midday stop in Lafayette to watch a softball game in progress. The group listened intently as the melody of the Cajun tongue rose in protest over a disputed call.

The group made a brief side stop in Baton Rouge, where they toured the Louisiana State University campus. They were especially impressed by the stated air of the occupants of the fraternity and sorority houses.

The group made camp at Paradis, on the outskirts of New Orleans. The boys spent the evening selecting their favorite clothes for the next day, when Chuck was to meet his mother. They showered and took extra pains to look their best. Chuck became more withdrawn than usual, feeling nervous at the close proximity of home.

CHAPTER XVII

The Rat

The dreaded phone book mocked him. It had all the power and he knew it. Although it may not have been the driving power of the evil which it delivered which it promulgated it enabled the evil doer to act without thought of retribution. As he watched it out of the corner of his eye it transformed itself. First a ghastly misshapen ghoul took shape which quickly morphed into an old man deformed bent powerful arms protruding from soiled and tattered remains of a blood and sweat stained undershirt. It was the hate in the eyes accompanied by that twisted smile which always caused the release the involuntary evacuation of his bowels and caused him to sit up, his sheets stained his horror increased. The nightmares were controlling his life dictating his every thought crowding out any vestige of normality. He looked at the clock it said five am. It was Saturday the worst day of the week but he had at least two hours to remove the evidence to avoid certain punishment for being a "dirty" little boy. He never questioned that was what he was even at ten. He just never thought to question because there was no control over where that might lead.

The door slowly opened and his mother tiptoed, as if through a mine field, into the room closing the door silently behind not wanting to awake the real monster in her bed. She had her arms tightly wrapped around her faded robe hugging herself comforting herself against the storm which raged around her which she called her life. She placed her finger to her lips warning him to not say a word. He was shaking uncontrollably now. Seeing his mother always increased his fear brought back the memories of that day the day she left him with "him" alone for a week. Her hands too were shaking and as they made contact, mother reaching to son and son to mother for comfort, their fear fused and for a moment they stared at each other with a wild uncontrollable despair which froze them. They sat on the edge of the bed clinging to each other the past, present and future nightmare of their life swirling around them taunting them laughing at their meekness their weakness. Terrified, the two forms sat with eyes wide and staring into the darkness awaiting their destiny. They were unable to remain still. Their ears were tuned to the slightest sound of him. Their hands clenched and unclenched. There was a constant pulling at hair and scratching restless appendages which signaled a need to escape from these bodies that drew so much pain to them.

His mother knew her son's night terrors. She too had them and could rarely sleep more than a few troubled hours each night always on the alert the look-out for danger. She silently moved the sheets away and took him by the hand leading him to the bathroom. There could be no lights for those would wake him. It was the same routine each time. Clean it up. Don't leave any clue that he had soiled his bed again because any evidence left was promise of certain punishment not just for her son but also for her. She knew now because she had been told so many times by him that she was equally as guilty as her son and therefore he should not be the only one punished. At first she didn't believe him but now after so many years she believed him. There was something wrong with her and with her son to cause such a fair man such a smart man to punish them. Knowing this was her penance for her failure as a mother she worked twice as hard and with no hesitation. Her salvation was in her own hands. She had no relatives that she talked to anymore. He had seen to that. Her family was his family now. He didn't like her family anyway too "snobby" he told her and she started to see it after a few years. The way her father treated him, her husband, was not right. The way his mother spoke condescendingly about him was wrong.

The two of them moved quickly now watching the clock knowing they had only until 7:30am exactly to have everything in place nothing amiss and his breakfast ready. She stripped him of his pajamas threw them in the tub where she would gather them later when she had cleaned her son. She washed him head to toe his hands last. It always made her cry silently inside to feel the anguish of her guilt when she saw his fingernails chewed to the quick. The fingers themselves damaged. They were both shaking now knowing that they had failed him again realizing their worthlessness to him who provided everything for them. They looked at each other both searching the others eyes for a solution for an answer to a remedy for their joint failures to meet his expectation. They knew the only control they had in this entire world was their ability to absorb the punishment, the blows and in doing so know that their sins were being paid for they were becoming better people for him which was all he wanted.

The small bathroom smelled of the mess the boy had made. That smell always reminded her of the first time. The time he had lost his iron like control and the monster had taken over. She had tried to protect her son but this just seemed to make him angrier. That day she would never forget. She had never been as afraid of him as she was then. After the first hit with the phone book to the side of her head she too lost control of her bladder soiling the carpet in the bedroom. Through a dense fog of pain she heard her son crying, "mommy, mommy, please don't hurt my mommy.

He was hiding under his bed when his father pulled him out by his hair. It was the monster that beat him and his mother that day. It was the monster that threw her down the stairs in a blind rage. She was in the hospital a week. It was a concussion. She explained to the hospital staff that she had tripped and fallen down the stairs nothing else. Of course he made it up to her later, flowers and promises of "no more monsters". But the monster hadn't left. He still prowled the halls and rooms searching for victims to vent his rage release his fury. She quietly opened the bathroom window to air out the room. She quickly and quietly dressed her son in clean pajamas and underwear and moved to the bedroom where searching under the bed she found the cache of clean linens which she hid there for times like tonight when they were all that stood between a tolerable day and a nightmare of brutal blows delivered with the compliments of the phone company. Her hands bumped into a hard object, long and hard. She pushed it out of the way without any concern about what it was wanting only the sheets, her salvation. She knew that if she could just be "perfect" all the punishment would end. He had told her so many times and she believed him.

Once she had managed to make the mess disappear she gathered the soiled laundry and tip toed quietly out the door. The hands of the clock on the bedside table said 5:30 and she knew she would have to hurry. A cold sweat broke out on her forehead under her arms and her hands grew moist. The boy could not stand still. His hands fed worn fingernails to his sharp little teeth. His head jerked one way and then the other at any sound any movement any sense of danger of the waking of the monster. She looked back at him in the darkness as she moved to the door and she saw his eyes grow wide with horror as the door opened. The phone book hit her directly in the face and the dirty sleepwear fell helplessly to the ground. She was out cold. He was on her like a cat grabbing a fist full of hair and pulling her to her feet. She could not see. She could only feel the pain. She could only concentrate on the pain of her shattered nose and only a weak cry could be heard escaping her. She wondered about her son. She knew he would be under the bed.

After the first time the boy was pulled from under the bed by the monster he promised himself that next time he would be prepared but he never seemed to be able to make that connection from being prepared to thinking about being prepared. Tonight he was prepared and before his father could come after him under the bed. The boy crawled out bat in hand and while his father was holding his rag doll mother by her hair he hit him in the head as hard as he could with the bat. And then he hit him again and again and again until the monster could not get up and the monster that was inside him grew tired satisfied with its inaugural appearance.

He would often think about those days out here in the woods around the campfire but even here there were monsters. There were monsters everywhere now and he would still wake up and find that he had soiled himself but it wasn't like it used to be those nightmares were gradually receding into the past. He knew how hardy the rat was. He knew how many enemies the rat had but he also knew the rat was a survivor because it was always on the lookout for monsters. It was always vigilant.

CHAPTER XVIII

The boys were up early the next morning, anxious to explore the French quarter and get a peek at Chuck's mom. The New Orleans city limits sign brought a cheer from the boys, who had crowded Chuck while he reread his mother's letter.

"What was that address again Chuck?" said Charlie, attempting to get Chuck's attention through the swarm of boys.

"Chucky, Charlie wants to know what that street address was again!" said Jerry from the edge of the group.

Chuck, rattled by the attention, fiddled with his letter. Duane worked his way through the wall of bodies to help extract the information.

"According to the map we should be pretty close now. I just need a street address," Charlie called out over his shoulder.

The old bus rattled into an exclusive neighborhood of tree-lined drives and hand-manicured lawns which framed the beauty of white pillared mansions and exhibited the elegance of southern wealth.

"Does your mother really live around here?" said Jerry.

"Is she rich?" said Danny, drooling over the display of wealth passing by his window.

The boys laughed nervously as they speculated on which house Chuck's mother lived in.

"This is the right street, but the address is 2207 and there doesn't seem to be a 2207," said Duane, looking from the letter in his hand to Charlie and trying to hold back a feeling of disappointment for Chuck.

"Let's try one more time, maybe we just missed it," said Charlie. He turned the bus around and drove back down the street.

Chuck squirmed uneasily in his seat, transmitting his discomfort to the others.

"She must have just written the wrong address by mistake. Did she give you a telephone number?" said Duane.

"Yeah, it's right here," said Chuck.

"We'll stop and give her a call when we get in the French quarter," said Duane. "How does that sound Chuck? I'm sure we'll be able to get her by phone. It would probably be better if she didn't have us all tramping through her home anyway. Nobody wants that. How does that sound to you?"

"Sure, that sounds alright," said Chuck guardedly.

"That sounds like a good idea to me too," said Charlie. "No sense all of us showing up at her house." Charlie's heart reached out for the boy. He didn't know what had happened with the address, but he did sense that Chuck's mother was not a resident of any of the palatial estates that had so recently turned up their noses at the unkempt group. He hoped that the boy would be able to see his mother, at least for five minutes.

The group arrived at the French quarter. The boys had outfitted themselves in their own personal costumes, all of which were intended to impress. Chuck found a phone and dialed the number his mother had sent. A strange voice answered and hesitated in order to recall a person there by the name Chuck had asked for. After several minutes and much discussion at the other end of the line, Chuck's mother was located and put on the phone. The short exchange that followed resulted in a meeting being set up at Lafayette Square that afternoon.

The group exhausted the next several hours wandering aimlessly through the historic section of Lafayette. Their favorite attraction was Lafayette Square, with its colorful collection of artists and various other personalities that could generally be labeled as eccentric. The boys fit in perfectly, for it was only on rare occasions that their own presence didn't have the effect of drawing stares and becoming the focus of unwanted attention.

Sherman acquired several new friends as the group lay sprawled in various positions on the grass, catching rays of sunshine escaping from the clouds. Jerry and Danny were captivated by the antics of a street juggler, while Keith, Roy, and Vince had joined a group of itinerant gypsies who were entertaining them. Duane and Charlie sat comfortably on a bench which offered the best view of the park. Chuck and Jerome stood huddled nearby, scanning the passing faces for a friendly profile or a knowing smile.

Charlie first saw her approaching from the far end of the park, looking about, obviously in search of someone. She was a thin, tall black woman in her early fifties. Charlie's first impression was of a no-nonsense woman and further study of her stern visage, unsmiling eyes, and no frills wardrobe, confirmed his intuition. She saw Chuck almost at the same moment he caught sight of her. It looked to Charlie like the meeting could have been in preparation for a wake—neither party emitted any visible sign of a happy reunion. Mother and son stood staring at each other, glued to the spot by the presence of some past sorrow.

Chuck neared his mother and she placed her hand carefully on his back. The two stood in silent communication. Chuck pointed back at Duane and Charlie, who were silently observing the scene from their seats. They waved self-consciously and Chuck's mother returned their greeting, her foreboding presence palpable even at that distance. She guided her son to a nearby bench and they sat shoulder to shoulder, their backs turned to the eyes of the counselors.

"I'm glad she came," Duane said, his eyes fixed on Chuck and his mother.

"Yeah, me too," said Charlie. "He was really excited to see her."

"You couldn't really tell. I mean, Chuck never get really excited, does he?"

"He sure doesn't, and it looks like it runs in the family." Charlie turned his gaze to the ground. "You know, we really don't know anything about these kids, other than what we've found out on a day-to-day basis over the last few months."

"Do you really think it would do any good if we did know what sorts of lives they had, what individual horror stories they have to relate?".

"I don't really know, probably not. It would probably just make things worse, create more rigid stereotypes, but sometimes I like to think that it would give us a key, something to work with."

"What you see is what you got my friend."

"What do you mean by that?"

"I mean that what we have to work with is what's in front of us everyday, and that's it." Duane finally tore his eyes away from the two figures to study Charlie's reaction.

"I guess you're right," said Charlie.

Charlie and Duane again turned their gazes toward the somber reunion of Chuck and his mother.

Chuck's mother took her son's hand and imparted a final message to him. Chuck's head hung low, his chin touching his chest. His mother silently studied him. She grasped Chuck in a maternal embrace. His head was still lowered, avoiding her eyes. They stood that way for some time as the group looked on, wishing that their mothers were there to hug them like that, even if only for a minute.

Chuck's mother retreated and looked back once more at her son, who stood riveted to the spot, tears welling up in his eyes as he waved goodbye, perhaps only until next year when he would return for a second hug, perhaps forever.

The day's festivities were quickly brought to an end as a thoughtful and unusually reserved mood came over the group. Chuck made no mention to anyone of his conversation with his mother and surprisingly everyone was too polite to ask.

The next day, as the group traveled to Pensacola, their next stop, Roy studied the object which Jerry had been chewing on for ten minutes from his seat across the aisle from the anxious boy.

"What's that you've got in your mouth Dino?" Roy called.

"It's just a balloon, that's all," said Jerry, his eyes darting about.

All faces turned to watch Jerry.

"Where'd you get it?" said Roy.

"I found it outside on the ground." Jerry's nervousness was exaggerated by the sudden attention.

"That's no balloon you little rat. That's a rubber," said Russ.

"It is not." Jerry threw the object aside as if it were on fire.

Jerome quickly dived for the rubber and held it up for the group's inspection.

"If that ain't a rubber then my name ain't Keith," said Keith.

The entire group, including Duane and Charlie, who, although endeavoring to remain neutral, failed miserably, fell into a fit of laughter. Jerry, realizing his unfortunate blunder, slinked lower in his seat.

Charlie pulled into a gas station in order to inquire into the cause of the knocking coming from the engine. The group had already waited several hours to find out how much it would cost for the bus to be fixed and when it could be repaired as Charlie listened for a return call from Mr. Johnson, whom he had been unable to reach earlier. Charlie's second call to the boys' ranch had been answered, however, and the people in charge there told had told him to have the engine replaced. Charlie had informed them that it had thrown a rod. He didn't know how it had happened—the oil had been checked continuously.

Charlie had only had minor conversation with anyone at the ranch and the impression he had received from the phone call left him with no desire to have another. Of course, his feelings were formed mainly from stories the boys had brought with them—stories of Thorazine injections by staff members along with the all the tales of sexual abuse by the bigger boys. There was no way of confirming the stories, but the fact that they were all Charlie had to go on put him in a negative frame of mind concerning the ranch.

Vince bounded into the bus from the telephone booth. "Charlie, it's for you. It's Mr. Johnson."

"Thanks Vince. Now you guys settle down in here and leave Jerry alone for awhile. He's had enough ragging to last a lifetime."

Charlie swung down from the bus. A renewed burst of laughter followed him to the phone booth. He picked up the phone.

"Hello Mr. Johnson. Yeah, everyone's fine, but the bus has a bit of a problem. Yes, he said he could fix it today. They've already located another engine, that's the quickest way to do it. Oh, we'll go ahead with it then." A long pause followed as Charlie listened intently to Mr. Johnson's voice, not sure he was hearing the social worker correctly. Sorrow suddenly came over Charlie's face.

Charlie turned slowly, still listening, and gazed at Danny in the bus. He was jumping up and down, waving the rubber under Jerry's nose and shrieking with delight.

"Yeah, I'll take care of it. No, I don't think there's anything else we need. Yeah, the trip's going fine. We're headed to Pensacola now. Yes, I will. I'll tell him as soon as I get off of the phone."

Charlie hung up the receiver, not wanting to move but aware of the responsibility that weighed on him. He slid from the booth and drifted towards the garage. He couldn't do it right now. Maybe if he had a few more minutes he would know what to say.

Charlie approached the mechanic, who was bent over a car.

"I guess you can go ahead and get that motor," said Charlie.

"We already did, figured you couldn't go any place with all those kids and no bus," said the mechanic flippantly, not even raising his head from the carburetor. He was obviously in no mood to aid Charlie in his dilemma.

Charlie turned and strode solemnly toward the bus. The boys' laughter had subsided and given way to a more relaxed harassment, with each taking his turn at teasing Jerry.

"Duane, could you come out here a minute please," said Charlie

Duane came quickly up from the back of the bus. The two counselors stepped outside for a few moments and conferred in low tones. Duane climbed back onto the bus, a look of concern arresting his features.

"Danny, could I see you for a minute please," Charlie called into the bus from the front step.

Danny continued to tease Jerry.

"Danny, I said I would like to see you a minute please," said Charlie.

Danny suddenly sensed the immediacy in Charlie's voice and ambled from the bus, a puzzled expression on his face.

"Yeah, what is it?" said Danny nonchalantly, even while a certain tenseness sounded in his voice.

"Come with me. I want to talk to you for a minute," said Charlie. He put his hand on Danny's back and guided him towards the back of the gas station, out of sight of the now curious boys, their faces pressed against the bus' windows.

Charlie and Danny rounded the corner of the garage and sat down on a low concrete wall facing directly into a pile of old tires. Charlie sat a few feet from Danny. He turned to face the boy and allowed for a slight pause before he began.

"I just talked to Mr. Johnson on the phone Danny, and he had a very sad piece of news for you," said Charlie.

Danny looked at Charlie, bewilderment coming over his face.

"It's about your brother," Charlie continued. "He's been killed in a car accident."

There it was, he said it. Charlie had no idea if he had prepared the boy sufficiently or if he had only blurted it out to relieve his own uneasiness. Danny's features froze in disbelief while his mind slowly registered the painful news.

"My brother dead, my big brother Dave, dead," said Danny. He began to cry and his body shook with grief.

Charlie moved closer to Danny.

"He can't be dead, he can't be," said Danny.

Charlie put his arm around Danny's small shoulders. He felt a sadness stir deep inside of him. It surged upward and forced tears from his eyes. He wiped them away with his free arm. Danny's shaking gradually became less violent. The silence grew to five, ten, fifteen minutes as the information gradually worked its way into Danny's psyche.

"Why Dave? Why did Dave have to die?" said Danny.

"No one knows that Danny. It was just his time to die, just like you and I will have our time. There's no escaping it," said Charlie.

The boy studied his counselor for a long moment, his red and swollen eyes questioning his brother's fate. A second silence followed. It seemed an eternity to Charlie, who sat facing the boy, trying to console him in whatever way he could.

Youth, however, is amazing in its acceptance of change. Charlie watched Danny absorb the news, devour it with grief, and come up for air.

"How are you doing?" said Charlie gently.

Danny's tears had slowly lessened. "I'm alright," he said in a melancholy tone. "What am I gonna tell the guys, though? Or are you gonna tell them?"

"That's up to you. You tell them when and where you want to. I won't say anything. Should we go back to the bus now? Do you think you're ready, or would you rather stay here for a while longer?"

"I'm ready." Danny wiped his tears with his shirt.

Charlie and Danny drifted back to the bus in silence.

Danny entered first, his head lowered, avoiding the curious stares. Charlie came in quickly behind him, announcing that it would be four to five more hours before the bus would be fixed. A chorus of moans accompanied the announcement, momentarily drawing attention away from Danny.

Duane leaned over the back of Danny's seat and whispered in the boy's ear about the bad news.

"How did you find out? Who told you that?" said Danny. He glared at Charlie, "I thought you weren't going to tell anyone. They all know about my brother, they already know."

Charlie's confusion immediately cleared when he caught Duane's guilty expression and deduced that he must have told the boys already. They had probably known before Danny did.

Charlie felt guilt weigh on his conscience. Danny's sobs returned, renewed in strength by the realization that the news of his brothers death had turned into gossip.

The next few days were warm and the crispness of the nights alluded to the impending Florida winter. The group made their way gradually around the west coast of Florida, past the whitest sand dunes in the world in Pensacola, then to St. Petersburg, Sarasota, Fort Meyers, and Everglades National Park.

The group gradually accustomed themselves to life on the road—the endless procession of new sights, sounds, and cultures. Charlie, Duane, and the boys discovered, much to their surprise, that many residents of certain parts of Florida were not so welcoming in their attitude toward blacks. The major cities offered few problems for the crew, but once in the rural areas they encountered a distinct strain of virulent southern racism.

The animals of the everglades fascinated the boys. The crocodiles and alligators proved favorites. The boys took interest in the "skunk trees," as they called them, as well—those groves the fragrance of which carried their memories back to a skunk roundup in Lake Whitney.

The journey up the East Coast began with a visit to a museum a short distance from the Atlantic. The museum was centered around exposition on sunken ships and treasures to be found beneath the sea. The subject aroused Duane and Charlie's curiosity and they sought to further explore it with the help of the museum attendant. The counselors' interest in ruins beneath the sea quickly faded with the group's sighting of a whale some two hundred yards offshore. Duane and Charlie attempted to mine their brains for all information on the behemoth. The crew's interest in sea creatures was in turn replaced by a fascination with the stars when Danny spotted a meteor the first night the group made camp in Miami.

Much to the group's delight, the campground was situated, at least it seemed to them from the proximity of yacht harbors and noisy boulevards, directly in the middle of Miami. The campground was surprisingly spacious and devoid of other humans.

The campsite was centered, as always, around the picnic table. A thick green turf, perfect for pitching tents, spread out for twenty yards in each direction. A dumpster was located twenty yards from the group's camp, at the end of the entrance road.

Slightly after sunset on the second night at the camp, as the group sat around the picnic table finishing a dinner of hamburgers and potato chips, they detected a pair of eyes in the dark. Suddenly the eyes became four, then six, then eight. Before the group could determine if the visitors were stray cats or some less domestic species, Danny identified the black bandit's mask, ring tail, and hump-backed gait of the raccoon. To their astonishment, the boys and the counselors found themselves ringed in by a band of at least fifty coons waiting patiently just on the edge of light cast by the Coleman lanterns.

The raccoons remained in place behind the dim line of light, biding their time. Danny was the first to venture forward to feed the scavengers, who were well acquainted with the eating and sharing habits of humans. What they were not aware of was the potential danger they courted by begging food from this particular group of campers.

"I don't want you guys feeding those coons too much. After the dishes are finished I want the lights out and everyone in bed," said Charlie. He got up from the table and moved slowly toward his tent. "I mean it now. I don't want anyone fooling around with those animals tonight." Charlie looked directly at Russ, who turned his head quickly and muttered under his breath.

"What did you say Russ?" said Charlie, stopping suddenly.

"Nothin, just that you always pick on me. You always think I'm gonna do something wrong."

"You just remember what I said."

Russ continued to curse under his breath.

Charlie crawled into his tent. He collapsed into his sleeping bag, barely mustering the energy to undress. His usual reading time was preempted by the need for sleep.

Duane experienced the same paralysis as he got into his tent. He undressed and neatly placed his clothes in a small area to the rear of the tent. He donned his pajamas, a habit he had been unable to break or even compromise despite the difficulty of maintaining clean PJs under the present circumstances. He removed his watch, a Bulova eighteen carat gold his father had given him upon graduation from high school and placed it carefully on top of his clothes. He gradually fell asleep as the last sounds of dinner cleanup sounded against his tent.

The boys came and went from the bus. They made their beds on the seats or carried their bedrolls to sleep on the grass under the stars.

Charlie drifted off to sleep, satisfied that the boys had taken heed of his warning.

The raccoons moved cautiously inward and crossed the now absent light barrier that had held them back.

CHAPTER XIX

At midnight, satisfied that the counselors had fallen asleep, Russ crept cautiously into the bus and located Vince in the darkness.

"Hey, wake up Vince. Come on, get up," said Russ.

"What? What is it?" said Vince.

"Come on man. The coons, they're all over the place, everybody's asleep," Russ whispered, his excitement stirring the air in the bus.

"What's going on over there?" said Sherman from across the aisle, peering over the edge of his sleeping bag.

"We're gonna catch some coons. You want to come?" said Russ.

"How bout Charlie, remember what he said?" said Sherman.

"Charlie's been asleep for three hours. It's midnight. If we're quiet we won't wake him. What do you say?"

Vince and Sherman quietly crawled from their sleeping bags, waking Keith, Jerry, and Roy in the process.

"I wouldn't do it if I were you," Roy warned while Russ, Vince, Sherman, Keith, and Jerry silently jumped from the bus.

Out in the open, Vince caught sight of an object in Russ' hand.

"What's that?" said Vince, making a grab for the object.

"This pipe is mine. You'll have to get your own," said Russ, yanking the pipe away, a savageness drawing his face into a long scowl.

The boys huddled in a small group some ten yards from the dumpster, from which an odd assortment of noises arose.

"They're in there. I've been watching them for the last couple of hours," said Russ.

Three coons walked along the edge of the dumpster, their eyes reflecting the light of the full moon.

Russ began creeping quietly towards the dumpster. The other boys watched while he slithered up to it and waited patiently. Within minutes a pair of nostrils emerged above the rim of the metal trash can, followed by a black mask and pointed ears. Russ waited, coiled like a spring. His response was so lightning quick that the raccoon had its skull crushed within a second of making eye contact. Russ let out a muffled cry as he grabbed the battered body, threw it to the ground, and pounded it repeatedly with the pipe. A dull thud, metal against meat, accompanied each blow.

Russ worked himself into a fury. The others sat motionless watching the brutal scene. Two more curious sets of eyes, tamed with years of handouts from animal-loving tourists, peeked over the rim to investigate the commotion. Russ quickly clubbed the coons to death and they fell back into the dumpster with dual thumps.

Russ' face was stretched in a self-satisfied grin. He picked up the first coon up by the tail and swung it over his head. A trickle of blood splattered the boys. Russ tossed the animal into the tall bushes behind the dumpster. He grunted in Vince's direction, threw him the bloody pipe, and jumped over the rim of the trash can. He landed in a pile of rubbish amid a half-dozen coons, too startled by the sudden intrusion to flee. Russ grabbed the nearest animal, wrapped his hands around its neck, and choked it to death.

Russ repeated the execution in rapid succession with two other raccoons. He emitted a series of low, animal-like sounds as he wrung the life from the raccoons. Those animals escaping strangulation by reaching the rim were efficiently clubbed by Vince, the other boys having gone to find their own weapons.

While Charlie, Duane, and the other five boys slept, a mass slaughter of the native raccoon population took place. Each animal was methodically killed, then grabbed by the tail and thrown far into the bushes, hiding all evidence of the murder.

The first rays of morning sunlight skimmed over the dew-laden grass. The morning was silent except for the wing beat of an osprey. A snake hung limply from its beak, streaking close to the ground.

Charlie woke with a start. His dream had been so real and his reactions so intense that he had twisted himself up in his sleeping bag. Laying calmly in the morning stillness, he searched his mind and pieced together portions of the dream. He clearly saw the canoes heading down the river—four of them. All the boys were there—or were they? He couldn't be sure. He remembered the river becoming a raging torrent and hurling the canoes forward through rolling waves and treetops that appeared suddenly out of the muddy depths. He heard a scream and turned to see a canoe capsize. The three occupants were dumped into the raging waters. Their heads bobbed and their arms flailed. Each in turn was sucked under by the current.

Then the dream had ended. There had been other times in Charlie's life, infrequent and unpredictable, when he had had similar dreams, with the same intense feeling of reality, along with a foreknowledge of coming events upon awakening. The other two times the dream events had come to pass. Charlie felt his stomach tense—a fear which warned of troubles ahead.

Duane's exhaustion had lulled him to sleep like an infant in the arms of its mother. He awoke feeling fresh. An unusual feeling of serenity coursed through his body. He was up, showered, shaved, and brewing coffee before Charlie poked his tousled hair, evidence of a labored sleep, out of his tent.

"It's about time you got up. What do you think we're paying you for, to sleep all day?" said Duane with a laugh.

"My oh my, aren't we chipper this morning. What did you put in your coffee?"

Roy, Chuck, Jerome, Danny, and David also rose. They shook the sleep from their eyes and dragged their stiff bodies into the morning sun.

Russ and Vince lay sprawled in their sleeping bags alongside the bus.

"It looks like somebody got a good night's sleep anyway," said Charlie, nodding his head towards the boys on the ground.

An hour later a breakfast of bacon and eggs simmered over the campfire. The five midnight ramblers still slept and showed no signs of rising before noon.

"Wake those guys up, will you Roy. I don't know what they were up to last night but they certainly aren't gonna sleep the day away," said Charlie.

Roy shifted uneasily. He averted his gaze from Charlie's concentrated stare. He quickly rose and moved with a shuffling gate. Roy kicked first one and then the other of the boys stretched out on the ground. Once he had ascertained that they were awake he moved to the interior of the bus. Voices were raised and insults traded as Roy went about the business of waking the rest of the dead.

The five late sleepers sluggishly collected themselves enough to sit down for breakfast. All were red-eyed and haggard. An uneasiness gripped Charlie as he examined the five boys. He couldn't seem to place his finger on it, but he felt that something was definitely amiss.

"You guys look awful tired this morning," Charlie began nonchalantly, trying not to arouse the boys' defenses.

The boys merely looked at each other over their fried eggs.

"I thought I heard some noises in camp last night. Were any of you guys up late?" said Charlie, looking directly at Keith, whose eyes shifted uneasily back to his plate.

"No, not me," said Keith.

"Me neither," came the replies from the other boys.

"Must have been the coons," said Sherman abruptly.

Charlie's curiosity piqued at Sherman's quick reply.

"OK, I'm just going to ask you once and that's all. Were you guys up to something last night or not?"

All eyes shifted to the group of red-eyed miscreants.

"I wasn't," Russ blurted out belligerently.

"Neither was I," said Vince.

The other boys followed in denying the charges.

"It was probably just a bunch of coons having a feast in the garbage can," said Duane, trying to dispel the fog of suspicion that had settled over the table.

Roy walked away muttering to himself. Charlie accepted the boys' statements as the truth.

The group spent the next few days driving north up the east coast of Florida. City limit signs rolled by rapidly: Fort Lauderdale,

Pompano Beach, West Palm Beach, Melbourne, Daytona Beach, Jacksonville, and Tallahassee.

The boys reveled in the countryside at Suwannee River State Park. The days reached into the mid-sixties. Sufficient warmth allowed for swims in the deep green running waters of the Suwannee River. Although the width of the lake was not impressive, no depth could be discerned by a submerged body. The unknown quantity of water rushing beneath the surface sucked at dangling appendages and attempted to wrest swimmers from their secure holds on the wooden pier. It was only with a great deal of reluctance that the group moved further west.

At Florida State University the pert young co-eds headed the boys' list of favorite attractions.

Danny, who had shown few signs of despondency since absorbing the news of his brother's death, appeared withdrawn and brooding as the bus crossed the state line into Alabama. Charlie, Duane, and the boys respected Danny's silence and by the next morning his spirits were revived enough to eat two bowls of cereal.

As the group passed through Mobile on their way to view a historic plantation home, the words "coons" and "Miami" escaped from the tightly huddled group of boys in the back of the bus and drifted toward Charlie at the helm of the coach.

Charlie jerked the bus over to the side of the winding, rather steep-sided road and pulled to a halt. He drew his mouth tight in an effort at self-control. He had been lied to, that was all he had to know.

The boys' eyes had automatically gone to Charlie following the jolting stop. He bolted from his seat and faced them, furiously studying their faces.

"Alright, I want to know what happened in Miami with the raccoons," said Charlie.

A tense silence pervaded the bus. No one responded. Jerry's thrust his fingernails into his mouth. Roy turned away from Charlie and sought Russ in the back.

"Go ahead Russ, tell him what happened with the coons," said Roy.

"Shut up Roy, you prick. Nobody said nothin to you, did they?" said Russ.

"We was just having fun Charlie, that's all," said Keith, faltering on the last words.

"What happened?" said Charlie.

"They were just a bunch of old coons, that's all Charlie. There were too many anyway," said Keith.

"Did you kill coons? Is that what you're telling me?" said Charlie, his body shaking.

"We killed a few," said Sherman.

"How many is a few?"

Another long pause passed as Vince, Keith, and Russ exchanged looks.

"I said, how many?" said Charlie.

"Thirty," was the barely audible response.

"Get out of the bus right now. Everybody who had anything to do with this, I want you out of the bus this minute before I throw you out."

No one moved. Charlie took a step towards the boys, his anger palpable.

Keith bolted for the emergency exit in the back, not wanting to walk past Charlie. Russ, Vince, and Sherman followed. The boys jumped clumsily to the ground.

"You too Dino. Get out here," Vince yelled from outside of the bus.

Jerry was curled up in a small ball in a corner of the bus, rooted with fear to his position.

"Let's go Jerry. Out," said Charlie. He leveled his hard gaze on the quivering boy. "Right now."

Jerry drew himself out of his cocoon and slinked out the back door.

The bus was parked precariously on a narrow shoulder, dropping off some thirty feet to a dried creek bed which offered an open expanse in the otherwise tree-studded area.

"OK, down the hill," Charlie ordered. His eyes bore through the boys.

"It's too steep," Keith whined, looking at the sharp incline.

"You need some help getting down?" said Charlie. He took a step toward Keith.

The boys went down the hill in a headlong rush. Jerry fell at the bottom and immediately got up, too anxious about Charlie approaching from behind to stop and check for injuries.

"Line up right here," said Charlie, drawing a straight line in the dirt.

The boys reluctantly shuffled into place, shoulder to shoulder, behind the line and facing Charlie, who had taken up position in front of them. Charlie paced back and forth.

The boys could feel Charlie's anger rise as he strode by. Russ, situated on the far end of the line, looked about nervously as if deciding which direction to flee. The others were rooted motionless to their spots, held by their fear of the inevitability of punishment.

"What did I tell you about lying to me?" said Charlie.

Keith's wiry, unkempt hair stood on end. He edged back from the line, seeking distance from Charlie.

"Get back up here," said Charlie.

"We didn't lie...I—" said Keith. His protest was cut off in mid-sentence by a slap to the face from Charlie. Keith whined but held his position.

Russ bolted frantically from the end of the line.

"Get back here Russ, or so help me," said Charlie.

Russ halted momentarily, ten feet from the line. He gauged his chances of escape. Charlie rushed toward him and delivered a swift kick to the rear. The others stood shaking. Another kick. Russ whimpered. Yet another and he took his former position in line.

"I told you guys once before," said Charlie, resuming his pacing and stopping in front of each boy, "the worst possible thing you can do with me is tell me a lie. If there is anything that is going to make me mad, that's it. If you don't believe I mean what I say, then I'll have to find some way to convince you."

Charlie stood and stared at the quaking line of boys. "Do you know that the worst thing you can do is tell me a lie?"

Sherman uttered a weak "yes." A succession of nearly inaudible answers followed.

"I didn't hear you."

The boys responded slightly louder.

"I still didn't hear you," Charlie repeated once more, this time loud enough to be heard by the thankful spectators in the bus, their heads stuck out of the windows, watching the excitement.

Charlie made the boys stand in place for five minutes while his anger gradually subsided. He studied the boys, hoping that they'd be more resolute in telling the truth in the future.

"One more thing, just to not let you think you're getting off easy. No allowance for the next two weeks," said Charlie.

The few moans and grumbles were instantly cut short by the sternness on Charlie's face.

"Now back to the bus." Charlie's order was less tense than before, devoid of the fury which he had so recently wielded over the boys' heads.

The boys quickly scurried back up the hill, relieved that they were still alive. The guilty parties filed quietly into the bus.

Charlie took his place behind the wheel. The image of a dead pile of raccoons came over him. He shook his head, feeling overwhelming sorrow for such a waste of life.

Duane and Charlie had chosen to pursue a different route on the trip home. In the evening, the group prowled west on Highway 98 outside of McLain, Mississippi. This particular stretch, as the counselors well knew, offered no campgrounds. Out of desperation the group pulled into a narrow gravel road immediately off of the two lane highway. A small clapboard church with a faded white steeple offered a driveway for the bus and a comfortable lawn in front to pitch tents. At night the group made dinner over the Coleman stove in the bus.

Early the next morning the campers awoke to the sounds of car doors closing and people moving about. Charlie poked his head out of the tent and saw the local black citizenry in their Sunday finery staring open mouthed at the gypsies camped in their churchyard. A few of the delegation were dispatched to investigate the intruders.

Charlie told them of the group's plight and they were more than understanding.

By the time the congregation poured out of the church the next morning the odd intruders in their decrepit bus had pulled up stakes and left. The only remaining signs of their stay were flattened areas in the grass where they had spent a peaceful night under the watchful eye of the lord.

The group passed the next two days burning highway in Mississippi. They followed Highway 98 into Highway 49 outside of Hattiesburg, then into Jackson and finally Vicksburg.

Duane spied the cotton gin first and suggested a tour of the plant. The boys took to his idea and were prepared to investigate. The plant manager felt kindly disposed to grant the group's request. His gaze fell on one wild boy after another throughout the extensive tour. He answered the boys' questions and a slew from Duane and Charlie with the utmost concern that a real understanding take place. The boys gained first-hand knowledge of the workings of an American business and gained exposure to one of that group of men that make business work.

The boys' favorite diversion during that portion of the trip was the Vicksburg National Military Park. They walked the battlefield, studied the monuments, and felt infused with the spirits of the dead as they charged up and down the hills emitting rebel yells while the few stray tourists scattered before them.

The boys were also impressed by the plantation home they visited. Of all the facets of the house, the hand-hewn beams, rafters, and support posts fascinated them the most. The wood itself, its surface marked by shallow, scallop-shaped indentions, served as a symbol of slavery. Sherman, Jerome, and Chuck were particularly curious, if not a bit disturbed, by the indentions from the repressive past era.

"You mean all the black people like me and Chuck and Jerome were slaves?" said Sherman.

"At one time that's the way it was in this country," said Duane.

"Well, why did black people have to be slaves?" said Jerome.

"They had no choice," Duane continued. "They were captured, brought to this country, and held against their will. They were treated very poorly in most instances, being considered more farm animal than human. Their owners had the right to buy and sell then, even kill them without having to answer to anyone."

Duane's explanation unsettled the boys even more.

"Why didn't they run away or fight?" said Sherman.

"They did a lot of that too," said Duane. "The problem was they were outnumbered and had the law against them."

"I'm sure glad I didn't live back then," said Jerome. "They must have been some crazy people."

"They sure were crazy and I'm glad I didn't live back then either," Duane concluded.

The topic of slavery recurred in conversation for the rest of the day and set a record for holding the boys' attention spans.

Three days later the group jolted along the entrance road to their home. The familiar presence of the fine powdery dust that normally filled the air was absent, a recent rain having dissipated it.

Mr. Johnson and Bud were both present to welcome the arrivals, who were glad to be home. The leafless Autumnal trees allowed for a clear view from the parking area of the canvas-covered bunkhouse and kitchen. The outhouse also stood out more prominently and could easily be seen from the bus. It still lacked canvas sides and a top, embellishments the group had as yet found unnecessary.

To the newly arrived group's surprise, four new aluminum canoes sat at the bottom of the hill, gleaming dully in the sunlight.

"How do you like them?" said Johnson as Charlie and Duane stood looking down at the canoes, neatly placed on the trailer's racks.

"They're great," said Duane. He shuffled down the hill for closer inspection.

A feeling of uneasiness came over Charlie as he viewed the canoes, but faded in his excitement to join Duane and the boys at the bottom of the hill. They were already unloading one canoe and climbing in just to get the feel. The scene of three boys and Duane seated in the canoe, paddles in hand, struck Charlie as being oddly familiar; nevertheless, he joined Duane and the excited boys at the bottom of the hill, grabbed a paddle, and took his place in the grounded canoe.

CHAPTER XX

That night, Bud, Charlie, and Duane gathered around the kitchen table.

"You look awfully tired. I think it's about time you had a vacation," said Bud as he studied Charlie's features.

Charlie knew Bud was right. He felt more exhausted than he could remember since he had started. Maybe it was because he finally felt safe enough to let himself relax. Bud was back and therefore, at least, on this night the responsibility for enforcing the boys could be passed on.

"I can't, in all truthfulness, say that I'm not ready for a vacation. But then again, I am gonna miss everybody while I'm gone, or almost everybody," said Charlie.

"What do you think about the Buffalo River trip Charlie? Sounds to me like it's gonna be a lot of fun," said Duane.

Duane looked tired to Charlie. The edge of his initial enthusiasm seemed to have been dulled by daily abuse.

"It sounds good to me. I've never even been in a canoe before, but I'm sure we'll have plenty of opportunities to get our feet wet before spring."

"I have a feeling there'll be a lot of wet feet before this gang learns to handle those canoes," said Bud.

"Where're you going on your vacation?" said Duane, all the while wishing that it was him leaving tomorrow, away from the bedlam which he found himself surrounded by.

"Just around really. I may take my girlfriend out to Arizona though. I talked to her tonight and she's been accepted into graduate school out there. She needs someone to move her out."

A wordless exchange took place between Bud and Charlie as their eyes met across the table. Duane noticed the counselors' communication and quickly excused himself from the table.

"I'm gonna miss you Charlie, and I know the boys will too," said Bud, directing a level gaze across the table.

"Well, I don't know about that. I think the guys are gonna want to celebrate as soon as I'm out of camp."

"Maybe a little party, that's all." A wide smile set off Bud's straight white teeth, which contrasted deeply with his dark brown skin. A healthy outdoor smile, one you could believe in, Charlie thought—one you wanted to trust.

Mr. Johnson drove Charlie into Longview early the next morning and left him standing on the westbound shoulder of Highway 20. Charlie's destination was Kilgore, then down Highway 259 into Houston and Tomball.

Charlie's first priority on his vacation was acquiring transportation. He had called home and inquired with a series of what he thought were circumspect questions regarding the '64 Continental sitting unused in his parent's driveway. It was the long, low, squared-off model that had the odd doors opening front and back in an opposing manner. He had used the car before on occasions very similar to the one he was currently in. He attempted not to dwell on the so-called incidents that accompanied the vehicle wherever it went.

Charlie had only been directly involved in two, maybe three, mishaps with the car. The other incidents, he told himself, were exaggerated rumor. The car was being borrowed less frequently, however, as the experiences of various drivers added to its eccentric reputation. Not one to ignore facts, Charlie contemplated the incidents with an unbiased air.

There was the time he had promised to give his friend a ride back to Lafayette. The car had refused to start and had stalled at his house, as it frequently did after sitting for longer than two minutes with the engine off. By that time, Charlie knew the specific remedy for the problem. Filling a coke can with gasoline and removing the air filter, Charlie explained how simple it was to pour the gasoline into the carburetor while he attempted to start the car. Suddenly, as

Charlie peered through the opening in the hood, flames shot up his friend's arm. Charlie's friend cast the can behind him in a attempt to escape the fire. The can landed in the neighbor's lawn and flames leaped up the side of their house.

Charlie remembered the last incident with the car and chuckled to himself with satisfaction. The car had been parked, as always, heading into his small house near the university. He must have been half asleep when he put the car in reverse, as his foot found the gas first and then the brake. The car bolted backwards and took off at twenty miles an hour. The car ran full hilt into a two feet high concrete intrusion and jumped on the curb. The back wheels of the car spun furiously as the bumper rested on the concrete curb.

Two days after Mr. Johnson had dropped him off, Charlie arrived at his parent's apartment in Tomball. His mother chided him from her position in front of the stove.

"What do you mean, you're leaving tomorrow? You just got here. You haven't even had a chance to rest yet. Look at you, you've lost weight, your color's bad and it sounds like you're coming down with a cold. No, it's just ridiculous to be thinking of running off again so soon. Besides, your father and I would like to see you every once and a while too you know."

It seemed to Charlie that his mother was always in front of the stove. The aromas of good home cooking constantly filled the apartment and raised impatient appetites.

"Where are you planning on going anyway that's so important that you can't even spend a little time with your parents?"

"I have to go to Austin."

"I knew it, I just knew you were going to see her. If I've told you once, I've told you a hundred times, that girl is no good for you. She's a hippy, going around barefoot. God what am I going to do?"

The question, although addressed to the heavens, was directed at Charlie, who stood shifting uneasily from one foot to the other, suffering the agonies of his mother's lecture. That girl, of course, as his mother so fondly referred to her, was Linda. Although he hadn't actually ever heard her name pass his mother's lips, he knew full well when she was being spoken of.

"Theresa, leave him alone. He has to find these things out for himself," said Charlie's father. He sat quietly at the dinner table, coffee cup in one hand, pipe in the other, carefully gauging the level of his son's discomfort by the numerous times he ran his hand through his hair.

"Oh OK, I'm not gonna say another word. I'm just his mother after all. What do I know. Go ahead, go to her tomorrow, let her ruin your life, but just remember that I warned you."

Charlie sighed. He said goodbye to his mother and father and made his way out of the apartment and toward the garage.

The continental purred as Charlie and Linda passed through Beaumont on their way to Linda's parent's house in Port Arthur. Linda snuggled up next to Charlie then turned her head and exhaled. The ashtray burst with half-smoked butts. Linda curled her legs up under her. She pressed closer to Charlie and sought other playthings.

"Don't you think it's a little late for that?" said Charlie, taking a deep breath as his body reacted to Linda's nimble fingers.

"No, not at all. In fact, I'd say it's the perfect time," said Linda.

Charlie knew his resistance, what there was of it, was no use, for Linda did exactly what she wanted, when she wanted, wherever she wanted to do it. It wouldn't be the first time, and Charlie knew better than to count it the last, that this fiery woman would have her way with him. The final mile to Port Arthur was covered in approximately the time it could have been walked, due to Charlie's difficulty controlling the car, not to mention himself, during the last stretch.

Charlie pulled into the driveway of Linda' parent's house, his eyes slightly glazed, giving Linda just enough time to freshen up—or freshen down—before the family reunion.

The house was just as Charlie remembered it, at least from what he had been permitted to see in the past, which had mainly been the front porch. It was an old, weather-beaten frame house, one of those that had settled in stages over the years, erasing all signs of perpendicular walls or level floors. Like most of the houses in Port Arthur, it was built up on blocks, allowing just enough crawl space under the house for rat and roach conventions. Both Charlie and Linda had learned to expect sudden infestations of roaches when Linda's mother sent packages. Even the cockroaches in Port Arthur seemed to be seeking a free ride out.

"Hi Linda, hi Charlie. You're a little late, we expected you an hour ago," said Linda's mother from the porch. She was tall and raw-boned, with a wild paranoia in her eyes. Her features were plain; she applied no cosmetics and paid little attention to her overall appearance. Charlie had to admit that she was civil to him, beyond that he understood little of the world that she inhabited.

"Well come on in. Don't just stand there gawkin. We got some Colonel Sanders chicken. Thought you might be hungry."

"Oh that's alright Mrs. Pierce. Don't bother, we're not hungry anyway, are we Linda," said Charlie.

Charlie felt a sharp elbow in his side and turned to see Linda pointing for him to follow her mother, who had already reached the screen door and was holding it wide for the two of them.

Linda had another cigarette out, attempting to calm the rage and loathing she felt upon coming home. She understood only too well Charlie's reluctance, as she had seen it many times on the face of her friends when they had come to visit. She had hoped and prayed to get away from the house for as long as she could remember. She could recall the desire to get out that had kept her awake nights, listening to rats running around, searching the debris on the floor for food. College had meant freedom for her after the years of hell she had spent in high school as a social outcast, a misfit spurned and ridiculed by all the "right people." Her clothes, her manners, and her home were different, and in the world of high school cliques, different wasn't acceptable. She drew hard on her cigarette. The smoke permeated her body, and, along with the conviction that she wasn't trapped anymore, and never would be again, calmed her mind.

Two disheveled children ran past Charlie and Linda.

"Frank, Mary, you settle down right this minute or else!" Linda's mother screamed. She smacked one then the other of her children across the face. The punishment resulted in an outbreak of even more erratic behavior.

"Damnit, I told you kids to shut up. Now you do what I tell you or else." Linda's mother grabbed for her children and came up with two handfuls of hair. "I said to leave your sister alone and I meant it." She smacked the boy again then held him by his hair as he squirmed and jerked to get loose. "Now go over there and say hello nicely to your sister and her boyfriend."

Linda was furious at her mother's attempt to link her more closely than she cared to be with her stepbrother and sister and even more so because she felt herself being pulled down into that pit which it seemed she had so recently crawled out of.

Charlie stood in the middle of the scene, trying to hide his disbelief. Linda watched him while he examined her family, judging them. What right did he have to judge them anyway? He wasn't poor, never had been really, not in the sense that her family was. The kind of poverty that breeds confusion, frustration, and finally desperation, and is seldom escaped.

Charlie adjusted his eyes to the darkness of the living room. Linda's mother directed him to the couch, where he was joined by Linda and the rest of the family.

Linda's mother passed out boxes of fried chicken, cold to the touch.

Charlie shifted uneasily. He got up and removed a shoe which he was sitting on. Other miscellaneous items in the shadows crowded him on the couch. The coffee table was piled a foot high with a heap of what appeared to be trash. Charlie moved his eyes from the coffee table to the floor. He knew that he had stepped on something coming in, and now that he could clearly see the floor, at least for a reasonable distance in front of him, he realized it was covered with litter. He recognized old bones, cat food cans, and boxes of chicken, the contents long ago eaten, among the layer of trash that lay forgotten all over the floor. In a far corner, only barely discernible, a mound of trash some four feet high was piled up.

Linda couldn't help but smile as she followed Charlie's eyes around the room, watching his face show first curiosity then astonishment, and, finally, ill-concealed disgust. What he didn't realize was that her mother had cleaned the place up for his visit. The huge mound of trash in the corner was the telltale sign, for her mother's method of cleaning was to rake the always present foot-high layer of trash that covered the floor into a pile in the corner. The least

Charlie could do was attempt to hide his emotions more successfully. For this household, it was truly the thought that counted. Linda reminded herself to reprimand Charlie for his insolence as soon as they were alone.

Charlie turned upon hearing Linda chuckle. The challenging look in her eyes was accentuated by her wicked grin. To Charlie her look said, "Yeah, you think you're so tough, how long do you think you would have lasted in a house like this?" Of course, she already knew the answer or she wouldn't have that self-righteous grin on her face. Of all the people Charlie had known, this skinny redhead could make him feel like shit quicker than anyone. Charlie turned from the accusation in her eyes.

"Come on kids, eat up now before it gets cold," said Linda's mother.

Focusing on his food, Charlie noticed a movement on the side of the box of chicken. He peeked around and saw a huge, silky brown cockroach crawl into his dinner. He strained to resist the urge to bolt out the door. Examining the couch more closely, Charlie saw that it was teeming with cockroaches, which didn't hesitate to crawl over his legs and up his arms. A quick, inconspicuous glance behind him revealed the living room wall to be a solid mass of swarming bugs. Despite the conditions, Charlie was not one to insult a host. He slowly and meticulously ate his dinner among wild, maniacal shrieks directed at the two children chasing each other through the rubbish.

Charlie's upbringing had not prepared him for the scene. The filth was unbelievable and the kids seemed to have inherited their mother's abhorrent traits. The exchanges that took place between mother and children were, for the most part, unintelligible, at least to Charlie's ear. Linda's mother had only one volume when addressing her offspring—loud.

Seizing the opportunity to move from the infested sofa, Charlie offered to help in the kitchen, aside from the fact that there were no dishes—the boxes, along with the remaining contents, joined the others on the floor. Linda informed Charlie later that absolutely no one was allowed in the kitchen because it was a "mess." It was frequented regularly by the dozens of cats kept on the back porch, who no doubt waded precariously through month old dishes, searching for edible morsels.

Charlie and Linda, after gathering together Linda's possessions, bid a brisk farewell, desiring to drive late into the night rather than be a burden. Reliving the scene at Linda's home during the drive, Charlie realized the overwhelmingly sadness of it. He felt for the three prisoners trapped in that dehumanizing environment and reevaluated Linda's personality in light of the bizarre experience. He promised himself that from then on, whenever he was confronted with her harsh, sometimes brutal character, he would remember her roots in that house and family.

The stretch of highway was dark except for a dim set of taillights blinking ahead in the distance. The red, pulsating glow of Linda's cigarette illuminated the car.

"You'll never be able to understand how much I wanted to get out of there until you've lived it," said Linda.

The smoke from Linda's cigarette curled lazily toward the headliner and down again. The wheels of the Continental hummed against the asphalt.

"I wanted to run away so bad, but I knew in the back of my head that the only chance I had was using my brain, and that meant school. So I was stuck there for a while, but now I'm not and that's in the past. You can bet your bottom dollar on one thing, this kid's never gonna live like that again."

Charlie gazed at Linda. Her eyes were fixed reflectively on her cigarette. He knew she meant it.

The left rear wheel of the car ahead flew off and into the darkness at the side of the road. Sparks shot up as the rear axle dug into the asphalt. The car swerved to the shoulder and came to a grinding halt, the rear fender resting against the pavement. Charlie had had just enough time to swerve around the disabled car and avoid an accident. His instinct to reach out and help compelled him to guide the Continental to the shoulder in front of the marooned vehicle.

The highway was deserted. The car clock showed 12:34 as Charlie started to go check on the occupants of the car. Linda remained in the front seat.

"Let's just go. Somebody else will come along and help them. It's none of our business," said Linda.

"Look, there're no one else out here and these people need help, whoever they are, and I'm gonna help them. Just lock the door while I'm gone. You'll be alright."

Linda watched Charlie approach the car. Two figures emerged from the vehicle, one from each side. To Linda, they appeared to be laughing. One of them, the driver, fell back through the open door. The other supported his shifting weight against the roof. Both were medium-sized black males dressed for a Saturday night on the town. Linda heard Charlie offer assistance, after which came the sound of a slurred, drunken acceptance.

"Open up will you," Charlie called to Linda.

The two men followed Charlie, supporting each other while stumbling toward the back door of the Continental.

As she reluctantly pushed the back door open, Linda wondered what Charlie had gotten them into. They were out in the middle of nowhere and there likely wasn't a town for miles.

The two men clambered into the back seat. A strong aroma of stale whiskey hovered around them and carried into the cold night air.

Charlie eased into the front seat. He turned and addressed the men.

"You'll have to show me where to go. I'm not too familiar with this area out here."

The two men slunk low in the backseat. One began to snore while the other peered through heavy lids at Charlie's charitably innocent countenance.

"That a way, just go that a way. I'll show you," said the conscious member of the pair, pointing with a long, bony finger back in the direction he and his friend had come from.

Charlie turned and drove back down the road, following the slurred directions of the two drunks.

"Turn here," the conscious drunk directed, pointing down a dark gravel road with a faint light in the distance.

Charlie drove down the road.

"That's it, this one!" said the man, pointing to a low, one room house on the side of the road, surrounded by a half-dozen identical houses.

Charlie stopped the car. A bare electric bulb at the door of the house illuminated the figure of a large dog bounding toward the car, barking as it approached.

"Wake up Bubba. Come on now, wake up. We're here," said the man who had given directions, shaking his partner, who responded with a grunt.

The dog had begun to bark fiercely as the two men stumbled out the back door. Gunshots issued from the backseat. The barking suddenly stopped. Bubba casually placed his weapon in his coat pocket and delivered a halfhearted kick to the dog laying at his feet.

The two men moved towards the light of the house, arm in arm, while Charlie watched, his eyes going from men to dog and back.

"God damned dog," came the words from the retreating figures.

"Goodnight," Charlie called after them, feeling sick.

CHAPTER XXI

Charlie looked out on the Arizona desert through the front window of Linda's house near the ASU campus.

"Bullshit," said Linda from the worn sofa across the living room. She was surrounded by cardboard boxes in various stages of being unpacked. "Those boys don't need you, and you know it. That's just an excuse."

It was a continuation of the argument that Charlie had listened to many times over the past few weeks. But this time Linda had become more urgent and insistent, perhaps because of his impending departure.

"I don't know why you think you have to be such a do-gooder anyway. What it really comes down to is, you're just a fool sometimes."

Linda's vindictiveness caused Charlie to slump over. He hung his head slightly as he weighed the validity of her accusations against what he supposed was her need to vent her frustration at his leaving.

"I'll bet that's not it after all. I'll bet it's not the boys you're going back for, but something else—a girl."

Linda watched Charlie's reaction to her words closely, gauging the degree of discomfort they were causing.

"Don't be crazy. There isn't another girl, we live out in the woods. There aren't any girls around, even if I wanted one."

"You mean to tell me that all the time you've been there you haven't met any girls?"Linda had laid the trap and Charlie saw no way to avoid it.

"I didn't say that."

Charlie and Linda exchanged glances and she knew instantly he had not been faithful. Even though she hadn't directly requested it, she had expected to get it out of him. The new development fired her resentment.

"You've been sleeping with someone then?"

The question tempted Charlie's honesty.

"Not exactly."

"Well, have you been screwing or have you screwed any females since you went to work at the camp, other than myself that is?"

"Yes, I have," said Charlie, feeling guilty. He could remember reacting the same way as a boy when a neighbor would come knocking on the door to complain that little Charlie had wrestled their little girl to the ground and kissed her again.

"I knew it was something other than the boys you were going back for. All that crap you gave me about how much you wanted to help the poor unfortunate little hoodlums. Bullshit. All you want to do is to go running back to some little whore you got hiding in the woods."

Charlie realized Linda's accusation was ridiculous, but he understood her need to distort his avowed attempts at goodness. It was a scenario which had played itself out many times over the years.

"What are you waiting for then? Go running back to the little bitch. See if I care. I'm sure I can find plenty to occupy myself with." Linda shot Charlie a sly smile and flipped her hair over her shoulder.

Charlie understood the threat, but it wasn't anything new. It seemed to be a wedge fixed permanently in their relationship. Aware of Linda's intractability, Charlie scooped up his bag, walked cautiously to the couch, and tried to kiss her goodbye.

Linda recoiled from Charlie's attempt with disdain.

"I'll call you when I get back," said Charlie as he stepped out into the Arizona heat.

"Don't bother."

Linda's words shot back at Charlie as he closed the front door. For the most part, aside from its ending on a sour note and Linda's bad moods, his vacation had been enjoyable. The weather in Mesa had been beautiful and exploring the campus at Arizona State had been interesting. The drive out from Texas had taken them through some truly beautiful country and there had even been times when he and Linda had enjoyed each other's company.

Due to the late start he had gotten out of Mesa, Charlie found himself falling asleep at the wheel on the outskirts of El Paso. After his second time running off onto the shoulder, when he was suddenly awakened by the crunch of dirt and gravel, he decided that he should pull off the road and get some sleep. He stopped at a roadside park situated on top of a rise which would have allowed for a panoramic view of the burning brown hills of Mexico had it been daylight. His clock showed 3:30 a.m.

When Charlie had bought the truck in Austin, after returning the Continental to his parent's apartment, he had thought the camper on the back a tremendously good idea and had pictured himself curled up in it in a trouble-free sleep. His daydreaming in the car lot that day hadn't included the incessant volume of motors being started, cars being parked, and doors being slammed that now kept him awake.

At five-thirty, Charlie dragged himself back behind the driver's seat and headed for Dallas, seven hundred miles away.

It had seemed like a good idea at first, picking up the hitchhikers. They had seemed friendly enough and they had been stranded in the middle of the barrenness of West Texas. It was only while contemplating their feet up on his dashboard that Charlie realized why he had found them where he had. He wasn't prepared to face another seven hours, regardless of what he told them about going all the way to Dallas. His desire to help his fellow man was losing ground against his own desire for peace and quiet.

Charlie pulled the truck over to the shoulder and eased it to a stop. The two hitchhikers looked quizzically at Charlie, then at each other. The landscape was barren. The empty, arid vastness lay broken only by miles of highway stretching in a straight line. An occasional car or truck swept by, sending little whirlwinds of dust up against the motionless truck.

"OK, this is it. The end of the line," said Charlie, looking over at the two hitchhikers, their feet still propped up on the dashboard.

"I thought you said you were going all the way to Dallas?" said one of the men.

Charlie felt his guilt conflict with his resolution to be firm and get what he wanted out of the situation.

"I am going all the way to Dallas," said Charlie. "But I'm going alone."

"You can't just leave us off out here in the middle of nowhere," said the other man.

"I found you in the middle of nowhere and I can leave you in the middle of nowhere. Now, I'd appreciate it if you would get your stuff and get out."

The sternness Charlie heard in his voice pleased him. The two hitchhikers reluctantly let themselves out.

Charlie accelerated slowly off the shoulder, not once looking back in the mirror. He luxuriated in the site of the foot-free dashboard. The hitchhikers had needed help and he had refused, but aside from the small voice of guilt, he felt much better.

Charlie turned off the highway onto the farm road heading into camp. He missed the boys and he had to admit that he hoped they felt the same.

Charlie rounded the first turn in the road and peered up. The boys were sitting on the roadside. They recognized their counselor's face behind the wheel and let loose whistles and catcalls. The boys swarmed over the truck and shoved toward Charlie. His smile let them know that he shared their happiness. The boys piled into the truck and the remainder of the drive was a shrieking, yelling reunion. Charlie never thought that such an intense uproar could actually be a balm for his tattered spirit.

Once back at camp, the boys jumped out of the truck. Charlie began to count heads.

"Where's Sherman?" said Charlie.

"He's in jail!" said Jerome. The other boys' concurrent replies confirmed his words.

"How did he get in jail?"

Each boy clambered to tell his version of the story first.

"He he he pulled a knife on the police," said Jerome.

"Yeah Charlie. We were at the movies and Sherman was outside by himself. Before Duane and Bud knew what happened they slapped his black ass in jail," said Keith.

As Keith delivered his exciting narrative, Bud came slowly up the path, hands in his pockets, smiling warmly.

"Welcome back Charlie, seems like you've been gone forever," said Bud. He removed one hand from the pocket of his snug-fitting black corduroy pants and firmly grasped Charlie's outstretched hand.

"Go on Bud, tell him how Sherman attacked the cop with that knife. He was just lucky he didn't get wasted," continued Keith.

"Keith, you wouldn't know the truth if it hit you between the eyes. Sherman didn't attack any policeman and he only had a small pocket knife." Bud gave Charlie a knowing look and shook his head.

"Well, they threw him in jail and Mr. Johnson and Charlie are gonna go and get him out. And he did too attack that cop," said Keith.

Keith's nagging persistence sparked Bud's anger.

"Keith, I'm only gonna tell you one more time. Keep your mouth shut, or I'll be on you like white on rice."

Bud's warning hit its mark and Keith held back his words.

"Yeah Bud, why don't you kick his ass? He's been asking for it," said Jerome.

"I'll kick your black ass if you don't mind your own business," said Bud.

"So Sherman's been in jail for two days? Where?" said Charlie.

"Gilmer" said Bud. "Johnson did think it would be better if you went in with him. He said you know Sherman better than anyone and that the two of you might have to do a pretty hard sell to keep the boy from being taken away from us. In fact, Johnson's coming out today to bring you in with him."

"I'll bet they won't let him come back, no matter what Mr. Johnson and Charlie do," said Keith.

"Keith, you better shut up, or I'll bust you in the mouth. Everybody's gettin tired of your attitude," said Roy.

Keith halted again.

"Looks like you've made a few enemies while I've been gone Keith. Is that mouth of yours getting you in trouble again?" said Charlie.

"It ain't me. Things just ain't been the same since you been gone. But now that you're back, there's gonna be some other guys that better be watching out." Keith glared at Roy.

"Well, we'll just wait and see what's going on. I probably spoiled you so rotten that Bud and Duane had to work twice as hard to get you to do anything at all. Anyway, bitching and all, I'm glad to be back, at least right now. I'm not sure I'll be able to say the same tomorrow morning."

Charlie's short speech helped alleviate the current of dissension that he felt running through the group. Bud looked tired and he snapped more readily than Charlie remembered. Keith appeared to be the center of trouble in the group. Duane hadn't even made an appearance yet and his name had hardly been mentioned. In the middle of his train of thought, in which he had begun to imagine himself as the all-knowing, perfect counselor come home to right the wrongs which had arisen since his departure, Charlie stopped himself. Perhaps roles had revised in the group momentarily while he had been gone—some appeared more tired, others less, some quieter, others noisier. But, all in all, if he were truthful with himself, he had to admit that they were just the same boys that he had left—no better, no worse.

CHAPTER XXII

M r. Johnson soon arrived and he and Charlie rode to Gilmer in the social worker's truck.

"The fact is that Sherman did pull a knife on a policeman in that alley," said Johnson. "Now, they don't really care how old he is or how scared he was. All they know is that he was wielding a deadly weapon and appeared to have every intention of using it. If they had been less patient with him and reacted on first instinct, I'm sure they would have shot the boy."

Charlie tried unsuccessfully to picture Sherman holding off a policeman in a dark alley with a pocket knife.

"They don't really even know why he ran when they spotted him on the street," Johnson continued. "They said he just took off like a jack rabbit. They, of course, were obliged to pursue. I do want you to know before we go in today to speak with the sheriff, that they have the power to put him away. I have no idea how they feel about the matter right now, but I do know they wouldn't let him back in our custody. So they're still undecided."

Johnson stopped the truck in front of the unpretentious stone edifice of the combination jail and police headquarters, located on the north side of the town square.

"Sheriff Collier, this is Charlie Rogers, one of Sherman's counselors," said Mr. Johnson as he and Charlie walked into the sheriff's wood-paneled office.

The room was sparsely decorated, containing a modest collection of books situated directly behind the sheriff's imposing oak desk. Citations hung on the wall in dark, unimaginative frames. There was no furniture other than the chairs occupied by Charlie and Mr. Johnson. Nothing much interested the eye, except for the sheriff himself, who sat leaning back in his leather armchair, scrutinizing the supplicants.

"You already know why we're here Sheriff," Mr. Johnson began casually, with an undertone of concern. "We would like to have your permission to take Sherman back with us to camp."

"I wish it were that easy. There's the matter of attempted assault with a deadly weapon hanging over the boy's head. We want to make sure that wherever we decide to put him he does no harm to anyone."

Charlie guessed the sheriff was in his mid-fifties. His crew cut was gray, and although his physique was that of a younger man, he was obviously of the World War II generation. His manner so far seemed to suit that of the county constable rather than the big city cop, paternal instead of rigid.

"That's exactly what we want for the boy too, and we think the best place for him is with us," said Johnson, leaning forward, his elbows on the smooth, wooden arms of the chair, his hands clutched together.

"I've heard some pretty strange stories about the goings on out at that camp. Even old Swanson, the ranger out at the park, says he's had to put his place off limits to your group a couple of times. At this point, I'm not really sure the boys are receiving adequate supervision."

The indictment had been made. Mr. Johnson and Charlie fidgeted under the steady gaze of the sheriff. Charlie took a deep breath and began, his voice quavering slightly.

"When I started working at the camp and first met Sherman and the other boys, I didn't know if I had what it would take to help them and maybe even now I'm not sure."

Charlie hesitated, wondering if he should continue. Then he began again, not knowing exactly where he was going, only wanting to make this man understand what he had come to understand about the boys. Mr. Johnson and the sheriff waited attentively, watching Charlie's emotions animate his features.

"I'd never met boys like Sherman before. Kids who'd never known what it was to have parents, a home, someone who wanted them and cared for them. I've learned that they've had to grow up fast and tough, with little or no education and no guidance from a system which locked them away with a bunch of kids just like themselves. I'm not really sure what I'm saying, except that Sherman does have all that now, because, speaking for myself anyway, I really care about him, about what happens to him and what kind of a man he turns out to be. I feel responsible for that and maybe I'm the first one who has ever cared that much and because I care I keep him in line."

Charlie leaned forward in his chair.

"I don't know what happened the other night, but I can guarantee you that, as long as I'm around, it won't happen again. I know the boys need as much as discipline as love and I don't hesitate to give it to them, and if you want to know the truth, they love it because they know I care enough about them to stop them from hurting themselves. I think it would be wrong to take Sherman from us, just because it may be the last chance he ever has to straighten his life out." Charlie stopped abruptly, beginning to sweat.

The sheriff remained silent, taking in Charlie's plea.

"Well," the sheriff began, lightly clearing his throat and turning his gaze from Charlie to Mr. Johnson, "it seems as if this young man has a good case for sending the boy back with you." The sheriff hesitated, then returned his attention to Charlie and began slowly and thoughtfully. "Charlie, I have to agree with you, not because of anything in particular you said, but just because I can see that you meant what you did say. I feel safe handing him over to you. I'll call down to the jail and you can go pick him up."

"Thank you sir. You won't regret this," said Charlie, still nervous and somewhat embarrassed by his outburst.

"No, I don't think I will."

Charlie and Mr. Johnson picked up Sherman at the jail. As soon as the door swung open he leaped forward to hug the two men.

"I guess I can't ever go on another vacation if you're gonna get yourself thrown in jail every time I leave," said Charlie, throwing his arm around the boy's shoulder.

"That sounds pretty good to me," said Sherman. He smiled first at Charlie then at Mr. Johnson.

Charlie, Sherman, and Mr. Johnson walked out of the jail and into the fading light of late afternoon.

CHAPTER XXIII

It was three weeks until Christmas and winter had already come to the backwoods of East Texas while Charlie had been gone. There had already been a few mornings with temperatures in the low teens. The pot belly stove in the bunkhouse had been kept constantly stoked on the coldest days and everybody had taken to sleeping in their clothes.

It had become increasingly apparent that something was going to have to be done about the outhouse. Each morning the boys had found themselves having to chip a thin veneer of ice off the seat before they could tend to business. After a great amount of bickering the group decided that the outhouse at least required a top.

The water supply situation had been vastly improved while Charlie had been away on vacation. Mr. Johnson had had a water line run into camp, which provided one official spigot for the group's needs and eliminated the tiresome job of hauling the fifty gallon canvas water bag.

A number of new construction projects were already underway. Vince and Russ were building their own shelter in the vicinity of the camp. The counselors and the majority of the boys, however, could not discern the progress of the project, as visitations were by invitation only.

Bud and Charlie decided to build a two bed bungalow. The project, the idea of which arose from a late night discussion, was so impelling to the two counselors that they were out in the early frost the next morning scouting prospective trees for the frame. The tent was to cover approximately a twenty-by-thirty foot area and was located at the apex of a triangle which included the kitchen and group bunkhouse.

Duane had departed for his vacation the day after Charlie's arrival. His face had been drawn tight and he had looked thinner than Charlie had remembered.

Although Duane was no longer the new counselor in the camp and had carved out some semblance of a niche, it was, to Charlie's thinking, a very uncomfortable niche. His lack of physical aggressiveness and general wavering character acted as a target for the group's abuse. On most days he received fourfold the amount of insults as anyone else in camp, yet he persisted in spite of the abuse.

Mr. Johnson promised that the Buffalo River trip would be one of the most memorable and enjoyable trips the boys would ever take. Charlie and Bud's group were to be the first to take the trip. In consideration, they had almost exclusive use of the four aluminum Grumman canoes. The first trial run took place at Lake of the Pines, where everyone learned how to enter and exit, where to sit, and how to paddle most effectively. As the canoes seemed to be designed only to go in circles, the boys complained and moaned for several hours before they made some progress towards holding a predetermined course.

The canoe is deceptive in appearance. Its simple curves conjure images of pleasant outings on crystal clear waters. Once seated, a soul with even the slightest desire for adventure begins to assume the proud bearing of an Indian warrior setting out on a journey into the wilderness. With each dip of the oar the hair seems to grow longer and darker; the muscles harden and the imagination quickens until one becomes a brave fighting for one's life as white water surges ahead. The only way of knowing what lies ahead is for one to let the roaring torrent carry one around the next bend, through the approaching cataract.

Yet the beginner is a long way from the brave in terms of ability. The canoe, as the group had not yet understood, has the uncanny ability to dump its entire contents, people and all, in a split second, merely through a slight shift in the load.

CHAPTER XXIV

The boys were looking forward to Christmas and feeling isolated from the holiday festivities that Texas, and the world, for all they knew, were enjoying. Their Thanksgiving had been uneventful, a quiet day in camp without a turkey, though Duane had prepared his much awaited ham in the hole, which had been declared by all to be a success.

The Christmas plans were special. There was to be a trip to the ranch for a Christmas party followed by a visit to Charlie's house for Christmas dinner and presents. The visit to Charlie's was a topic of conversation that drifted through canvas doorways throughout the days. Charlie overheard, on one occasion, a discussion among the boys regarding what they should buy his mother. He was left with the impression that they were stumped, but he knew they would come up with something.

The bus was packed with forethought in the manner that had become routine to the veteran travelers: tents, ice box, and sleeping bags stored in the back, accessible from the emergency exit on the inside, cooler stored in a manner that would allow easy access—not, however, for the purposes of random snacks, as it had been a stern rule from the beginning to stay out of the icebox unless you were fixing a meal. Early on the group had discovered that unlimited access to snacks quickly led to starvation for those who had not partaken.

Each boy's personal belongings were his own responsibility, including his tobacco. Although the thievery of the past had for the most part subsided, there still occurred infrequent disappearances of caches of smoke.

Bud had chosen to take a vacation during the holidays and David went with him. Bud was replaced by Tim, a nice recruit from the other camp. Tim was in his early to mid-thirties. He wore a bushy, dark mustache and horn-rimmed spectacles. His overall build was slight and he appeared more fit for a clerkship than for handling juvenile delinquents in the woods. Charlie noticed, however, that Russ' behavior seemed to become more congenial and less erratic under the counselor's influence. Charlie envied Tim's ease with Russ, as he had still been unable to get through to the boy himself.

The bus was once again on the road. The sound of the group's impromptu rendition of "He's got the whole world in his hands" filled the inside of the coach.

"Hey Charlie, you think Bud will adopt David?" said Keith from his seat midway to the back of the bus.

"I really don't know. They sure seem to like each other's company, that's for sure," said Charlie from the back of the bus.

"I wish he would adopt me," said Chuck from his position near the front, where he sat with his legs stretched out and his head turned to survey the rest of the group.

"Me, too," said Jerome.

"I wouldn't mind getting all that stuff he does. Watches, cigarettes, money," said Keith.

"Yeah, me too," said Danny.

"How come you guys never say you'd like for me to adopt you?" said Charlie, feigning disappointment.

"You're too poor," said Keith.

"You're too mean. You'd beat us all the time," said Russ, enjoying the heckling that Charlie was getting.

"I may have a million dollars in the bank and I just act poor."

"If you had that kind of money you wouldn't be out here wasting your time with us," said Keith.

"Maybe I'm just a masochist. I like hurting myself."

"I doubt that too," said Keith. "You get too cranky when things don't go your way."

"Oh, yeah. Come back here and say that."

"Alright, I will. Come on Roy, Sherman, let's show this guy who's tough."

The boys moved to the back of the bus and piled on top of Charlie. The counselor's laughter broke from the growing mass.

Tim navigated the bus onto a tentacle of road leading past a ranch-style residence on the right and a cluster of squat, stucco buildings in front on the left.

"So this is the ranch. Looks like a pretty good place to live to me," said Charlie.

The boys pointed out the stucco buildings as the bunkhouses and identified the school room and the girls' section.

"It may look pretty good to you, but you sure wouldn't want to live here," said Roy. "They don't let you do anything here and that Janice is mean."

Charlie knew from the boys' numerous stories that Janice, a matronly woman by description, dispensed her punishment most often at the end of a needle. Her reputation, from what Charlie was able to discern from the various stories, was a mixed one. The boys spoke of her as a heavy-handed disciplinarian, yet always maintained a note of warmth when bringing her up.

Tim pulled the bus to a halt in front of the boys' dorm. The grounds and buildings appeared abandoned except for a few boys lounging outside of doors. Charlie wondered where the welcoming party was. The boys scattered to various parts of the ranch, scouting up old memories.

The adults that Charlie briefly came into contact with could only stare. When asked where he was from, and as he received a head-to-toe examination and rejection, Charlie's reply failed to elicit any recognition. He gradually sensed from his surroundings and the stiff reception that the ranch was not a place he cared to linger for very long. He already yearned for the fresh country air, the leafless oaks, the blue jays strutting from branch to branch, and the cool waters of Wolf Creek. They all meant freedom, the antithesis of what he sensed in the empty hallways of this institution.

Charlie assumed as much responsibility as anyone for the trouble that soon followed. His attempt at discipline was much more suited to a rural setting than to the bureaucratic ranch.

A boy and his two cohorts were engaged in harassing Jerome as he tried to leave his dorm. Charlie came to Jerome's aid from his position on the sofa across the room.

"Fuck off," said the leader of the group as he pushed Charlie away.

The boy shoved Jerome.

Charlie stepped in between Jerome and his tormentors. "I'll say it one more time—leave him alone."

"We we're just having a little fun with the nigger," said the leader. "Why don't you get lost before we have to kick your ass too."

Charlie's patience was broken by the threat. "If anybody does any ass kicking around here, it's gonna be me." He grabbed the leader by his shirt front and pulled him closer in order to make the warning understood.

Charlie shoved the bully back firmly, releasing his hold. The boy stumbled slightly against his friends.

Jerome was watching the standoff with a smile.

"You can't put your hands on me like that, I'm just a kid. I'll show you asshole," said the bully. He stormed out the front door, his friends following behind.

Charlie sat down on the sofa again. He put his legs up and tried to get interested in a copy of Road and Track.

A while later, Charlie looked up to see the group of bullies and a staff member in the lead approaching him.

"Hi, I'm John Cunningham, senior counselor, and I've been told by Billy here that you were physically abusive to him."

Charlie remained seated. "What exactly do you mean by physically abusive?"

"He said that you roughed him up. In short, that you physically assaulted him."

"Yeah Mr. Cunningham. He grabbed me and choked me, then threw me against the wall. My buddies here will tell you how it happened," said the lead bully. He looked to his two companions for confirmation.

"I certainly won't deny that I grabbed him," said Charlie, "but it was only to reinforce a point that otherwise wouldn't have been taken seriously."

Charlie's blunt admission momentarily set the group back. The senior counselor cleared his throat.

"I'm not sure how you discipline the boys at your camp, but here we have very strict rules that expressly forbid excessive physical abuse."

"You can be sure it wasn't excessive, but only appropriate."

"That's not for you to decide at this point. It's merely your word against his. From now on, please keep your hands off of the boys."

"If they keep their hands off my group then I'll keep my hands off of them. Is that fair enough?"

"It's not your business to decide what's fair. We have rules and they're meant to be obeyed."

With that, Charlie's first encounter with the power structure of the ranch came to an end. His rebellious behavior left a bad impression on the authority of the institution. The second encounter that same afternoon served to illuminate the disciplinary tactics used at the ranch. Charlie was lying on the couch in the common room of the boys' dorm when Keith first brought the news.

"One of the kids is saying that he had a pack of cigarettes stolen, ready rolls. Everybody seems to think it was someone in our group that did it," said Keith.

"Why don't you find Roy and get the other guys together. Bring them in here and let's see if we can straighten this out," said Charlie.

"They just left to tell Janice about it. There'll probably be a big commotion."

"Then get moving. The faster we move the better off we are."

Charlie swung his legs around and planted his feet firmly on the floor, a position better suited to the protection of his interests. Keith and the rest of the boys soon entered. They herded together as the room quickly began filling with boys of every size, shape, and color—more activity than Charlie had seen since the group's arrival earlier in the day.

The surge gradually subsided and the room teemed with thirty to forty restless, suspicious boys. The senior counselor carved a path through the room and grabbed the attention of the mob. His speech was overly lengthy and convoluted, considering the extent of the crime: one pack of cigarettes assumed to be stolen. The offender was to be given an opportunity to redeem himself while still concealing his identity. If the cigarettes were not returned, all further extracurricular activities for the evening would be curtailed. Of course, the only activities of that nature which Charlie knew of were the plans his group had made to go into town to a movie.

Mr. Cunningham enacted a plan to allow the guilty individual to come forward. Within the large common room, where everyone was gathered, there was a bathroom accessible by two doors. A small basket was placed against the inside wall, at such a height that anyone passing through could reach up and drop an object, a pack of cigarettes perhaps, inside the basket.

Each boy and counselor was to pass through the first door, closing it behind him, and leave through the rear door, doing the same. As the last boy made his exit, the senior counselor would enter and check the basket for its contents.

With each full pass through the bathroom, as the basket came up empty again and again, Charlie and the boys saw their chances for a night on the town recede further and further from possibility.

The group eventually overcame their disappointment with thoughts of the next morning's Christmas party. Even the counselors were supposed to receive a present from the ranch. Charlie visualized a twenty dollar bill or something of equal value as a just recompense for his dedication to the group.

The next morning the common room was once again full of life. This time the atmosphere was festive. All attention was fixed on the tree and the presents heaped under it. Even Santa made an appearance. Several of the ranch boys commented on his striking resemblance to Janice's husband.

Charlie waited anxiously in the rear of the room, trying to appear unconcerned as the gifts were distributed. Neither he nor Tim had received even the slightest nod of recognition and Santa's bag was almost empty. Charlie felt his anger rise as he looked at Tim and attempted to gauge his reaction.

Charlie heard his name being called and looked up to see Santa holding a gift high in the air. He sighed deeply. He knew wouldn't be forgotten. He could forgive the staff now for the shoddy treatment he had received.

Charlie attempted to repress a self-satisfied smile as he ambled up the aisle and took the gift. Tim rose as well and strode towards Santa's outstretched hand.

Charlie took the gift back to the couch and started to unwrap the package. He threw off the final pieces of paper and stared down at a quart milk carton with Gumbos Malted Milk Balls emblazoned on the front. Charlie's stomach twisted and his hands became clammy.

Tim sat down next to Charlie and unwrapped his gift.

"Well look at that. We got the same present. I guess we'll have plenty of malted milk balls for awhile. I don't even like them. You can have mine if you want Charlie," said Tim. He laid his carton down on the couch next to Charlie, who sat staring dumbly at the carton in his hands.

"Gumbos Malted Milk Balls," Charlie muttered to himself.

"Did you say something?" said Tim, a queer expression on his face.

Charlie choked back his disappointment.

"Hey Charlie, what'd you get?" said Vince from behind the couch. He stared at the Milk Ball carton. "What's that anyway? Malted milk balls? That's kind of a weird present."

Charlie eyed his carton in frustration.

"You know what the counselors here at the ranch got?" continued Vince.

"What?" said Charlie wearily.

"Keith told me they all got a twenty dollar bill. Maybe they put a twenty in the bottom of your boxes and you have to eat all those balls to get it." Vince chuckled out loud.

Charlie threw his carton down next to Tim's.

Later that day the counselors and the boys gladly said goodbye to the ranch and made their way to Charlie's parent's apartment in

Tomball. They arrived just as Charlie's mother was finishing Christmas dinner. She greeted the group warmly and herded them to the kitchen.

The ranch was only a bad memory to the boys as they sat around the kitchen table, savoring the smell of fresh cooked turkey and fixing their eyes on the succulent bird. Stomachs churned as plates were passed and heaped full of potatoes, corn, bread, and stuffing. Despite powerful urges toward gluttony, the group managed to retain their manners. Charlie was the only exception, as the combination of home and good food made him forget his etiquette in his haste to subdue his hunger.

After dinner, the counselors, the boys, and Charlie's parents moved to the living room to open presents. Amid the commotion of gifts being handed out and opened, Russ ducked quickly into the bedroom and returned with a package neatly wrapped in brown paper.

Russ approached Charlie's mother with the gift. "This is for you Mrs. Rogers. It's from all the guys. I hope you like it," he said nervously.

The boys gathered around, anxious to see the response their gift would elicit. Charlie and his father, in the back of the group, exchanged looks. Charlie shook his head, indicating his ignorance of the contents of the present.

Mrs. Rogers unwrapped the gift. She pulled a vase out of the paper and held it up for everyone to see.

"Oh, it's beautiful. It's really lovely," said Charlie's mother, examining the vase.

"We weren't sure if you'd like it," murmured Roy.

"I think it's beautiful. Every time I see this vase I'll think of you boys." Charlie's mother looked from the vase to the boys. "That way I'll always remember you."

"You want to know where we got it?" said Russ, wanting more than anything to tell her.

"Let me tell her, I found it," said Keith.

"We three found it," said Roy firmly, pointing to Russ and Keith. "But you can tell her Keith."

"We found it in a trash can and do you know what it had in it?" said Keith.

"No, what did it have in it?"

"You can tell her that part Russ," said Keith.

"A snake, we found a snake in it," said Russ.

"Yeah, but we washed it real good before we wrapped it up. It doesn't even smell anymore," said Roy.

Mrs. Rogers smiled. The gift, along with the story, would be cherished for years to come.

A snake in a vase in a trash can, Charlie mused. He knew the boys would come up with something, but he had completely under-estimated their sense of the dramatic and their ability to please.

Charlie positioned himself in front of the living room and attempted to find the best angle for a group picture. Jerome refused to have his picture taken. He stood behind Charlie.

"Come on, take the picture already," said Jerome.

"De de de, can't you talk right Jerome?" said Chuck.

Chuck's mimic of Jerome's stutter made everyone smile, including Jerome.

"You boys leave him alone," said Charlie's mother from behind Charlie, where she sat happily surveying the scene while sewing a new patch on Roy's hat.

Charlie found his shot and clicked the camera. The Christmas tree was pictured on the left of the frame, draped with conspicuously misaligned tinsel and twinkling bulbs. The poinsettia was positioned directly in front of the tree and over Keith's right shoulder. Keith, his hair neatly plastered into a gelled wave, was seated nearest the camera, on the floor. His face was stern, but an inward glow seemed to illuminated his features. Chuck was seated to Keith's immediate right, closest to the television set, solemnly studying the barely visible box in his lap which contained the model car that he had received.

Danny was crouched behind Chuck. He too had a model car in his lap, but in contrast to Chuck's stiff countenance, he was smiling warmly. Roy, "Love" emblazoned across his yellow shirt, was kneeling directly behind Danny. His blonde hair was low over his fore-head, accentuating his somber, shaded eyes. Sherman was standing upright behind Roy, his darkness in stark contrast to Chuck's more subdued color, wearing a white turtle neck and gray sport shirt. He was smiling and clutching a gold teddy bear to his chest.

The two remaining figures were Vince, and Charlie's father, who were sharing the rocking chair in the center of the picture. Charlie's father was smiling affectionately, his arms wrapped around Vince's middle. Vince was leaning against Charlie's father's chest, his long blonde hair held in place by a red bandana.

The photo would always be a favorite of Charlie's as the years passed, never failing to elicit warm memories of the Christmas of 1971.

CHAPTER XXV

As winter moved on, a succession of new counselors passed through the camp.

One new recruit was a writer who had explored the farthest depths of the Amazon in search of treasure. His main hobby at camp was resting his huge bulk on any convenient bunk and shielding himself from the reality of camp life with a magazine. His strongest contribution to group activity was his occasional intimate conversations with Russ in which he would enchant the boy with tales of adventure. He lasted not quite a month, somewhat less time than Tim, who also departed after five weeks.

Arthur, a black man in his mid-thirties, sported a wooden leg. This anomaly, together with his warm yet subdued nature, made him especially popular with the boys. They were particularly interested in his leg, which became a topic of endless speculation. Shortly before his departure three weeks later, Arthur gave the boys a gave a demonstration of the mechanics of his wooden limb, which they listened to attentively. Though they genuinely liked Arthur, the boys were even more ruthless in their taunts than with Duane, who could at least manage himself with the smaller boys.

As counselors came and left the camp, the boys endured, knowing that they held final judgment over the mutability of any particular candidate. They had grown used to Duane, Bud, and Charlie and perhaps had no desire for anyone else to lead them. Russ and Vince completed their small shelter in the woods, exulting in their new independence and privacy.

Keith spent some time in the hospital after a late night prank which ended in broken eardrums. Everyone had gathered in the bunkhouse and surrounded the wood stove in an attempt to absorb its precious heat when Keith appeared with a Q-tip protruding from each ear. Nobody was able to say why—perhaps it was just a mild case of cabin fever which made him act the part of Frankenstein with his blue and white electrodes. Roy snuck up behind the would-be monster and slapped him simultaneously on both sides of his head, driving the Q-tips deep into the boy's ears. Keith screamed as two rivulets of blood flowed from his ears.

The episode had its lighter side for Keith. In the hospital he met a group of young candy stripers whom he loved to entertain with his stories of his life in the woods. It was later discovered that he had been able to leave his room through the window at night to visit one of his most interested listeners. He would return in the small hours of the morning and vow to extend his hospitalization as long as possible.

The other group too spent the long winter battling the effects of cabin fever. One night, Nathan, by far the largest and strongest boy in either camp, for no clear reason, lost touch with reality and terrorized the camp for an hour, waving a large club at whoever approached, and destroying portions of the campsite. Bud and Charlie finally managed to talk the boy back to sanity.

Above all, the boys' restlessness in winter was due to the curtailment of the physical activity necessary for their well being. The group took a weekend canoe trip and several limited hiking expeditions, but these were not enough to satisfy. Only the Buffalo River canoe trip, when the spring rains would swell the waters and carry the canoes on their long journey, would appease the boys' need for adventure.

The first signs of spring began showing around the camp. With the increasingly sunny days, the counselors began construction on their bungalow. Intended to ensure privacy for the adults, it became one of the favorite hangouts of the boys. They usually came alone, seeking attention. Jerome would frequently creep into Charlie's tent, catching him unaware, and pounce on him as he lay absorbed in a book. The two would grip each other in mock combat, laughing and cussing. The wrestling match inevitably culminated in Jerome's exclamation of "Uncle" as Charlie exerted pressure on one of the boy's limbs.

Charlie and Jerome's relationship had grown stronger and closer with each passing month of winter. Jerome's outer shell of animosity had begun to dissipate, as had Charlie's sometimes irascible emotions. Even Russ, with the special attention he had received from Tim and the other new counselors, had become more frequently happy and at ease.

On a sunny Saturday morning, Charlie, Duane, recently back from his vacation, Mr. Johnson, and the boys began to load the bus for The Buffalo River trip. Although he had checked and rechecked the list of necessary items for the trip over the last week, Charlie still felt anxious. A heightened cautiousness goaded him from his usual "everything will take care of itself" attitude to an almost pedantic obsession with details.

"Duane, would you check that trailer hitch one more time and make sure those canoes are secured?" said Charlie. "Roy, you and Sherman double check the paddles and life jackets. Jerry, you and Russ make sure we have enough rope and watertight bags. And while you're at it, make sure we have those waterproof matches, will you?"

"Are you sure everyone has a lifejacket? I expect you to make sure that everyone wears one at all times," said Mr. Johnson. He seemed just as nervous as Charlie, never missing an opportunity in the last few days to remind the counselor about the jackets.

"I think we've got just about everything Charlie. The trailer looks good, the food's been packed according to instructions, and that just about does it," said Duane. His eyes darted from Mr. Johnson to Charlie. Duane's eyes had watered profusely since he had come back from his vacation fitted with new contact lenses. The timidity in his look was still visible, constantly scouting for impending dangers.

"OK you guys, let's get on the bus and get going. We're going on a canoe trip!" said Charlie.

Charlie's announcement drew a chorus of yells from the boys.

"I hope you fellas have a good trip," said Mr. Johnson. "If everything I've heard about the river is true, you should have a lot of fun. Just be careful and remember the—"

"Life jackets," Charlie and Duane simultaneously interjected, leaving Johnson with an appreciative smile.

"I should trust you by now," said Johnson, his glasses catching the reflection of the morning sun.

"We'll be fine, don't worry," said Charlie as he shook Johnson's hand.

Charlie and Duane stepped aboard the bus.

"Get the fuck out of my seat Jerome, or I'll beat your ass," said Roy.

"Go to hell, this is my seat," said Jerome.

"Cool it you guys," said Charlie. "This is gonna be a long trip and you'll both have plenty of opportunities to sit in that seat. Now, you have ten seconds to decide who sits there first. If you don't, neither of you will."

The finality of Charlie's statement called for a sudden compromise. Jerome remained in the seat, grinning devilishly.

"Oh you little nigger. I'll get you," said Roy. He lumbered to the rear of the bus.

Charlie slipped behind the wheel and closed the door on the tall, wiry figure of Mr. Johnson, who stood calmly watching the group board. Charlie watched Mr. Johnson recede in his rear view mirror as he started the bus on the journey to Buffalo City, Arkansas.

The Buffalo began below The Norfolk Dam, on the Arkansas side, in the midst of the Ozarks National Forest. Johnson had claimed that this river hidden deep in the rural countryside of Northern Arkansas would offer a true white water experience.

The aluminum Grumman canoes that the ranch had supplied were, at least, according to Duane, in his knowledge of the sport, the best available. "Unsinkable" was the word Duane had used, which Charlie recalled whenever he felt an uneasy premonition regarding the trip.

Bud had been conscripted by the other group for the time. His services were much needed, as the boys had relentlessly driven one new counselor after another away. Bud had very much wanted to come on the trip, but Johnson, having the final authority, thought he would be more useful elsewhere.

The group headed directly north, taking Highway 257 to 30, which would carry them through Texarkana, Arkadelphia Hot Springs, and Little Rock. From there, Highway 65 would lead the adventurers due north into the Buffalo back country. The culmination of their road journey was to be the bend of the river at Buffalo City. For ten days after that, the waterway would be their trail. Although the group was anxious to proceed directly to their destination, they traveled at an unhurried pace, as their itinerary included no rigid timetable, but was subject only to the day-to-day whims of their natures.

In Hot Springs, Arkansas, the boys were fascinated by the groups of the elderly that roamed the streets and haunted the bath houses, seeking youth in the steaming mineral waters.

"I hope I never get that old," said Chuck, his face pressed hard against the window of the bus, scrutinizing the ancient specimen apparently asleep on a bench.

"You won't say that when you get older," said Duane.

"Me neither," said Russ, wrinkling his face at the prospects of old age.

"You'll see things a lot differently as you get older. You're not always gonna think the same way. Even your bodies are gonna wear out someday," said Duane.

"Bullshit Duane," said Roy. "Nobody can tell me about my body. I can kick your ass now and I'll be able to kick your ass when I'm ninety."

Roy's summation set the other boys to howling and flexing their youthful muscles in defiance of time.

The counselors made arrangements with a local man to have the bus driven down river to a prearranged location, where it would be deposited, ready to carry the travelers home again after their journey.

The trip was beginning to sound idyllic. Even the river itself, when viewed on the map, seemed to be unimpressive. It did seem to have a noticeable absence of straight stretches, but after all, that was what the trip was about—floating contentedly downriver wherever the water would lead.

The group were soon to discover that river travel was an unusual mode of transportation. The simple matter of where one was at any time could be perplexing. Normal roadways supplied innumerable indicators of position, both qualitative and quantitative: Dallas, 35 miles, Miami, 10, turn right here, dead end there, two-way traffic. The only directions worth knowing on a river were upstream and downstream, and, invariably, as time passed, one's position moved downstream; yet downstream was not always downstream, as rivers had the uncanny ability to double back on themselves while hiding this secret from their travelers.

The group stood together on the shore of the river, observing the complacent waters below.

"It don't look bad to me at all," said Danny. "I bet I could even stand up on the bottom, right there in the middle."

"There's a few rapids right there," said Keith, pointing some twenty yards downstream to where the current was constricted by two boulders jutting out.

"That ain't nothin. Look, it spreads out right on the other side. It's a piece of cake," said Russ.

The group pulled the canoes up to the water's edge. All food had been waterproofed and bound, along with the cooking pots and pans, to the boats. The boys and the counselors sported bright orange lifejackets with what seemed to be a million buckles and clasps. The smaller boys, Jerome, Danny, and Jerry, were swallowed up by their vests.

"Let's get moving," said Charlie, scanning the boys' faces. Despite their overt enthusiasm, Charlie discerned a sense of finality in their looks, stirred by this apparently docile section of river.

"OK now. I want you all to remember the order that we're going to travel in and that means for the whole trip," said Charlie.

"We already heard all that. Let's get going," said Vince. He fidgeted in the confines of his jacket, anxious to move. Duane appeared to be the only one who wore his vest with any degree of comfort.

"This thing is for sissies," said Vince, digging at the straps and buckles of his jacket.

"Sissies or not, you're going to wear it. Now, since you know so much, you tell us about the order," said Charlie.

"You, Roy, and Jerry first, then me, Russ, and Keith, then David, Sherman, and Jerome. And last, Doofus, Danny, and Chuck."

"Good. Now make sure you stay that way. No matter what happens, always try to keep the canoe behind you in sight. If anyone gets in trouble, just call for help and we'll be there. Alright?"

"Sure, yeah, alright," came the replies from the row of nodding heads.

"I think we should say that all canoes should be in sight of each other at all times," said Duane, obviously nervousness about being the last canoe.

"We'll sure try to, but if we can't, then we'll have to do second best. Now get those canoes in the water."

Charlie, Roy, and Jerry scurried for their craft and maneuvered their boat towards the placid departure point. They waved goodbye to the bus and headed toward the minor rapids ahead.

The river took an abrupt turn to the right on the far side of the boulders. Before anyone knew what had happened, the boat had capsized beyond the entrance to the boulders, still within sight of the bus.

Vince's group nearly encountered the same fate, but righted themselves at the last minute, avoiding drifting broadside to the rushing current as the first boat had.

Charlie, Roy, and Jerry stood thigh-high in water, attempting to right their canoe. Kool-Aid drifted downstream from the overturned boat.

"What's the matter with you guys? You're all wet. Maybe we should lead this and show you how to do it," Vince jeered.

"Just get that Kool-Aid," said Charlie, furious at his own stupidity.

The third boat headed for the opening and met with the same misfortune as the first.

Duane's group, learning from the mistakes of the others, quietly glided through the opening and passed the six floundering mariners.

The two submerged groups finally righted their canoes. All four trios gathered back at the shore and again readied their boats for departure.

"OK, let's try this again," said Charlie.

"You sure you wouldn't rather ride with us Roy?" said Vince. "Old Charlie looks like he might be a pretty dangerous guy to be around on this trip."

"Screw you Vince," said Roy.

A marked difference in attitudes now divided the group. Those who were still dry mocked and momentarily held power over those who were soaked.

The voyagers soon discovered that little physical exertion was required on the river, as the current supplied all the necessary power. The primary concern became staying dry.

After several test runs, the group developed a strategy to protect against future capsizing. The person at the bow of each canoe became almost as important as the helmsman, as this person could scout all approaching sections that appeared troublesome. They would then pass on valuable information concerning unexpected turns, hidden boulders, or shallow spots in the stream bed to the helmsman, who would respond in an appropriate fashion.

The team work approach soon became a fluid process which, with each successive white water section, brought an increased confidence among each crew. The four boats were beginning to stay together nicely, losing site of each other only when the river made abrupt turns. The river bottom could be seen easily, as the water was crystal clear and the stone-paved stream bed excluded any chances of its being muddied by sediment. The sounds of oars dipping, wood creaking, joints snapping, and muscles stretching mixed with the teasing of the breeze against leaves, the belly flop of frogs, and the other light noises along the river as the novices adjusted themselves to the waters.

Vince brought his canoe alongside Charlie's. The river had widened, slackening its pace as the bottom receded and deepened.

"You guys dried out yet?" said Vince.

"I'll show you who's gonna be wet," said Roy. He smacked his paddle sideways against the water, splashing Vince, Russ, and Keith.

Charlie yelled and splashed along with Roy.

"Let's get em!" said Jerry as he splashed with glee.

"You sons of bitches!" said Russ.

"Come on you guys, cut it out. I'm getting soaked," said Keith.

"That'll teach you to keep your mouth shut," said Roy, laughing and glaring at the dripping victims.

"I'll get you for that, I swear!" said Vince, paddling fast. "You just wait and see."

The other two canoes had kept a safe distance behind, not wanting to become involved in the water fight.

"We got those guys didn't we Charlie?" yelled Jerry. Roy followed with a deep bellow.

The rancor which had beset Charlie's group since their first capsizing suddenly dissipated with the playful act of revenge.

The group encountered the second difficult section of the river shortly after noon. Once again the channel narrowed, passing through a four foot opening in the rocks. Approaching the rapids, the river swung to the left. A grove of water maple obscured the view beyond that point. The canoes had become more widely spaced now, with the second boat drifting peacefully some thirty yards back, oblivious yet of the chute that the first canoe was being sucked into.

"Whoa, hold on," Charlie yelled as the rocking boat hurtled through the opening, striking a submerged rock.

"Watch out Charlie, it's turning again!" said Roy above the rush of water.

Jerry sat motionless in the middle, his paddle in the canoe, his knuckles white with the effort of holding on.

"Shit, help!" Jerry screamed as the canoe slammed into the rock abutment that turned the current suddenly back to the right again.

"Whoa," Charlie hollered as he flailed with his paddle in an attempt to line bow and stern with the main flow.

A third turn loomed ahead where white turbulence crashed against a wall of stone.

"Hold on!" said Charlie.

The river narrowed to three feet. The force of the water thrust the canoe irrevocably forward.

"Turn, turn!" said Roy.

"Right side paddle, on your right side," Charlie called in response to Roy's directions.

The canoe slithered around the turn, once again crashing into submerged boulders. Almost as suddenly as it had appeared the raging cataract transformed itself once again into a quiet, subdued force.

"Let's get out of here and watch the other guys go through that," Charlie gasped, his body still shaking with excitement.

Charlie, Roy, and Jerry beached the canoe and ran back upstream. They positioned themselves atop the rocks on the second turn.

"This'll be great. We'll get to see them coming right into it. They'll never suspect it's here, just like us. It's one hell of a turn," said Roy.

"I can't believe we made it. I was scared shitless," said Jerry.

"Here they come," Charlie called.

The group turned their eyes toward the canoers hurtling directly towards them.

The second crew had just come successfully out of the first sharp turn when they too had skidded against the imposing cliff on their right side. The three onlookers watched as Vince, Russ, and Keith headed for the perilous second turn. Vince was the helmsman, his view obscured by Keith directly in front of him and Russ in the bow.

It was Russ whose wild screams could be heard above the torrent. He shrieked with joy as the canoe was catapulted forward, rocking and twisting in the stream. He threw his hands up and let loose a Brave-like yell as the craft raced for the stone wall. Keith's eyes bulged and his hair stood on end. Vince's countenance remained concentrated. Charlie had to give it to the kid—he was doing a great job so far and he appeared determined to stay dry.

Just as the crew appeared clear of the last turn, a submerged rock reaching toward the surface caught the craft on its exposed belly about midway. The canoe tipped precariously and water gushed over the side and into the boat.

It looked to the observers as if the canoe would be swamped until Vince, moving quickly forward and shouting instructions to Keith, managed with help to dislodge the craft. The boat burst out and the boys glided into the relative serenity of the next section. The crew yelled in triumph as they beached their craft. They raced to join the spectators and arrived just in time to see the next canoe round the first turn.

Unnerved by the first turn, David, Sherman, and Jerome were about to meet the second completely unprepared. Their paddles lay idle inside the boat as they held on for impact. The canoe was thrust forward. The bow hit first, then the bottom. Metal sounded against stone. The boat capsized and dumped all three occupants into the turbulent waters. The flotsam, canoes, and paddles floated a short distance to calmer waters.

All three boys emerged from the water, shivering and shaking from fear and cold. They huddled together on the warm beach, trying to compose themselves as the last canoe came flying around the first turn.

Duane's face turned white as he assessed the second turn.

"Come on Doofus, you can do it!" said Vince from the rocks.

Vince's encouragement inadvertently averted Duane, Chuck, and Danny's attention, almost causing them to come to an identical end as the previous canoe.

Duane's group successfully made passage after the near mishap. The four crews gathered to salvage the items from the wrecked third boat that had floated downstream.

The group made the decision in mid-afternoon to camp for the night and assess the situation while allowing everyone time to dry out. A fire was started and those who most recently capsized were granted the closest positions to the heat.

"Man, did you see us come around that turn," Russ squealed, "we were hauling ass. I thought we were goners there for a second."

"We're the only ones who haven't gone in yet," said Vince.

"Shut up, will you Vince," said Chuck. "I'm tired of hearing about how great you are."

"Yeah, I knew we'd make it," said Keith. The fear he had shown on the river had suddenly evaporated.

"You looked scared shitless to me when you were taking on water," said Roy.

"I ain't gonna ride with Doofus no more," said Chuck.

"Look Chuck, before this is over with, everybody's gonna wind up in the river," said Charlie.

"Not us," said Vince and Russ simultaneously.

"I don't care. I just don't want to ride with him. Why can't I go with Sherman and Jerome?" said Chuck.

"They tipped over too," said Charlie.

"That's alright. I'd still rather be with them than Doofus."

"It's alright with me," said David. "I'll go with Duane. Chuck, you can have my place."

No other attempts were made to change positions.

"When are we gonna get off this river anyway," said Chuck, still unsatisfied.

"We just started Chuck. You got at least nine more days," said Charlie.

"Well I'm tired of it. This ain't no fun. Why can't we just go back?"

"What are you gonna do? Paddle upstream Chuck?" said Sherman, attempting to dry his hair by running his pick through it.

"Nobody asked you nigger," said Chuck.

"Alright Chuck, that's enough from you. We don't need you pissing everybody off," said Charlie.

"Fuck you," said Chuck softly.

"What did you say?" said Charlie, getting up slowly and walking toward Chuck.

"I didn't say nothin."

Charlie eased up to Chuck. "I could have sworn I heard you say something."

"He said, 'fuck you, Charlie.' I heard him," said Sherman.

"Nobody asked you Sherman. So why don't you mind your own business," said Chuck.

"Why don't both of you just shut up," said Roy, standing bare-shirted and absorbing the heat.

"I didn't know I was taking a bunch of babies on this trip. You get a little wet and you're ready to go home to momma crying," said Charlie.

Charlie's words stung Chuck. He eased himself off the sand and walked toward the forest to find solitude.

"Come on Chuck. Cheer up. It's not that bad. It was kind of fun and nobody was hurt," said Duane.

"Screw you Doofus," said Chuck as he continued toward the woods.

The group returned their eyes to the leaping flames which were devouring the drift wood.

"We did lose some food today," said Duane, "but mostly Kool-Aid, hot chocolate, and a few more extraneous items. Nothing to worry about really. We should have plenty of supplies for the rest of the trip." Duane looked across the rising heat to where Charlie stood, hands clenched behind his back, apparently mesmerized by the fire.

"Yeah, we'll be fine," said Charlie unenthusiastically, not taking his eyes from the blaze. "Did you have a chance to check the canoes out? I know a couple of them took some pretty hard hits."

"Just a few dents here and there but nothing to worry about. I told you those things were unsinkable."

All eyes turned toward Duane at his last word.

"That's yet to be seen. This was only the first day," said Charlie, the feel of rocks pounding the bottom of his canoe still fresh in his memory.

Toward dusk, as Chuck ended his self-imposed exile and returned to the group, he noticed an increasing number of clouds gathering to the north.

CHAPTER XXVI

On the second day, the group began to get a greater sense of the patterns of the river. The depth and width of the stream bed, the type of terrain passed through, and the direction of the flow became understood as signs of what could be expected next. True to Mr. Johnson's description, the river had an abundance of white water sections of varying difficulty, and all were fun.

The group observed an abundance of wildlife on the river: beavers, rabbits, snakes, king fishers, flying squirrels, trout, skunks. Numerous other creatures too sly and wily to be seen alerted the travelers to their presence with rustling leaves and splashing water.

As their confidence increased, and due to the bulky discomfort of the contraptions, the boys began to shed their lifejackets. Chuck's mood had improved with more experience on the water. The seemingly invincible team of Vince, Keith, and Russ capsized for the first time and were finally humbled by the river.

The group beached their crafts in late afternoon in preparation for making camp. Charlie rustled through his gear and produced a fishing line and hook.

"I don't know about any of you guys, but seeing those trout swim by the last two days has worked up my appetite for a fish fry," said Charlie.

"How you think you gonna catch any fish without a fishing pole?" said Danny, eager to participate in the experiment.

"I see plenty of poles around here. In fact, that one over there looks just about right." Charlie walked toward a tree and broke off a branch. He held it up and gave Danny a knowing smile.

"You ain't gonna catch nothin with that stick," said Russ. "You don't even have any bait."

"Bait? That's the easiest part of the whole thing." Charlie laid down his fishing pole, to which he had secured the line and hook.

Charlie walked downstream, keeping his eyes to the ground. Danny and Russ watched as he bent over and darted his hand toward the ground. Charlie stood up and lifted his closed hand to his face. He approached the two boys.

"That takes care of the issue of bait," said Charlie, opening his hand to reveal a small, green frog. "Looks like you better get a fire started."

"There ain't no way you're gonna catch any kind of a fish with a frog and a stick," said Keith from his nearby seat on a log.

Charlie hooked the frog through the loose skin on its back. "Well, we'll just let the fish decide if they want to be caught or not. How does that sound?"

Before the stream narrowed about ten yards down, it formed a wide expanse of shallow, pure, and clear water, rippling over a bottom laden with smooth stones. Charlie's intuition suggested that if there were any fish to be caught, this portion of the stream just where the turbulence began would be the best place to look. Charlie carefully threw the frog-line into center stream and let it drift to a settled position. The frog skipped over the ripples as a subtle force pulled it slowly back upstream. Charlie hoped this illusion would fool whatever fish happened to be looking for a frog dinner.

Keith, Chuck, Danny, and Russ positioned themselves behind Charlie, where they kept up a constant murmur of disparaging remarks about his particular method of fishing.

"Everybody knows you got to have a rod and reel to catch fish," said Keith.

"Whoa, it's trying. There she goes, I got one!" said Charlie. The water splashed around the frog as a slim brown trout struggled against the line.

"Wait, I'll help, no let me!" said Danny and Russ simultaneously, their jeers now halted by the immediacy of their hunger.

Charlie quickly captured a second trout with the same technique. The fish were cleaned and skewered with a sharp stick, then stuck in the ground to roast over the fire.

The boys curled up on the river bank and watched the stars late into the night. David observed a group of clouds moving north, the light of a three-quarter moon illuminating their passage through the sky. The sounds of running water eventually lulled the boys to sleep. Roy was awakened by a creature that ran over him as he lay in his sleeping bag. From what he could deduce, it was about the size of a skunk.

The third day began with an early morning drizzle. The wet was only enough to occasion a damp face and a trickle of water down the neck and into the warmth of a sleeping bag. The light rain lifted towards nine and the day presented an array of colors; blues, yellows, browns, whites, off-whites, oranges, reds, crimsons, grays, and blacks all harmonized into intricate patterns in the spring landscape.

That morning, as they rounded a bend in the river, the canoers observed the first sign of civilization they had come across since first departing on their journey. The narrow banks of the river suddenly receded, allowing for a view of a horse ranch spread out along the stream for perhaps fifteen secluded acres. Horses raced along the river bank, their tails whipped by the breezes of the valley. A man with a rancher's garb, Stetson, chaps, and western shirt, sat on horseback. The boys waved and whistled, seeking signs of acknowledgement as their boats sped by.

For Charlie, that vision of a simpler life on the ranch passed too quickly. He would have enjoyed pulling over and learning something of the retreat. His yearning was subsumed, however, as the group drifted deeper into the wilderness. Once civilization was well behind them, the crews beached their canoes. Duane and Charlie began to check the food stores.

"Where in the hell are those cookies we had?" said Duane. "I know we had a five pound bag of cookies in here and now they're gone."

The other caches were checked and still nothing.

"I know we had them," said Duane.

"Who was in that boat anyway?" said Charlie.

"That's Chuck, Jerome, and Sherman's canoe," said Duane.

All eyes turned to the suddenly silent trio.

"You guys don't know what happened to those cookies, do you?" said Duane. "Sherman, you know anything about those cookies?"

Sherman looked to Jerome and Chuck for assistance, both of whom kept their eyes to the ground.

"Well, I, uh," said Jerome.

"What? Let's hear what you know," said Duane, a rare firmness in his voice.

"Chuck ate em," Sherman spoke up.

"You and Jerome ate em too Sherman. Don't be blaming it all on me."

"You mean that you guys ate five pounds of cookies this morning? Is that what you were doing lagging back this morning? Stuffing your faces with cookies?" said Duane.

The trio couldn't help but laugh at the memory of their delight in devouring the treasure they had discovered earlier that day.

"No more cookies for you guys for the whole trip," said Duane.

"No more for anyone," Keith interjected, "those were all we had."

While the canoes were being launched, Danny pointed to a row of mature beech trees. He turned to Duane with a puzzled expression. "What's all that stuff in the limbs of those trees?"Duane followed Danny's finger. A jumbled collection of branches lie up in the trees.

"I'm not sure how that stuff got there, but I've noticed it for the last several days," said Duane.

"It looks like water lodged them there, which would mean that the river gets that high sometimes," said Keith.

"It seems pretty hard to believe that this river could be that much higher at times," said Charlie, craning his neck in an attempt to gauge the height of the branches.

"I can't think of any other explanation for how all those branches and sticks got up there, can you?" said Duane, his arms folded across his chest, trying to imagine the surface of the river flowing ten feet above their heads.

"I'll tell you one thing, I sure wouldn't want to be in this valley when the river got that high," said Keith. "Count me out of that one. I like it just the way it is right now."

Toward evening the setting sun became obscured by a thick bank of clouds which transformed the purple and golden hues of dusk into steel-gray tones.

The group established camp that night on a sand bar which rested in mid-stream. The island provided sufficient kindling and sandy stretches for a comfortable stay.

The fresh country air and the continuous exercise during the subsequent days gave everyone generous appetites by night. The group would huddle around the campfire and fix their eyes on the embers for long stretches of silence, only seldom broken by attempts at conversation which seemed superfluous against the fullness of the night. The boys would unroll their sleeping bags as close as advisable to the fire and fall asleep with the heat glowing on their faces.

On the morning of the sixth day, a dark layer of clouds had gathered to the north, upstream from the camp. A sense of urgency hung over the group at breakfast, rendering the meal little more than a short prelude to the morning's launch.

A light shower began falling around mid-day. The boys, bare-chested, their life jackets long ago stored away, reveled in the warm rain as it accompanied them downstream. The river, from all appearances, wasn't gaining any momentum as a result of the rain and the group were content to continue their voyage under the gentle showers.

Around three, the showers became more insistent. Sheets of rain began to sting the boys' bare torsos and the canoes began to take on uncomfortable amounts of water.

Charlie pulled his crew to the shore, where they waited for the other boats.

"Pull over here!" said Charlie through the rain to the other canoes.

The rest of the crews pulled their crafts to shore, near Charlie's. The group clung to the few bushes on the otherwise barren rock face defining the shoreline.

"We need to stick together and start looking for a dry place to spend the night!" said Charlie over the downpour.

"Sounds good to me!" said Duane.

The crews once again headed their canoes downstream, searching the cliffs for shelter.

"There, to the right, up that incline!" said Charlie. His words were inaudible to all but Roy and Jerry, who shared his canoe, but all eyes followed his extended arm toward the cliff.

The crews paddled fervently for shore. Roy leaped ashore and grabbed the bow of his crew's boat, keeping it from slipping back into the current. The other boats followed the same procedure, until all four canoes were lodged half in, half out of the water.

The eight-foot-wide strip of shoreline allowed passage back upstream toward the caves high up on the cliff face. Charlie led the way on foot. Rain pelted the boys as they hacked a path through the underbrush. Twenty yards upstream, the caves once again came into view, hollowed out depressions in the cliff face forty feet above where the huddled group stood. Charlie, Duane, and the boys the climbed up the rock face, aided by make-shift footholds along the way. Charlie reached the largest cave first and stood dripping wet under its overhang. He watched the others pick their way up the incline. The group stood shivering together under their new shelter.

The cliff was formed in the shape of a crescent, the back wall having been scoured out at the deepest point to perhaps five feet, narrowing down the farthest point to no more than two feet. The surface that the group stood on ran the length of the cliff and varied in width from four feet to a two foot path at the farthest end. The scalloped cliff presented a series of hollowed-out depressions accessible by the ever-diminishing ledge.

"First things first. Danny, you and Jerry get a fire going," said Charlie as he studied the boys' worried faces.

"But there won't be any dry wood," said Jerry, shivering beneath the light T-shirt that clung to his skinny chest.

"You look hard enough and you'll find dry wood. Now get going. The rest of you go down to the canoes and get your stuff up here," said Charlie.

"Where's Duane anyway?" said Jerry.

"When I last saw him he was down unloading a canoe," said David.

"Here I am," came Duane's voice from behind a rock outcrop at the top of the incline. "I was just telling everyone to get down and bring the food and other essentials up. Also, make sure those canoes are secured. You don't know how high that river's gonna come up tonight."

The dripping figures turned and looked out from their covered shelf high above. The almost sheer cliff obscured the river and allowed only for a view of the shoreline.

"Let's get going then," said Charlie.

The group made their way down the cliff one by one, retracing their steps. This time Duane led the way down as Charlie brought up the rear.

Charlie approached Duane and the boys. The shoreline had narrowed to less than half its previous width. The group stood looking down and across the now swollen river. A lone canoe lay lodged between the opposite shore and a fallen, projecting tree. It rocked to and fro, buffeted by the billowing current.

"What happened?" said Charlie, staring at the stranded craft.

"I'm not real sure," said Duane in an unsettled tone. "But I think we've had a flash flood. I had our food laying here on the shore next to the canoe and now it's nowhere to be seen and the canoe's over there."

"You mean all our food?" Keith cried.

Duane slowly nodded, looking like he wanted to cry.

The group stood on the bank, attempting to come to terms with the flood that had come so quickly and threatened their trip so thoroughly.

Charlie shook himself free of his reflection and looked at the boys. "Roy, you and Sherman come with me. We have to get that other canoe."

"There's no way you can get across this river and bring it back!" said Duane as the river crested in midstream.

"We're gonna have to try. If we leave it there overnight it'll be lost. This river's gonna get even higher before this storm's over with.

Now get those other boats secured and get everything up in the caves. Come on Roy, Sherman, let's go."

The stranded canoe lay some fifteen yards downstream and twenty yards across the river itself.

"You guys are going to have to paddle harder than you ever thought you could. We'll be going against that current and if you don't give it all you've got plus some you might as well kiss it all goodbye," said Charlie.

A large limb caught in the river twisted in the grip of the current. Charlie and the boys set off. In order to keep from being forced too far downstream they had to paddle perpendicular to the current. The water rolled off their bare chests as they thrust their paddles deeply and swiftly into the torrent. Once they reached the other shore, the trio tied the two canoes together.

"Let's change ends now," Charlie panted above the rain and thunder as the two canoes tied in tandem rocked back and forth against the shore. Roy and Charlie crossed paths in mid-canoe so that Roy would be in the bow and Charlie in the stern.

"Are you rested enough?" said Charlie.

Sherman and Roy took deep breaths and nodded. The rest of the group huddled together on the far shore to lend support.

"Alright, let's go. Go go go!" said Charlie from the stern.

Charlie and the boys worked their muscles against the pull downstream. They halted the backward progress and, inch by inch, pulled forward against the flood.

"Go go, you can do it!" said the others from the shore. The group's rooting coupled with Charlie's commands from the stern drew the two tied boats closer and closer to the far shore. Six pairs of hands grabbed the bow of the occupied boat when it approached. Charlie, Roy, and Sherman slumped forward onto land.

Later that evening, the group stood around the fire in their shelter, listening to the onslaught of rain against rock outside.

"What are we gonna do now?" said Duane. He moved closer to the fire. Flames danced against the cave walls. The echo of a great horned owl seeking shelter rolled through the trees.

"The only thing we can do is move on," said Charlie. "Except for a box of oatmeal, we're out of food. You know as well as I do that we lost everything we had."

"I don't see how we're gonna be able to get out on that river tomorrow. You saw what it was like today. Somebody's liable to get hurt or even worse," said Duane.

The circle of faces, each reflecting the light of the campfire, turned in unison toward Duane.

"I just don't think we should try it. I get the jitters just thinking about it," continued Duane.

"We did alright today and we'll do alright tomorrow. There's nothing to be afraid of," Roy interjected, sounding convinced if not for the last minute worried expression he cast in Charlie's direction.

Charlie sat cross-legged, leaning into the fire. He probed the burning embers with a stick. "I don't really see any alternative to moving on. The oatmeal will be finished in the morning and after that there isn't anything." The statement sounded as matter-of-fact as he had meant it to be. He carefully scanned the attentive faces, trying to gauge the advances that fear had made on the group's defenses. If he were entirely truthful, he would have to admit that the uncertainty he felt was much greater than any he could discern on the tired faces in front of him, except, perhaps, for Duane's and Jerry's. He did know, however, that he had to keep everyone moving and not give them time to become frightened.

"Now, I suggest that everyone find a place to stretch out for the night and get a little sleep. You're going to need all your energy for tomorrow," said Charlie.

"What are we gonna do if we don't find any food?" cried Danny. "I'm hungry already."

"Shut up will you Danny. You're just a cry baby," said Sherman, his own uneasiness causing him to attack at the first sign of frailty.

"We'll just have to find some food. Kill some maybe," said Russ. "I'll bet we could kill some rabbits easy."

"Yeah, me and Russ could do the huntin," said Vince.

"We'll just have to deal with that when we get to it. Now let's get some sleep," said Charlie.

Charlie raised himself on stiff legs and stretched upward before the fire, attempting to work out the soreness of his cold, tired muscles. He picked up his bed roll, tucked it under his arm, and headed for the ledge. The main camp area was capable of sleeping only eight on its rock surface. The rest of the group would have to sleep on the only other flat surface available, the narrow ledge that Charlie now traversed. The kerosene lamp he held was barely sufficient to penetrate the darkness and guide his feet.

Charlie chose the farthest point on the ledge and laid down his bed roll. The flat, stone surface would not be comfortable but it was all that was available. Charlie positioned a string of rocks near the edge of the cliff, so that if he were to become too close while asleep he would send a stone plummeting over, which in turn would awaken him. The precaution turned out to be a hindrance, as Charlie lay awake all night frittering with the placement of the rocks. Jerome, who had curled up behind Charlie, slept soundly, free from the anxieties of the adult mind, his snores reverberating against the rock face.

The group awoke and consumed the last of the oatmeal. They trudged once again down the steep rock incline.

The river had risen overnight another five to six feet, bringing it to some ten feet above its previously accommodating level. Great billowing crests formed in mid-stream and submerged obstacles created gnarly swells. Limbs, branches, and tree trunks of all shapes and varieties rushed headlong downstream.

"I don't know about this," said Duane.

"There's nothing to know," said Charlie. "Let's get going and try to stay together. If you get too far behind, wait for the canoe behind you. We have to be extra careful today." Charlie presented a determined face to the group, his skin drawn tight from the sleepless night. "Now remember, the first sign of civilization we see, we're getting out."

"You mean a house or something like that?" said Jerry.

"I mean anything—road, house, whatever."

Charlie, Roy, and Jerry shoved off in their canoe. The boat quickly picked up a speed in midstream that was twice what it had been on any previous day.

Jerry looked back. The other three crews pushed off, one by one, until all four were caught in midstream, catapulted forward by the tremendous power of the Buffalo at flood crest.

From his position in the last canoe Duane could see Russ and Vince whooping and yelling, having a good time. "Fools," he muttered to himself as drops of sweat stood out on his forehead, his full concentration on the unruly river grabbing at his vulnerable boat.

The group carried on their habit of going without life jackets as if the river were as friendly as it had been the previous four days. An observer standing on the banks of the river, watching the crew race downstream, would come to the conclusion that the crew had lost their senses.

The river now flowed through treetops, the trunks of which stood rooted to submerged sand bars. The intermittent rapids of prior days had completely disappeared, replaced by an entire river rushing headlong through all obstacles. Aside from the tops of trees trapping any objects which drifted within their vicinity, the river was highly navigable. The true danger awaited those unfortunate enough to capsize, as the river held no more sympathy for the helpless swimmer than for the rubble which it swept away.

Charlie's first priority was reaching a point of debarkation and ending the journey as quickly and painlessly as possible. The increased speed of the river worked to the group's advantage, as they were covering vastly more territory than they could have before. The only real worry that continued to upset Charlie's confidence was the lack of life jackets. It was short-sighted really that he hadn't made everyone don the one precaution that was available to them, but if he had he knew something would have been missing. Perhaps it was the excitement of risking everything. He could sense that the boys felt it; the confrontation with nature, bare survival, and the prospect of death, demanded every bit of their fearlessness and courage, and inspired within them, for the first time, the youthful desire to test themselves against the world. It would have been wrong to have taken that away.

Around midday, Charlie began to notice his canoe's increasing distance from the others."Roy, have you seen anybody else recently?

It seems like quite a while since I spotted that second canoe!" said Charlie over Jerry's head and the noise of the river. He dreaded Roy's answer.

Roy looked back over his shoulder, keeping one eye upstream. "No. I haven't seen anyone back there for a while now. I think maybe we lost them."

"How about you Jerry?"

Jerry's nervousness, which he had managed to keep in check all morning, flared up. His eyes shifted erratically. "Not me, I ain't seen nobody."

"Alright. Let's find a place and pull over. We're gonna have to wait for them to catch up," said Charlie.

Within five minutes, the trio stood on dry ground, their canoe tied securely to a tree.

"I wasn't really paying any attention to anybody behind us. I don't know when we lost them. I was having too much fun," said Roy, his guilt making him look vulnerable.

"I should have been keeping a better eye out myself," said Charlie. "But I guess I was just enjoying the ride. The only thing we can do is just wait till they show up. Jerry, what time do you have?"

Jerry quickly checked his watch, a gift from Christmas at the ranch. "It's eleven-forty. Do you think anything happened to those guys?"

"I don't think so. Probably just slow is all," said Charlie.

With each sweep of the minute hand the group grew more anxious. Fifteen minutes stretched into thirty, then an hour, and Charlie's composure began to crack as he imagined the worst.

"I can't sit here any longer," said Charlie. "Something must have happened. I'm going back upstream. I want you guys to stay here. If you see any of them come by, tell them to pull over here and wait, OK?"

Roy and Jerry nodded. Charlie turned and strode upstream.

CHAPTER XXVII

Charlie trudged upstream, scanning both shorelines and the river itself. The river bank had flattened out as the sheer granite walls receded farther and farther back into the underbrush. The most prevalent plant life on the shore, aside from the wild blackberry, interspersed with occasional sprigs of poison oak, were the huge, old oak trees, their gnarled limbs silhouetted against the slate gray sky. Many of them had long, thick vines, some the size of large ropes, which hung down from the tops of the oaks and dangled out a few feet from the ground.

"Charlie Charlie, here we are, over here!" came voices from upstream.

Charlie could barely make out three figures approaching from upstream on foot.

"Over here Charlie, here we are!" came more shouts, closer now as Vince, Keith, and Russ came into view. The trio were running and from their soaking wet appearances and lack of canoe Charlie could tell there had definitely been a mishap.

The three boys stopped before Charlie and caught their breath.

"What happened to you guys?" Charlie blurted out. "Where in the hell's your canoe? Where are the other guys? How'd you get wet?"

"Our canoe sunk," said Vince.

"We hit a tree," said Keith.

"We were lucky to get to shore. That current's terrible," said Russ.

The three boys stood shivering, attempting all at once to explain what had happened.

"Where are the others?" Charlie asked again.

"We don't know, we lost them about an hour ago, we haven't seen anybody," said Keith, his teeth chattering. His hair hung in wet strands over his forehead.

"Are you guys alright? Anybody hurt?"

"Naw, we're fine. But I don't know about that canoe," said Russ.

"Yeah, remember when Doofus said they wouldn't sink? Well this one sunk," said Vince.

"You two get back to camp. Vince, come with me and show me where that canoe's at," said Charlie. He directed Keith and Russ downstream toward Roy and Jerry. "Keith, tell Roy to get his ass back up here and you guys get a fire going. It looks like we're gonna be here for awhile."

The two pairs started off in opposite directions, both wondering what had happened to the other two crews.

Vince stopped a ways upstream and pointed at a stand of submerged trees about ten yards from he and Charlie. "It went down over there." Vince shook from the chill of his wet clothes.

No canoe was visible near the trees.

"We drifted in sideways and got swamped. Before we knew what happened the whole thing turned over and sunk. I know its there. I could feel it underwater when I fell out."

"We're gonna need that other canoe for this. Come on, let's get back," said Charlie.

Vince and Charlie met Roy on the way back and returned with him to he and Keith's makeshift camp, where the other three boys had already the beginnings of a fire started.

"I'm gonna need one other person to help get Vince's canoe out," said Charlie, scanning the boys as they nursed the fire.

"Wait, what's that?" Keith shouted, pointing upstream.

Duane's canoe came rushing headlong down river.

"It's Duane! They're alright!" said Keith.

"Duane! Duane!" said the whole group, throwing up their hands. "Here we are, come over here!"

"He sees us now. I think he sees us!" said Russ.

Duane's group beached their canoe. Danny and David jumped ashore, followed by Duane.

'Where 's the other canoe?" said Roy. "Where's Jerome, Sherman, and Chuck?"

"I don't know. It's been awhile since we saw them," said Duane. Deep wrinkles had formed across his forehead from worry. His eyes were ringed with dark circles and his hands shook visibly.

"But you were supposed to be last. How did you pass them?" said Charlie impatiently.

"Don't yell at me. We just did. They were fooling around going slower and we just passed them, that's all."

Charlie could sense Duane's guilt, similar to that he felt himself.

"Duane, I'm going to need your help to get a canoe that sunk. I think with you, me, Roy, Keith, and Vince, we can get it," said Charlie.

"How about me?" Russ cut in. "I'm gonna go too. You'll need three people in both canoes to get them up and back."

Charlie considered the boy's argument.

"OK Russ, you too," said Charlie. "Let's take one canoe upstream. David, you, Danny, and Jerry stay here and keep that fire going. If you see the other canoe coming downstream, let them know where you're at."

The six made their way upriver in the canoe until they reached the spot where Vince had indicated his group's canoe had sunk.

"You sure that's it now?" said Charlie, eyeing the water that pulsed through the tree limbs.

"Yeah, you can ask these guys, they'll tell you," said Vince defensively.

"Yup, that's it," said Keith.

"Sure is," said Russ.

"You mean they actually sunk a canoe?" said Duane.

"That's what they say, and we have to go get it," said Charlie.

"How do you intend to do that?" said Duane, a frantic edge to his voice. His guilty conscience was trapped back upstream with the missing boys.

Charlie quickly stripped off his shirt and jeans. He stood on the shore in his underwear and tennis shoes.

"What did you do that for?" said Duane, looking at Charlie's bare figure silhouetted against the muddy current.

"I just want to make sure to have something dry to put on when I get out of the water. I see no way of raising that thing that doesn't involve getting wet. It's gonna take four of us out there, two in the water and two in the canoe. Who else wants to volunteer to get wet?"

Roy shot his hand up. Charlie nodded and Roy began stripping to his briefs.

"Duane, you and Vince can stay in the canoe," said Charlie.

"What about me," Russ interrupted, "I don't want to just stay here on shore."

Charlie had to concede that there was no valid reason why Russ shouldn't participate. Keith hadn't expressed a desire to accompany the group on the water—he evidently felt fine just watching from shore.

Charlie, Roy, Vince, Duane, and Russ, launched their canoe upstream and directed it toward the submerged trees.

"Grab that branch, quick. Let the bow go downstream," said Charlie.

Charlie, Roy, and Russ grabbed tightly onto the tree limbs.

"Now hold on," said Charlie.

The canoe rested its axis parallel with the current. Its midpoint was bisected by the clump of trees that tilted downstream as the current swept through. First Charlie then Roy left the relative safety of the canoe and gained footholds among the limbs. They climbed from one branch to the other, their feet just inches above the torrent. Charlie lowered himself waist deep into the water, bracing himself against the limbs, which kept him from being swept downstream. He probed the water with his hand and felt the metallic smoothness of the drowned canoe.

"It's there alright!" said Charlie above the rush of water. The current sucked at his limbs as he moved to the edge of the craft, trying to discern its position.

Roy followed directly behind Charlie, also waist deep in water, and stood on the bow of the submerged craft.

"See if you can feel where the nose is Roy. If it's wedged or something. It seems like everything's free here," said Charlie.

Roy carefully reached down until his head was parallel to the water. "It feels like this end is wedged between a couple of trees."

"Will it move?" Charlie yelled from the far end of the canoe, clinging to the projecting branches to maintain his position.

"I think maybe both of us could get it out." The arteries in Roy's neck stood out as he exerted his total strength to move the bow.

"Wait and I'll help," Charlie called, making his way to Roy.

"You guys need any help?" Duane called from the canoe.

"No, I don't think so, not yet anyway. Just stick around though and be ready with those extra paddles," said Charlie.

Roy and Charlie bent their heads to water level and grappled for a strong hold on the boat.

"Ready?" said Charlie.

"Ready," said Roy.

The combined strength of the two moved the bow slowly upward and out of its wedge.

"Alright!" said Charlie.

"Yahoo!" came the shouts from the others as the boat popped to the surface like a cork and immediately righted itself.

The boat had suffered only one heavy dent that ran crosswise on the bottom, making the bow and stern ride only inches high out of the water. Other than that their was little damage; the cooking utensils and pots and pans which had been secured inside still dangled on the end of their rope.

The group baled water from the righted canoe. Charlie and Roy manned the paddles.

"We'll meet you guys back at base," said Charlie. "Keith, you get back to camp!" he yelled to the far shore.

Soon after, Charlie and Roy stood once more around the fire, this time nude except for their clinging briefs and soggy sneakers.

"What do you think's taking Duane so long?" said Roy, glancing upstream. "He was right behind us, wasn't he?"

Cries came from upstream. The small group turned toward the river.

Duane's canoe shot past the group. The counselor was kneeling in the middle of the boat, gripping the sides.

"Help! Help!" said Duane.

"I don't believe it," Charlie muttered to himself. "Come on Roy, let's get him."

Charlie and Roy bolted towards their canoe. They pushed it into midstream and began paddling with deep, powerful thrusts. They quickly gained on Duane's runaway boat.

Charlie and Roy thrust their hands out and grabbed the side of Duane's canoe.

"Get over here!" Charlie shouted at the stunned counselor.

Duane face registered a blank at the request. The two canoes sped through the churning waters side by side.

"Get your ass over here!" said Charlie.

Duane leaped to Charlie's canoe. The impact of his body rocked the craft dangerously.

The two canoes remained side by side, hurtling downstream.

"Grab it and pull it up and across!" said Charlie, gesturing with his head while his hands were occupied in keeping his craft in midstream, out of the danger of treetops.

Duane and Roy struggled to lift the craft out of the water. They yanked the boat up until it rested crosswise across their canoe. The piggy-back canoe cut the boat in half and obscured Charlie's vision downstream.

"We're heading for shore!" Roy yelled back to Charlie.

The craft cut diagonally against the raging current. The hull of the canoe ran on dry ground. Roy jumped ashore, followed by Duane, who pulled the boat to safety.

"Get this thing out of the way," said Charlie, shoving the piggy-back canoe toward Roy and Duane.

Roy and Duane slid the canoe off the boat and onto safe ground.

Charlie leaped ashore and turned to Duane. "What happened to Russ and Vince? Where are they?"

"We ran into another bunch of trees and they fell out. I think they're upstream. I don't know for sure. I didn't look back," said Duane with a ghastly expression.

"Alright, let's get back to camp and make sure everyone's alright. We still don't know about Sherman and those guys. Then we'll have to look for Russ and Vince," said Charlie.

Charlie, Duane, and Roy bounded upstream toward camp. The mad dash to save Duane had taken the trio seventy five yards downstream.

Back at camp, Charlie sighed as he saw Chuck and Jerome sitting by the fire, soaked from head to toe, their teeth chattering.

"Chuck, Jerome, God it's good to see you. Where's Sherman?" said Charlie.

"He fell overboard. We don't know where he's at. Our canoe's upstream but it's alright," said Chuck.

"Did you see what happened to Sherman when he fell out?" said Charlie, trying to weigh the chances of survival in the fierce current. He knew Sherman couldn't swim.

"Da da da da" said Jerome, attempting to answer through his stutter. He cocked his head sideways and squinted in concentration, but the words still wouldn't come.

"The last we saw of him was his head going downstream. Then we held onto the canoe and it got tangled in branches along the shore. When we got out we didn't see him anywhere. We yelled and he didn't answer," continued Chuck.

"OK," said Charlie. "Duane, you and Roy take a couple of these guys and go upstream to look for Sherman. Work your way up to their canoe and keep yelling all the way in case he made it to shore and he's lost. I have to go find out what happened to Vince and Russ."

Charlie once again raced upstream, taking long strides. He stopped to catch his breath.

"Charlie Charlie, here we are, over here!" came voices from nearby.

Charlie turned toward the river. At midstream, Russ and Vince clung to the highest limbs of a small stand of trees

"Thank God," Charlie cried aloud to himself, "at least they're safe."

The boys were positioned some fifteen yards across the river. Charlie ran a mental check of the available rope among the group's things. There wasn't sufficient length to bridge the distance. An image of the long, strange vines that hung down nearly to the ground from the oak trees came into his mind. Maybe, just maybe, he thought as he raced for the nearest strand of gnarly vine.

Charlie grabbed the free end of the vine and exerted his full strength in an effort to loosen the giant tentacle from its uppermost hold. A sharp crack pierced the air and Charlie rolled backward, clutching the broken-off vine.

Charlie jumped to his feet. He carefully considered the vine. It was certainly long and strong enough, but there wasn't any way to tie it to the boys' end.

"I'll be right back, hold on!" Charlie said across the river.

Downstream, Charlie encountered Roy and David proceeding upstream and yelling for Sherman.

"I found Vince and Russ hanging onto a couple of trees in mid-river!" said Charlie as he ran past the two boys.

"What do you think happened to Sherman?" said David to Roy after Charlie had gone.

"I don't know, but from what Chuck and Jerome said, it doesn't sound very good."

"I'll bet he drowned, and if he did, old Charlie and Duane are gonna be in deep trouble. If Bud had been here this wouldn't have happened. You can bet your ass on that. It's Charlie's fault, with all his big talk. We shouldn't have been out on the river and now Sherman's probably dead because of it."

"You don't know that for sure. Charlie did what he thought was right and Sherman may be alright."

The two boys continued upriver. They soon came across Russ and Vince, clinging to the tops of the trees.

"Looks like you two got yourselves into a mess!" said David. "How do you think you're gonna get outta that one?"

"Charlie's gonna get us out!" said Vince and Russ in unison.

"Sure, and we're gonna have steaks and fries for dinner too!" said David. He laughed over his shoulder and once again joined Roy to look for Sherman.

The two trapped boys watched the receding figures. David's laughter echoed off the water.

"He'll get us out, you just wait and see," Vince said to Russ.

A figure crashed through the brush downstream. Charlie emerged from the bushes, followed by Keith and Chuck.

"Charlie!" said Vince and Russ.

Charlie looked toward the boys. "Hold on!"

Charlie produced a strand of small rope and tied it to the length of vine that he had broken off the oak tree. The trio dragged the vine close to the water's edge. Charlie held the end of the rope. He gave instructions to Keith and Chuck, then turned toward Vince and Russ.

"I'm gonna throw this end over to you. Try to grab it and pull until I say stop. Then tie the rope to a strong limb over there, as high as you can safely get it!" said Charlie.

Charlie momentarily turned to Chuck and Keith, then back to the stranded boys.

"You got that?" shouted Charlie.

"I think so!" said Vince.

"Alright then, here it comes!"

Charlie had secured a stone the size of an egg to the end of the rope. He threw the rock overhand toward the boys while he held the balance of the rope in his left hand. The stone landed over the edge of a branch and Russ grabbed the rope.

"I got it!" said Russ.

"Pull it in until I tell you to stop!" said Charlie.

While the boys in the treetop pulled, the crew on shore fed them a continuous length of vine until the vine hung suspended over the torrent, spanning the distance.

"Now tie that end of rope real tight on a limb over there!" said Charlie.

Russ tied the rope to a limb and pulled on the knot to test its strength.

"It's ready!" said Russ.

Charlie once again turned to his helpers to issue orders. The three then grabbed their end of the vine and pulled it tight, digging their heels into the sand. The vine formed a swinging bridge from the shore to the trees. It ran diagonally from the treetops at a height of about fifteen feet above water, to the shore, where its closest point to rushing water was only four feet.

"Alright, one at a time now. Grab the vine and come on over!" said Charlie.

Vince and Russ hesitated before the vine.

"Come on!" said Keith. "What are you, chickens?"

Keith's jeers motivated Russ to grab the suspended vine. He hung down and proceeded hand over hand toward the shore. The team of rescuers strained to hold Russ' weight. His physical strength made the climb look easy.

Russ dropped to shore with agility. "It's a cinch!" he said back to Vince.

Vince looked less than convinced as he followed Russ' example and grabbed the vine. He paused twice on the way down, kicking his legs up and wrapping them around the vine to rest. Five feet from shore his grip slackened and he fell. Charlie and Keith rushed forward and dragged him to safety before the current could grab him.

The boys and Charlie gathered together on shore. Charlie slapped Vince and Russ on their backs. "Welcome back."

Charlie and the boys returned to camp in late afternoon. The group split into pairs to look for Sherman. They searched up and down the near and far shores, calling his name against the coming night. Following an exhaustive effort that covered a two mile strip of river, the group called off the search as darkness descended.

The teams returned one by one to camp, each bearing the same news. The possibility of Sherman's death hung heavily over everyone. Only the river seemed unperturbed, ready at any moment to snatch another victim from the group that had finally gained a deep respect for its power.

There had been no food since the oatmeal at breakfast and the boys were starving. The only food left was a Hershey bar, which Duane divided into eleven postage-stamp-sized pieces and distributed to each boy.

Duane and Charlie found a private spot at the edge of camp to consider their predicament. The two counselors squatted with one knee on the ground. They were both anxious to mention Sherman, the subject foremost in their minds.

"How long do you think it's gonna be before we find civilization?" said Duane.

"I don't really know, but I would think in a couple of days anyway. The way that river's flowing we're bound to make good time again tomorrow."

The pair were silent for a moment.

"What are we gonna do about Sherman?" said Duane, his voice cautiously probing the unthinkable.

Charlie cast a forlorn look toward the river. "We're just gonna have to keep looking for any signs of him tomorrow. We may come across a piece of clothing or even…"

"How about food? I don't know how long these guys can subsist on nothing but water," said Duane, changing the subject.

"If we haven't reached civilization by noon tomorrow, maybe we'll try and kill something."

The idea seemed preposterous to Duane but he failed to say so.

"I guess we should all just get to bed. There's not much else we can do tonight. Goodnight Charlie," said Duane.

"Goodnight."

Duane raised himself wearily and moved towards the boys gathered around the fire, who had been talking quietly among themselves ."OK you guys, let's get some sleep. We're gonna get going early in the morning."

"Is Sherman dead?" said Jerry, the words issuing forth from between the fingernails he was gnawing.

"I don't know, but he might well be," said Duane.

"David says it was Charlie's fault that he drowned. He said Charlie's gonna be in real trouble when Mr. Johnson finds out," said Jerry.

Duane looked across the fire. David grinned back at him

"It was an accident. It wasn't anybody's fault, no matter what David says," said Duane.

"That's what I said," Keith interjected. "They won't do anything to Charlie."

"If Bud was here, it wouldn't have happened. You can bet on that," said David.

"Come on you guys, let's get to bed," said Duane.

The group broke up and found their sleeping bags. Charlie remained up, squatting in the same position that Duane had left him in, his eyes fixed on the rushing river.

At midnight, Charlie drifted across camp and into his bed roll.

The thought of what had happened to Sherman kept everyone tossing and turning into the night, except for David, who slept soundly imagining Charlie being reprimanded for Sherman's death and finally getting his due.

The group awoke red-eyed early the next morning. With no breakfast to eat, the crews quickly manned their crafts and resumed the search for Sherman. This time everyone wore their bright orange lifejackets. Despite the previous day's misfortune, the boys still grumbled over the necessity of the cumbersome and uncomfortable contraptions. A good deal of the complaining, however, was due to the boys' ever-increasing hunger.

The crews kept their eyes fixed on the passing shorelines and exposed branches, both wanting and fearing to find some trace of the missing boy.

Around noon, Duane and Charlie called a halt to the search and the group assembled on the shore to discuss the issue of food.

"All we have are rocks, so that's what we'll have to use to kill," said Charlie. "Keep a few in your pocket and have some ready in your hand. Rabbits would be the best, but I guess we should take anything that moves."

Charlie noticed a slight glimmer in the boys' eyes as he explained the plan. In this kindling of primitive hunting instincts, Charlie saw the first cracks in the shroud of grief which had smothered the group since the previous afternoon.

"It's probably better if we spread out in kind of a circle and drive anything we see into the center. Let's start over there," said Charlie. He pointed to a small meadow bordered by pine and oak, containing an abundance of clumps of brush and fallen logs that presented good prospects for rabbits.

The group carefully chose their necessary supply of rocks and fanned out towards the field. They soon closed in on a couple of cotton tails, but the rabbits quickly escaped, much too smart to have their lives ended by stones after having developed strategies that had worked against guns for centuries. Though the rabbit hunt failed, the excitement had livened the boys' spirits.

The hunters discovered some wild turnips and managed to kill a snake. The group quickly ate the turnips, but no one ventured to try the snake, even after it had been boiled sufficiently.

Charlie, Duane, and the boys once again headed blindly down-river, hoping for some reprieve from their seemingly endless journey.

The afternoon passed into dusk, forcing the voyagers ashore. Another uneventful night passed amid the rumbling of empty stomachs.

Mid-morning the next day the group came upon a one lane bridge that spanned the river. The sight brought a chorus of cheers from everyone. The disheveled crews dragged their boats ashore and made their way up the steep hillside, toward the bridge.

The group crossed the bridge onto an isolated stretch of country road that twisted out of sight in both directions. What remained of the once bright-eyed adventurers ready to set out on their river voyage only a few days before now trudged along an abandoned blacktop somewhere in Northern Arkansas.

After an hour trek, the group came upon a small roadside café, the lone outpost of civilization along the road. Duane pushed the screen door open and the momentum of the boys pressing at his heels carried him into the center of the small diner. The boys stood staring at the gleaming countertop, which held a variety of homemade pies, carefully guarded from flies by plastic covers. A middle-aged matron stood stiffly behind the counter, scrutinizing the unkempt lot.

Duane sensed the woman's fears. "OK you guys, sit down and act civilized and maybe we can get something to eat."

The boys found a table while Charlie and Duane remained at the counter.

"We'd like to get some food for everyone. It's been a while since we've had anything to eat," said Charlie in as smooth a manner as he could manage under the circumstances.

The matron stood square-shouldered behind the counter, her arms folded.

"Can you pay?"

"Sure," said Charlie.

"We'll even pay in advance," said Duane in an attempt to speed the proceedings.

"That won't be necessary. Just let me know what you want," said the woman curtly.

In a few minutes the group decided on the contents of their feast: hamburgers, French fries, and milk shakes.

"Make that two for everyone," said Charlie, turning from the taciturn owner to the boys' salivating grins.

Duane turned to Charlie at the counter, where they sat side by side, inhaling the scent of cooking hamburgers. "I guess we better get a hold of Johnson and let him know as soon as possible about Sherman."

Charlie conceded to get the inevitable call over with. "Yeah, I guess you're right."

"What are you gonna tell him anyway?"

"The truth."

Charlie whirled around in his chair and hoisted himself up. He headed for the payphone mounted at the end of the counter. The diner was so small and the telephone situated so near to the tables that it was impossible to carry on a private conversation.

The cafe patrons turned their ears toward Charlie as he dealt with a succession of operators. The familiar voice of Mr. Johnson finally came on the line.

"Charlie, how are you? I was just thinking about you and the boys the other day. I hope you're having fun."

Charlie hesitated. Johnson faltered then fell silent as if he were intuitively aware of the forthcoming message.

"We've had a little trouble Mr. Johnson. It's Sherman. We lost him upriver two days ago. He fell from a canoe and that was the last we saw of him. The river was real high and we searched and searched, but no word."

Mr. Johnson remained silent.

"You're not sure if he drowned or not then? I mean, you didn't find a body or any traces?"

Johnson's voice contained the same glimmer of hope which Charlie had tried to nourish in himself, until had been extinguished by the thorough search.

"With the river conditions and the search and all, I have to assume he's drowned."

Meanwhile, behind Charlie's back, Duane was absorbed in dialogue with the owner of the café. Duane was becoming increasingly restless as he listened to the matron. He sprang from his seat and moved quickly toward Charlie, who was castigating himself for his foolish negligence of Sherman's life.

"You'd better listen to what this lady has to say," said Duane, grabbing Charlie by the arm, "I think it's Sherman."

Charlie looked from Duane to the stern matron behind the counter, trying to comprehend what was happening. Johnson called Charlie's name from the line. Charlie turned to the receiver and asked the social worker to hold.

Duane turned to the owner. "A family up the road…you said they found a boy, a black boy, about fifteen, stocky build, a couple of days ago…and he's alive?"

Charlie, the boys, and the customers strained in anticipation.

The owner nodded slowly, her countenance remaining rigid.

Charlie closed his eyes and sighed together with the eavesdropping patrons. The boys cheered.

Charlie turned back to the receiver. "Mr. Johnson, um, it seems that a boy was found who meets Sherman's description. He's alive."

Charlie was overjoyed when the sheriff's car pulled up to the front of the cafe and deposited Sherman, smiling as he was suddenly hugged from all sides. The family whose house he had wandered to after reaching shore and running as fast as he could away from the river had taken exceptional care of him. While the remainder of the group had gone hungry and mourned his death, he had eaten delicious country meals and slept soundly in a real mattress. Sherman had charmed his hosts so thoroughly that they had extended an invitation for him to return that summer, which he did.

CHAPTER XXVIII

The Buffalo River trip was not the last wilderness experience for Charlie, Duane, Bud, and the boys, but it overshadowed and set the benchmark for all those that followed. Even the two week backpacking excursion into the Pecos wilderness of New Mexico, when Chuck's burning his only shoes in the campfire in a failed effort to forestall the trek resulted in his scaling the Truchas peak barefooted, seemed anti-climatic in comparison to the river trip.

In discovering the fruitfulness of persistence and determination, the boys had begun to mature, though instances of brutality and emotional instability continued into the end of the summer of 1972, when the group finally broke up.

Keith, Vince, Chuck, and Roy returned to the ranch, where they were integrated into a new routine of textbooks and teachers. Little Danny was reunited with his mother, who had after all married a wealthy gentleman who was prepared to take his chances with the changed boy. At Bud's insistence, David remained with the small group in the woods, which included Sherman, Jerome, Russ, and Jerry. It seemed as if the relationship that had developed between Bud and David might turn out to be a lifetime commitment on Bud's part. The other four boys who remained in the woods were promised only a short delay before they too could return to the ranch and a more normal existence. Charlie and Duane departed in early fall for school.

Six months after Charlie left, the entire camp was being closed down. Only Jerome was to remain at Wolf Creek forever: the little snot-nosed stutterer who had spent his short life being passed from one pair of un-wanting hands to the next had finally found rest. Charlie had not been surprised that Jerome's death had occurred on the Buffalo River, where a second expedition had gone, as Charlie had a personal knowledge of the potential for death which lurked in those waters.

Charlie visited Jerome's grave, which stood on a small rise between the vacant cook tent and Wolf Creek. The site was marked by a crude cross, hand-fashioned by Jerome's friends. Charlie stood motionless over the small grave for some time, recalling the furious little boy who had declared war on the world. The image soon changed to a moon-faced kid whose eyes and cheeks were aflame with laughter as Charlie held him down, tickling his sides.

In the years to come, Charlie would often say that he had been the real pupil, while that wild band of homeless but loveable boys had been his teachers.

CHAPTER XXIX

I t was 1979. In late afternoon, Charlie sat hunched over his desk at The Red Cross, studying the fundraising charts laid out before him. His phone buzzed and the button lit up.

Charlie picked up the phone and rested it against his shoulder and cheek, not taking his attention away from the work on his desk. "Charlie Rogers."

"Hey Charlie. Do you know who this is?"

Charlie leaned back in his chair, struck by the familiar voice. His memory raced back through the years and finally stopped on an image of an impromptu camp in the Texas wilderness.

"Vince, where in the hell are you?" said Charlie.

"I'm here. I'm in town."

"In town" could mean any number of places in Los Angeles, Charlie thought.

"How in the world did you ever find me?" said Charlie.

"I've been looking for you for a long time. Your mother told me where you were and now it looks like I've finally caught up with you. You sure move around a lot."

"Where exactly are you now?"

"I'm in Carson, staying at my girlfriend's mother's place. We're getting married."

The conversation was easy, the kind that comes from two parties sharing an intimate knowledge of each other's beings.

"Can I see you tonight? Would it be a good time for you?" said Charlie.

"That would be great, but I don't have a car."

"No problem. Just say where and when and I'll be there."

"I'd like for you to meet my girlfriend, too. I've told her so much about you and the guys and all the things we did, but she doesn't believe me."

"Well, she better believe you. Unless, of course, you're lying again, like you used to."

"Who me, lie? Never."

Charlie and Vince laughed remembering the ways things used to be at Wolf Creek.

The two met up at a bowling alley later that night. Charlie met Vince's girlfriend, a quiet cutie whom Vince had obviously swept off her feet. Vince, having grown much bigger through the years, insisted on an arm wrestling contest, which Charlie won only by cheating and grabbing the edge of the table.

Vince had turned into a handsome young man who exuded self-confidence, though his life was still far from what most consider ideal. He and Charlie met several times after that night, before Charlie lost contact when he moved once again.

Charlie never forgot Vince's words the first night they met at the bowling alley; in the years afterward, they often spoke to the doubts that arose in the former counselor's mind about his ability to meet life's challenges.

"You know Charlie," said Vince, his bride-to-be standing proudly by his side, "after everything we went through out there in the woods, I know there ain't nothin I can't do if I really want to."

CHAPTER XXX

The Miracle

The funeral was over. The well-meant speeches about how wonderful the deceased was and how much she would be missed were delivered with varying degrees of sincerity. The preacher who knew Viola Hart for over forty years as a member of his congregation from The Bible Baptist Church was able to clearly sketch with his bellicose language the steadfastness of her love of God and her family. What no one was able to explain rationally was the arrival of her only son in her home in her sixty seventh birth year after waiting so long and so patiently for a child. There were many who said that she and her husband Joseph were too old to have children but she would have nothing to do with that nonsense. She knew a miracle from the Lord when she saw it and this boy was the miracle which her and her husband had prayed for so many years.

The only two people who had lived the miracle in the entire congregation of over two hundred God fearing souls in attendance at the services were Joseph Hart and the couples' son Sherman. They sat in the front row heads bowed by their inconsolable loss by the invisible cloud of sadness which had descended over them. Joseph was now eighty five and still the same determined and willful soul who married Viola right out of High School. They had been sweethearts since the fourth grade and knew with the surety that innocence brings that they would someday be married and have many children. Joseph took over his parent's farm after his father passed and he was now the third generation of Harts that worked and cajoled the rich Arkansas river soil until it produced year after year its bountiful harvest. The character of their material life was defined by the seasons and the storms or floods or pests which, in bad years, tortured their crops into infertility and a shedding of their nascent abundance before fruition. In good years when the seasons smiled on them and all was right in Heaven and on earth the Harts flourished.

In 1971 the year that Sherman first came into their lives looked like it would be a lean year starting with the floods in the Spring and ending in hard baked mud in the Summer but that all changed when their son arrived on their door step just as a dinner of meatloaf, mashed potatoes and green beans, was set down on the table and Viola and Joseph joined hands to thank God for all he had given them and as was always their last request to bring them a child. Joseph knew, despite those biblical tales which said otherwise, that there was no chance of a child for them now. He knew that all they really had was this prayer, this ritual, this entreaty to God to bring them a child on whom they could lavish the abundance of love which they had to give. Joseph did nothing to erode Viola's immovable faith in the Lord. He made no attempts to explain logically the complete and utter futility of her prayers knowing that his logic any logic had no place where true faith reigned.

On that fateful evening they had finished their prayer and looked knowingly at each other. Joseph feeling only the infinite love he had for his wife and Viola knowing Joseph's lack of faith and sincere concern for what he thought was only a hopeless dream caused her to love him even more. She loved him deeply but her love was endless it seemed and only a child a child in need of her bottomless love could accommodate the enormity of love which she had to give. Joseph thought back on that day of their sons' arrival as he left the Church his hand firmly grasped by the Preacher as he descended the steps his son towering over him at his side.

There home was rustic. The front porch, like the rest of the home, was simple perhaps even austere. It invited guests into the heart of the home and enveloped them with the love of its owners as soon as they placed their feet on that porch and knocked on the screen door to gain entry. It was on this porch that the miracle became reality. In conversations over the years between the three of them the story was told over and over again and they never tired of it. They would often sit on the family sofa, Viola in the middle and Joseph and Sherman on either side of her and they would hold hands while they told their part of the story. Joseph and Viola, their worn and weather beaten hands gently enfolding each other his larger and rough, hers small with long fingers but strong as only a farmer's wife's hands can be. On the other side Sherman's hands were large, twice as large as Viola's and they completely enclosed her hand as a mother hen surrounds her eggs with her body carefully thoughtfully and always conscious of the fragility of the egg the intrinsic delicacy of the small hand. The most glaring contrast was not in the size of the hands but in the stark contrast of Viola's translucent alabaster skin and Sherman's deep black skin died darker each year by hard work under an unforgiving sun. It was this stark contrast of color of culture of prejudice which always drew the most stares from the locals, who took years to become comfortable with it to outsiders who often cast derisive looks and words in their direction. These furtive looks were hardest on Joseph as he was most conscious of them. Viola had only love for her son and the knowledge of a miracle fulfilled. She had no time for bigotry, ignorance or hate. In these final years of her life after being patient for so long and never doubting her Lord she only had time for love.

The two men entered the farm house and stood silently in the entryway somehow expecting to hear Viola's voice, "You men get yourselves cleaned up, suppers ready" she would call from the kitchen. It was this call to supper that was the keystone the iconic symbol of her love for them and theirs for her. She was there to care for them and they were there to care for her and the call to dinner reminded them every day of that fact. But today was different for she was gone forever and they would never hear her call again. Sitting on the sofa and looking through the screen door beyond the porch to the edge of the river visible some forty yards to the West Sherman recalled his arrival.

The river trip had been exciting, scary and finally horrifying to Sherman. At fifteen he still did not know how to swim and the water had been so powerful so angry. It pulled at him and pushed him under its churning surface dragging him through submerged trees and slamming him into hidden obstacles. He knew he was going to die and he was terrified. He took in great gulps of flood water. He choked and coughed and cried and screamed but no one came to save him. Charlie and the other boys had disappeared and it was only him alone no mother no father forever the orphan leaving this life as he had entered it by himself. He was awakened by the cold wet clothes that clung to him as he had clung to the last breath of life that he thought he would breathe before he was swept against the river bank. His body was caught by submerged trees as the flood waters churned voraciously pulling at his legs trying to pry him loose.

He saw the porch light as he lay exhausted on the ground his nose inhaling the rich scent of the dark rich soil for which the Hart's farm was famous. He stumbled in the fading light and collapsed on the porch where he turned over and threw up the muddy river water. The Harts heard the commotion, for life in the country had distinct sounds animals in the night but this was something different something they were unfamiliar with and they moved cautiously from their dinner to peer out the door. Sherman lay face up on the worn boards. His scratches and cuts bled freely making his face a black and red mask which hid the child beneath. Joseph wanted to go get his shotgun but Viola saw beyond saw a child and her love went out to him like a giant wave sweeping all concern all fear before it like so much dust in the wind.

"Sherman", "yes Pa" he answered as his Dad moved slowly around to the front of the sofa holding a cup of coffee gingerly as he sat himself down next to his son. "You know how difficult it was for your mother and me to adopt you?" he asked already knowing the answer for this was one of the stories they liked telling the most. "I know Dad," Sherman responded remembering how those months were such a torture for him. His two days with the Hart's and then taken from them with their promise that they would come for him that they wanted to adopt him. He was not aware then of the obstacles which stood in their way. The most obvious was the race difference and then a somewhat distant but distinct second obstacle was their age and the boy's age. "Well you know that if it wasn't for your mom's perseverance and faith it would not have happened at all." "I know Dad, I know what mom did" Sherman responded his mind still caught in those terrible months of waiting of doubting of hurting. "You know how much she loved you son and how much she did for both of us. But what you don't know what she did not want me to tell you until she was gone was what you did for her." Sherman turned his head slowly towards his father until their eyes met. His father was holding an envelope and he handed it to his son. On the outside in his mother's handwriting he saw his name, To Sherman, God's gift to me. LOVE Mom.

He turned it over in his hands sensing its importance to her knowing with all his heart that she had saved him that she had rescued from a "life without true love" the love of a parent for their child which is without limit. He removed the letter and held it in his hands hesitating to know its contents. He didn't want anything to ruin this life he had with these people these two wonderful human beings who had taken him in and taught him about love. "Read it son, she wanted you to know."

My Dearest Son: If you are reading this then I have passed but I know I am with God now and the only other place I would rather be is with you and your father. If you are mourning me do so sparingly and then caste an eye toward heaven and your mourning will become joy for I am there forever watching and protecting both of you. When God brought you into my life it was the fulfillment of a lifelong promise which he made to me as a child. I had such a huge portion of love to give. I could feel it trying to burst out of me at every seam until you arrived and then it did not need to burst for it had found its rightful receptacle in my son my miracle child who fulfilled my every dream of what I wanted my child to be. Strong, courageous, righteous, compassionate and loving you are all of those things. Your generous nature and pure heart surrendered itself to our love for you and for the first time in our lives we all three of us finally and completely felt the wonder of infinite love. I want to thank you son for your patience with me when I did not understand you, for your abiding love for all people in the face of prejudice and hate, for your mercy which you bestowed on the lowliest of animals and men without judging their acts and for finding me and your father who had prayed so long and so hard for you. I know your Dad had lost faith but I knew you were out there and that you would find your way to our door step. You are a good man. You will be a wonderful father and you are and always will be my loving son my miracle from God. Remember I am watching. Love Mom

He had to wipe his eyes with the back of his shirtsleeve during the reading of his mother's letter. It did not contain anything new or that she had not told him before. There was no doubt in his mind that his presence in this family was a miraculous thing, a holy thing. Sherman looked at his Dad who had been peering over his coffee cup as his son read the letter. What do you think she meant by "I am watching?" he asked his Dad. Well your mother had some crazy idea that when she went to heaven and she never doubted that she would go to heaven that she would watch over both of us. I always let her believe what she wanted to believe because it made her happy so I never argued. "But do you believe it?" Sherman asked. "Not really" he answered, I guess I just don't have the kind of faith your mother did.

The two men rose from the sofa simultaneously and looked toward the kitchen listening for the dinner call and then climbed the stairs to their rooms. Half way up the stairs they stopped abruptly and simultaneously and turned their heads in the direction of the kitchen. They looked at each other wide eyed and then smiled a knowing smile a loving smile. "What was it you heard" Joseph asked his son. "I heard mom calling us for dinner" That's what I thought I heard he said a curious look on his face. "That old girl is still watching over us strange as that may sound" he mumbled to himself shaking his head slowly from side to side. "You know her Pa you know she wouldn't let a little thing like dying stop her from loving us."

THE END